I0673464

The Beauty of Fragile Things

Emma Hartley

For Christine and Brian,
whose love even blooms in the desert

"So we beat on, boats against the current,
   borne back ceaselessly into the past."

-F. SCOTT FITZGERALD

———

"It is not in the stars to hold our destiny,
   but in ourselves."

-WILLIAM SHAKESPEARE

O n the floor of her bedroom, Margot DeWitt sat alone with her back propped up against the foot of her bed. With the airy fabric of her bridal veil draped over her arm, Margot studied the familiar designs for the thousandth time. Passed down from mother to daughter for generations, this priceless family heirloom had been worn many times by many brides, all on the happiest day of their lives.

Though the designs in the lace appeared substantial, they were fragile as a spider's web. Lace lied. It tricked the eye. It lured one near to marvel at its beauty, its solidity, its permanence. Margot, however, had finally perceived the truth: there was almost nothing there, a network of empty spaces connected imperceptibly by an insubstantial matrix, an identical deception to her well-constructed former life.

She could still see her wedding day clearly, the vision not dimmed by time's passing. Sunshine had glittered playfully on the water as Margot gazed across the bay. The lace veil fluttered and billowed in the gentle July breeze, the Calendar Islands rose up like old friends and congratulated her. Set against the sea, Kevin was resplendent, confidently waiting for her in his satiny black tux, stark against the blue-on-blue backdrop. The love he had for her, so evident in all he did, was as powerful as the crashing waves, as firm as the ground beneath her feet. Margot felt her father's loving presence as well, as though the sun itself was his blessing on Margot's marriage, manifested in light.

When the musicians began the wedding march, Margot's mother kissed her on the cheek. "I love you, Margot."

"I love you too, Mom," Margot said, her voice thick with emotion.

Her mother gently took Margot's arm and walked her down the grassy aisle.

Kevin's voice wavered with emotion as they spoke their vows. His eyelashes glittered with unshed tears. Though their joined hands had trembled with the intensity of the moment, nothing could have been stronger than the commitment they made.

The echo of their vows still lingered in Margot's broken heart.

Margot clutched at the delicate veil, its intricacy blurred by tears. The Point de Gaze lace was airy, its gossamer patterns and complex details hung suspended in an atmosphere of single thread netting. Elegant flowers and leaves were swept up in a tangle of swirls, yet the symmetry of the piece was precise. An inherent expression of mathematical universals had billowed out from creative psyches, the only outlet of the day for absolute feminine genius. Women had spent so much time creating beautiful things for themselves and for their daughters to be treasured for generations to come.

Margot's grandmother, a Belgian immigrant, had sung to Margot in her low, sweet voice the pride of the old country, as her lace needle flashed. Throughout her childhood, Margot had marveled at how her grandmother could draw designs into existence from nothing but thread and imagination. It had seemed to Margot like slow-motion magic. The creations sometimes took years to complete, but her grandmother's patience never waned. By the time she was old enough to learn, however, Margot had chosen a different form of self-expression.

As her passion for music took root, her fascination with lacemaking dissipated in equal measure. The value in preserving the old ways was lost on the teenager, whose punk rock sensibilities could no longer muster interest in her grandmother's lace-making tutorials. Lace was dinosaur-stuff, best left in the past. When her grandmother passed on, her knowledge passed on with her.

Oblique sunlight blazed against the gauzy lace, highlighting the intricate trace-work of threads over Margot's skin, white-on-white. Lately, the pattern had become a physical part of her, etched not only into her psyche, but into her *self*, like a scarification. Too much time alone had stripped her of the ability to judge whether this was a crazy thought or not.

Margot meant to box up the veil for good this time, to wrap the delicate antique lace in white, acid-free tissue, to cocoon it against the ravages of time and the elements and her own desperate compulsion to relive a moment that was forever gone. The ghosts of her ancestors clung to it somehow, still perceptible, grieving with her, for this veil had seen its last bride. In the fading light, yellowed with age and proximity to night, the veil reminded Margot of all she had lost, of all she continued to lose.

The pain in her heart, in her deepest places, was acute, as she kissed the fragile lace, held it to her cheek, and closed the box. She had christened it with her tears all too often these last months. It was time to put the veil aside, to let it join its memorial counterparts in the past. Margot's scars and lingering anguish were her only mementos now. She had no idea how to box those away.

In her pearl-white bedroom, Margot stood before the vast walk-in closet—such a selling feature when she and Kevin had looked at the house—and gazed up. With the bedroom's high Victorian-era ceilings, the top shelf of her closet rose to a staggering height of nine feet. Margot hoped it would be enough of a deterrent to her constant perusal of the veil, for her fixation with it was becoming disturbing. She climbed up and teetered unsteadily on the top step of the ladder she'd lugged up from the basement. While tucking the box safely between Kevin's winter sweaters and a tote of family photographs from her childhood, she almost lost her balance. With her heart racing, Margot grasped a shelf to steady herself, took a deep breath, and climbed down. She couldn't imagine doing that again any time soon.

As Margot awkwardly reinterred the stepladder in the basement, she bashed her hand against the cellar doorframe, bruising herself to the bone.

"God damn it," she called out, dropping the heavy ladder and rubbing her hand. The physical discomfort jolted her from her mire of emotional anguish so she focused on it, relishing it, surprisingly thankful for the momentary abatement of grief.

Recently, bodily discomfort would induce an immediate change in her emotional state. It came coupled with a distinct sensation of relief. It was disturbing. Why would one pain erase the other, even temporarily? After massaging her bruised hand, she picked the ladder up once more and returned it to its place in the basement.

The remainder of Sunday, with its burgeoning twilight, fed Margot's melancholy as the ache in her hand was supplanted once more by the only other emotion she seemed capable of anymore. The cable bill had lapsed long ago, resulting in a large TV in her den with nothing on it. Its black hole of a screen mocked her whenever she entered the room, so she rarely did. Instead, she sat in the formal living room, with its white walls and white trim and white couches punctuated with hints of pale color, exactly as the design magazines had suggested. The stark beauty of the space was devoid of human feeling, which is why Margot gravitated here nightly with her cooling mug of tea. She sat in silence with her memories until ten, when she forced herself to stop looking out the window at the streetlights beyond and get into her cold white bed.

Staring at the ceiling, Margot remembered how happy she'd

been with the house, with her careful attention to the details in every space. How proud she'd felt when Kevin complimented her taste. How meaningless it all seemed now that she was alone, surrounded by white walls and white duvets and white curtains, shrouded in an elegant tomb of her own design. At least Monday would bring work, and with it, the distraction she had come to crave.

Forensic accounting sounded more glamorous than it was. The numbers kept her mind busy at least, and Margot found some comfort in the ocean of statistics she sorted through each day, looking for patterns in the static. By late Monday afternoon, Margot felt thankful the day hadn't dragged by as badly as some days did. Margot turned off her computer, but as she did so, dread settled like lead in her belly. The last thing she wanted to do was meet her friend Ginny for drinks. Unfortunately, Margot had backed out of meeting Ginny too many times recently to do it again.

Outside, Margot reluctantly traced the same path she walked each morning and evening, past a vintage clothing store, past an inordinate number of restaurants, past the tattoo shop next door to the bar. Her heels usually clicked purposefully against the brick sidewalks, unwavering.

Lately, however, the tattoo shop had begun luring her in. Pausing at its window for a little longer each evening, Margot studied the fascinating images: daggers driven through bleeding hearts, bouquets of sentimental lilies and roses, lurid pin-ups, and leering skulls. Between the pictures against the glass, she sometimes caught a glimpse of the tattoo artists inside, working at their craft. Margot had missed the first wave of tattoos that had swept through her circle during college. Now, she couldn't even imagine getting one.

People of every description came and went, flaunting their newest works of art. Margot could almost feel their judgement hot against her skin, like they knew she was a coward. Still, she silently catalogued the graphics in the window. The people, the artwork, the place itself, all seemed surreal, parts of a fluid museum she did not have an invitation to, a language she could not understand.

Margot dallied before the window display once again, intentionally delaying her inevitable date with Ginny by analyzing a page of vintage swallow drawings, her forehead resting against the cool glass. The startling sound of clanging bells heralded the emergence of a young, pink-haired woman from the tattoo shop. The woman stopped on the threshold and stared at Margot with disdain. Was it Margot's fine, blush-pink blouse, combined with her overcast bearing, that gave the woman pause? When their gazes met, Margot spoke without thinking.

"Does it hurt?"

The pink girl smiled and said sarcastically, "Yeah, *Mom*. It does."

"Good," Margot had replied softly, unintentionally insulting the girl who, looking pissed, turned on her heel and strode away. The word *Mom* twisted in Margot's heart, as she stared back into the shop window. The pink girl, who couldn't have been more than twenty, had meant it as a derisive indication of Margot's age, a ripe thirty-two. The insult, however, had burned deeper than the bloody daggers she now regarded.

As she steadied her breathing and brushed a stray strand of hair from her forehead, one of the tattooers exited the shop, eliciting a gentler tinkling of bells, and leaned against the doorframe. Margot watched his reflection in the window glass. Unruly brown hair framed his handsome face, the sleeves of his tattered flannel shirt were rolled up, myriad designs mapped his muscular arms. With a distant expression, he watched the passersby. Reflexively, he patted his shirt pocket, as though looking for a cigarette. He seemed to realize his mistake and gave up in an instant, his hand falling idly to his side. Margot accidentally caught his glance for a startling moment as he looked her way. When their gazes met, it was like she'd been electrocuted. Knowing her anguish was all too obviously written in her expression, she dug her fingernails into her palm and headed into the bar next door.

The vintage neon light in the entryway glazed Margot's skin a deathly blue as she entered. The coveted window booth was available, so she sat down, noticing then avoiding her own reflection in the window glass, her emaciated frame mirroring her decimated spirit. She was more like a ghost than a woman.

When Ginny finally walked through the door, her lively golden curls made Margot feel even deader inside than she already had. Her heart was not in this visit, if she even had a heart anymore. The empty smile she proffered was reflected in Ginny's darkening expression.

"You don't want to be here."

"Hello to you too, Ginny," Margot replied, trying for her friend's sake to muster her energies.

"I shouldn't drag you out. But I worry about you." Ginny reached out and squeezed Margot's shoulder before taking the seat across from her.

"Nothing to worry about. I'm still breathing, right?"

Ginny sighed. Pity oozed from her skin, from her lacquered pink nails, from her expensive handbag. Even her lengthy eyelashes seemed to say, "You poor thing. You have nothing."

"You want your regular?" Ginny asked, trying to sound light.

"Yep. Thanks, next round is on me."

Ginny went to the bar and returned with a tall scotch and soda for Margot and a neon-yellow lemondrop martini for herself.

"Is that top new?" Margot asked, trying to make small talk.

"Nope. In fact, I think I wore it the last time we went out."

"Sorry. How's work?" Margot asked.

"It's work. It pays the bills until I find a man to pay them for me."

Margot cringed. "Why don't you do something you like better?" she asked, trying not to show her feelings about

Ginny's attitude regarding men. "You could easily find another job."

"Why bother? Running the agency is as good as anything else and at least I already know how to do it. People are so full of shit, though. You know?"

"I guess. Some of them are." Margot thought of Kevin. He had only been full of shit some of the time.

Ginny took a long sip of her lemondrop, then set the glass down next to the cardboard coaster instead of on top of it, which annoyed Margot. She looked back out the window, but felt Ginny staring at her. She lifted her glass to her lips, trying to avoid Ginny's gaze.

"You ready to double date with me yet?" Ginny said loudly.

"Fuck no," Margot replied, nearly spitting out her scotch. "Please don't ask me things like that. You know I'm…"

"Yeah. I know," Ginny said, absently swirling the sugared lemon rind into her drink. "But I keep hoping you'll rejoin me on this side of the veil, Margot."

"Don't hold your breath."

Ginny took a long swallow. "Fine. You know I'm here if you ever…"

"I don't." Margot looked out into the night. "No amount of talk can bring him back, Ginny."

"No," her friend agreed. "But it might bring you back."

Silence settled between them as the crowd thickened. The scotch was corroding Margot's empty stomach. The discomfort gave her courage. She leaned back in the booth and stared up at the strange, curved ceilings that made it seem as though they were inside an antique train car. Margot liked this bar. It was living proof that punk rock existed, once upon a time before Greenday. The bartenders here weren't afraid to play the real deal, thereby ensuring that the casual businessmen wandering in after work only stayed for a single drink, freeing up the bar for the regulars. Margot strained through the ruckus of the revelers to catch a few bars of an old, familiar song, involuntarily humming along. *Fine day, if you're not me...*

"How's your work?" Ginny asked, clearly hoping to change the subject.

"It's a whack-a-mole. I'm always busy." Margot drummed her fingers absently on the table along to the beat of the song.

"Tax season's over, why is it still crazy?"

"I landed a big corporate audit. They're all freaking out, and rightly so. Somebody hasn't been exactly honest, and I'm going to figure out who."

"Number detective." Ginny smiled mischievously.

For a moment, Margot could almost see the girls they'd been, so long ago.

"Numbers are incapable of deceit. The truth is in there somewhere," Margot mused aloud.

"Good. I'm glad you're busy."

"It helps." She took a sip. The scotch burned Margot's throat on the way down.

While they talked, Ginny unabashedly scoped out the scene at the bar. From her expression, however, Margot surmised she wasn't finding anyone appealing enough to hit on.

"Slim pickins," Ginny murmured with chagrin.

"Your dating sites aren't pulling in droves of rich hotties?" Margot asked, watching her friend watch the bar.

"Nope. Apparently, there's a serious dearth of available dashing lawyers or rich brokers in Portland. It doesn't seem possible that they're all taken, does it?"

"Wait ten more years and you can clean house on divorcees."

"They have to pay alimony. It's not worth it."

Margot had been joking, but Ginny's response made it clear where her friend's priorities lay lately. "I thought Robert and you were getting closer lately."

"I guess, but it never hurts to keep your options open." Ginny looked at her phone. "I'm meeting him for dinner, actually. Gotta go." Downing her drink and gathering her purse, she hopped out of the booth and came over to Margot's side. She bent down and kissed Margot on the cheek. Then she whispered, "Margot, you know I love you but maybe antidepressants would help. You might feel better." She straightened back up. "You've gotta do something. I want my friend back."

Margot regarded Ginny sadly and said, "See you soon."

Ginny walked out of the bar, waving behind her. She was not the same person Margot had known when they were teens. She wanted her friend back too. All through high school, college, and into their twenties, Ginny had been a joy to be with, vivacious and bubbly, the life of any social experiment. Now, she was more preoccupied with finding *the right man*. Maybe she wanted to settle down. Maybe she even wanted kids. Maybe she was right about the antidepressants. Maybe Ginny was on them. It would account for her newfound air of detachment.

Over a decade before, they'd shared a tiny apartment in a rundown part of Dorchester before it got gentrified. Ginny had always been outgoing and boisterous, bringing the introverted Margot along to parties. Margot, in turn, had introduced Ginny to all her musician friends. Ginny had snagged a few of them over the years. On more than one occasion, Margot had awoken to a hungover bando in her kitchen, helping himself to the coffee.

For ages, Ginny had been like a sister. When Margot had moved to Portland with Kevin, Ginny was not far behind. She was one of the only people from Margot's old life who knew her for the surly little punk she used to be. Time had changed Ginny into someone unrecognizable, though. Time had changed them both.

Outside the window, the show went on. People in suits rushed past, late leaving work, dreading the wrath of a spouse upon returning home. A couple of perennially drunk people fought with each other, a hunched man with a shopping cart full of bottles shuffled by, and the paintings in the galleries across the street glowed in their own tiny spotlights.

When a waiter finally wandered over to Margot's table she ordered another drink, despite the risk. The term lightweight had taken on new meaning since she'd barely eaten in the past year. The drink was good, though, and the alcohol was beginning to have its intended effect. The red pleather seat emitted an indelicate noise as Margot relaxed in her booth. Her limbs felt disconnected, her consciousness dimmed enough to dull the anguish.

Suddenly, an angry woman stormed past the bar; tears streaked her pretty face. She was followed by a big guy. It was the same man Margot had seen standing outside the tattoo shop earlier. He called to the furious woman plaintively, his expression alarmed, his words muffled by the bar window. The woman turned on him and yelled, then shoved him aggressively. He tried to reach out and pat her arm, but she flung it away, said something else, and with a last nasty glare, she stomped off.

As the woman left, Margot noticed the man's posture deflate. His expression transformed as sorrow washed over him. As he turned back toward the tattoo shop he chanced a glance upwards, inadvertently meeting Margot's gaze. Margot's own sadness must have showed, for he was her mirror in that moment. Then he was gone.

A feeling she hadn't experienced in ages welled up within Margot. It was gratitude. Even though it hadn't been forever like she'd prayed and hoped it would be, her relationship with Kevin had been peaceful, loving, and respectful. Had she taken it for granted that everyone could be so kind? The gratitude was a welcome change from her usual gnawing grief, and she reveled in it for as long as she could, allowing it to momentarily warm the frozen recesses of her heart.

Not long after, she threw back the remainder of her drink, paid her tab, and left. A lonely electric guitar strummed out a haunting melody from somewhere above as Margot stood outside the bar. She took a breath of sea air and looked around. The tattoo shop was dark inside, but its presence lingered with her as she walked home, filling her thoughts with images in dark ink, their patterns swirling and connecting through her mind like living things.

As she entered her house and locked the door behind her, the delusion of gratitude still clung to her like gossamer. She almost called out in greeting, but the truth wrapped its cold tendrils around her heart, aborting the "Hello" before it left her throat.

Grief hit Margot so hard it knocked the wind out of her. She struggled for breath as she staggered into the foyer, her heels scrabbling unsteadily on the marble floor, echoing lonely in the cavernous dark.

Margot sank to the floor and was swallowed up by the chill stone beneath her. It was never supposed to be like this.

TWO

Cassidy stormed away and Chase wondered what he'd done to deserve this. She was a nightmare. How had he been lured in? How had he missed that she was a total train wreck? Cassidy had dated him because of what she thought he was, not because of who he actually was. With his tattoos and his lifestyle, he fit in with her idea of a cool boyfriend. She had never bothered to look any deeper. Frankly, neither had he. She was hot and flirty, so he'd asked her out. It represented an unfortunate pattern in Chase's recent love life. Was he so emotionally fucked up that he couldn't see the truth about people until it was too late?

He turned back toward the shop, and as he did so, he caught the gaze of a woman sitting in the window booth at the bar. She had been outside his shop earlier. It was the same woman; Chase was sure of it. From her high perch, she'd been watching him fight with Cassidy. She'd seen the whole exchange, and from her expression, she understood how much it hurt. Chase couldn't bear the deep sadness in her eyes. For some reason, it made him feel ashamed.

Back in the tattoo shop, he cleaned up a few things Cassidy

had knocked over in her rage. When the place was presentable once more, he locked the front door from inside and turned off the lights. He grabbed his sketch book from the cluttered steel desk as he walked past it and headed up the back stairs.

Thankfully, business was pumping lately, even if his personal life was a disaster. Tattoo culture in Portland had taken off in the last couple of years and he was building a following. More and more people knew his work. Wasn't that what he'd wanted all this time? To be an artist and make a living at it? Then why wasn't it making him happy?

Chase grabbed a beer from the fridge, turned on his amp, and sat on the wide ledge in the front windows, trying not to think of how Cassidy had used him. How was he supposed to avoid that kind of shallow, meaningless relationship? The last time he'd been with someone real, someone he loved, he'd been eviscerated. The pain hadn't been worth it in the end, but a series of meaningless short-term relationships weren't satisfying either. What did he even want in a relationship? In a woman?

Playing guitar made him feel better, only until he thought about the state his band was in. There was so much fighting, so many disagreements, all revolving around Bryce. He'd been such a promising drummer when Chase had met him two years ago, but his behavior was spiraling in direct proportion to his drug use. The band wasn't going to last, and Chase found himself on the precipice of change once more. It was always uncomfortable.

Chase dreaded the process of starting a new band, or a new relationship, for that matter. He always seemed to float along on someone else's momentum with these things. He needed to be more purposeful, more intentional with his desires, but people always sucked him into their own stories, their own projects. Chase was too good natured, or maybe too weak to resist. It was depressing to think of himself as a weak person. Did he crave connection so badly? He'd never learned to discern whether the connections he forged were worthwhile. Then he got hurt, again and again. It was a shitty cycle.

Chase played a song he'd written a few months ago but had never shared with the guys. No punk rock band would play a song like this. It was sad and sweet and had too many of his early musical influences in it. His dad had loved Simon and Garfunkel. Their melodies and harmonies had infiltrated Chase's musical language early on. He could find traces of them in almost everything he wrote, despite having told his dad he hated them. As a teen, he'd stomped up to his room, slammed the door, and blasted The Decedents in direct defiance of his dad's musical preferences. By that time, Chase had tuned out everything his dad tried to share with him. They fought constantly. It nauseated Chase to think about now.

His dad would have liked this song, though. It was musical and complex. He sang some words softly, wishing for a person to sing the harmony with.

From high above the street, Chase watched the sidewalk below as the lady from the window left the bar. For a moment she paused, as though she was listening, before moving on. Then, she strode away with a steady and purposeful gate, and she didn't look back. Her tiny solitary form moved down the darkened street and disappeared, leaving Chase and his memories and his music behind.

Eventually, he made a burrito out of leftover meat and veggies from the night before and ate a quiet dinner. As usual, he sketched as he ate. When he realized what he'd been drawing, however, it jarred him. It was her. The lady from the window. There she was, sitting too close to the glass, a pale contrast to the shadows around her. The window framed her, dark space surrounded her, while she was suffused with light. He'd sketched a wreath of flowers around the window, encircling it lovingly in lilies, roses, and carnations. Like all his drawings, it was a little memorial to a perfect moment, lost in time.

Chase was about to get sucked down an unwelcome vortex of memory. He knew this sensation well. Best to end it before it went too far. For a moment, he traced his finger thoughtfully along the edge of the drawing before closing the sketchbook firmly. No good ever came from him dwelling on the past. It was time to move on.

THREE

Kevin's job offer at the Portland Medical Center had been the best bit of news. He'd come home to their tiny Cambridge apartment beaming. Margot had been engrossed in making dinner and wasn't expecting anything out of the ordinary. The moment she saw Kevin's expression, however, she knew something was up.

"What is it, babe?" Margot had asked him cheerfully, wiping her hands on a dishtowel.

"Portland."

"You got Portland?" she squealed. "That's incredible. Congratulations!"

Kevin picked her up and swung her around, right there in the kitchen. He'd applied for jobs as a cardiac surgeon all over the northeast, but Portland had been their first choice. It was city enough to feel cosmopolitan, and small enough to raise a family safely.

"I'm so proud of you, Kev," Margot said once her feet were back on the floor. "You did it."

"We did it. I couldn't have gotten through even half of this without you." He snuck a grape tomato out of the salad she'd been making and popped it into his mouth. Then, he grinned wide.

"I'll send my applications out as soon as I can," Margot said, playfully slapping his hand away from the bowl before he could grab another tomato. "I've already figured out which firms I'd fit in with, granted there aren't too many to begin with, but I can always start my own eventually if I'm not happy."

"You know you won't have to work, Margot." Kevin never wanted her to feel pressured.

"I want to. I really do. It's part of how I make meaning in the world."

Kevin sidled up to her, put his hands around her waist and asked sweetly, "What if we have a family?"

"Then I'll reconsider," she said.

"Okay." He kissed her on the head and grabbed a bottle of champagne from the fridge. As he uncorked the bottle he asked, "Should we drive up and scope out the housing scene this weekend?" Kevin's excitement was infectious.

"Definitely. I love you, babe. So proud of you."

"I love you too."

A realtor had shown them several crappy houses, and Margot was analyzing how much money and time a gut job would take when the realtor said, "I have one more to show you but it's in a higher price range than you're looking at."

"Can't hurt," said Kevin.

The moment they'd walked into the bright, airy house in Portland's West End, Kevin said, "This is it. It's so close to the hospital I can walk."

"It's too much, Kevin," Margot had countered, even though she loved the place. The accountant side of her brain was doing the math. Payments would be high. She'd grown up in a middleclass house in the suburbs, so this would be a major splurge.

"We've worked so hard for this, sweetheart. We can afford it now."

Margot knew how much Kevin wanted it, so she couldn't say no. Besides, sunlight flooded the space all day through tall Italianate windows, antique woodwork adorned every doorway and mantel. It was her very own palace.

As soon as they'd settled in, Margot said, "This feels like home. I love it."

"I love *you*," Kevin answered, his eyes full of desire for her. They made love in almost every room in the house, for good measure.

For nearly seven years, Margot and Kevin loved everything about their home. They loved their life together. They loved their marriage. Though Kevin's schedule was grueling, Margot hadn't minded. She worked hard as well, bringing work home with her when she knew he'd be gone for a long surgical rotation. When they were together, though, everything else disappeared. Kevin focused on her, babied her, gave her everything of himself. He was fully present when he was present. Margot was thrilled to be the object of his deep adoration.

Waking up now, with the freezing marble floor against her cheek, against her breasts, against her legs, taken by a cold so bone-deep she could barely move, Margot remembered crying herself to sleep on the foyer floor the night before with revulsion. Kevin would be appalled at her inability to get a grip. To control herself. To move on.

Standing unsteadily, she leaned against the empty foyer table, where flowers had always graced their entryway, and gazed up the elegantly curved stairway. Only a warm bath would help, so she made her way to the second floor. Twenty minutes later, Margot was marginally warmer, enveloped in a hot, soapy, fragrant bath. She closed her eyes to the elegant marble-tiled walls of the bathroom and tried to clear her mind. Her arms floated away from her body as she breathed in and out, drawing comfort from the warmth of the water. The problem was, all she could envision were Kevin's hands on her slippery body, his weight against her, as they'd made love in the extravagant tub.

They'd chosen the bathroom tiles on a sunny Saturday afternoon. Margot was shocked at the price they were quoted, but Kevin's income as a surgeon was astronomical. It seemed too luxurious, but everything in their new life had seemed that way at first. Little by little, Margot acclimated to their lifestyle. Her job at the accounting firm was lucrative as well, although not in the stratosphere of Kevin's income.

Margot's mind was made for numbers, her boss Jim told her, looking mystified at her neatly ordered spreadsheets. Margot spotted patterns easily and had therefore pinpointed the discrepancies in spending that led to investigations, illuminating fraudulent actions by high-up people in big companies her firm represented. Her talents resulted in the firing of more than one heavyweight, sweaty-faced, incredulous man who couldn't believe his life had been ruined by a petite, towheaded, blue-eyed angel like Margot.

Numbers had always been a refuge in her mind, so to keep herself from dwelling on the memory of Kevin's fit, muscled body against her own, she softly recited the list of prime numbers as far as she could remember. "…131, 137, 139, 149, 151, 157, 163, 167, 173, 179…" The audacious clattering of her alarm clock in the adjacent bedroom jolted her from this numerical meditation. Rising from the bath, her body steaming in the cool morning air, Margot stepped out of the tub. Shrouded by fog, she moved across the bathmat with soap bubbles still clinging to her, a matrix of distended iridescent circles against her alabaster skin. She took her towel down from the rod and wiped them away.

"…181, 191, 193, 197, 199…" she continued, ignoring the panic threatening to bubble up and consume her once more.

In the walk-in closet, Margot glanced up at the box containing the lace. It hung there in constellation with the other objects of her past, out of reach. Driving it from her mind, Margot returned her attention to her wardrobe. From an array of neutral, stylish clothes, she chose an oyster-colored top, a pale rose pencil skirt, and nude heels.

Dressing automatically, she forcibly ignored the dissipation of any curvature her body once had, as the skirt slid too far down her hips. She cinched her belt one hole tighter than usual to keep it from falling down all together. As she applied her make-up, light pink blush masked the translucent pallor her skin had taken on, mascara made her large, sapphire-blue eyes look marginally less haunted, and a tinted gloss brought her lips back to life. At the very least, Margot hoped she wouldn't frighten clients away.

Margot made coffee, grabbed her travel mug, her handbag, and her light jacket, and headed out the door.

Despite the fact she wasn't meeting Ginny, Margot stopped by the bar once more on her way home from work. It forestalled the inevitable slide into frozen despair at least, so this time she stayed for three drinks. The comings and goings at the bar were even more distracting than her work had been that day, and certainly more entertaining. Courtship rituals transpired in full view of the world. Girls flirted with guys who were flirting with the bartenders, who were fed up and desperately wanted their shifts to end. Men in tight jeans and ironic t-shirts leaned against the wall, women with heavily outlined eyes and full pouty lips sat on high stools.

A woman at the bar loudly complained of her ex-boyfriend's hours working, how he never paid attention to her, how he hadn't even fought to keep her when she'd dumped him. It was the same woman who had harassed the guy outside the tattoo shop the evening before. Even without knowing the couple, it was obvious the tattoo guy was a gentle, kind person, while this chick at the bar was a raging bitch. Fury at the woman rose up in Margot. Maybe it was the scotch talking, but Margot was consumed with the urge to kick the woman's ass. Ten years ago, punk rock Margot would have.

Eventually, the woman slammed her empty glass on the bar

and stormed out the door, her friends' eyes wide as they watched her go. Margot was glad to see her leave. A moment later, however, Margot's seat in the window booth afforded her the perfect view to a dramatic new scene outside. The guy from the tattoo parlor had chosen the worst possible moment to walk out of his shop. He marched headlong into an argument with the irate, and now drunk, woman. This time she got violent, shoving the guy and hitting his chest.

Margot snatched her purse up from the seat beside her, took two twenties from her wallet and left them on the table under her glass. Outside, she dove into the fray as the woman pounded her fists against the man's broad chest and beautiful face, shouting obscenities.

"You fucking asshole. You're in love with Alicia. I know it!"

"Stop, Cassidy," he said, straining to stay calm, his arms up, protecting his head from her blows. "You don't know what you're talking about. I already told you I'm not in love with anyone. Stop it. You're making a scene. Again."

Boldly, Margot inserted herself between Cassidy and her target. As aggressively as she could, she shouted at the woman, "Enough. Go home before you get yourself arrested."

"Who the fuck are you?" Cassidy demanded, her voice raw, her cheeks red from her exertions.

"I'm nobody. I just don't want to see you end up in jail for assault."

"Are *you* sleeping with him now? You fucking whore!" Cassidy turned her fists on Margot, who, though shocked, effectively dodged the first punch. The second, however, she took square on the mouth. The force of the blow knocked Margot backwards into the man's arms. Gently but swiftly, he guided her away from Cassidy and moved his own body between the women. He thrust his arms out to the sides protectively, shielding Margot.

"That's enough," he yelled, finally raising his commanding voice. He removed his phone from his back pocket. "I'm calling the police now, Cassidy. That's the final straw. You can't go assaulting strangers on the street."

Cassidy, her pretty features contorted in rage, finally realized she was in trouble. She spat on the ground at Margot's feet, turned around, and staggered away.

"Shit," the guy said, putting his phone back in his pocket and turning around to survey Margot's split lip. He reached for her, but she backed away from him with eyes wide, unwilling to let him touch her again. His expression registered shock at Margot's reaction, but she ignored it. Blood trickled from the cut and onto the front of her blouse, the crimson spatter a gory contrast to the elegant material.

"I am so sorry that happened. Why did you get involved? She nailed you," he said, looking miserably at Margot's lip.

"What is wrong with you?" Margot shouted, still full of adrenaline. "Why would you let anyone treat you like that? She's out here all the time fighting with you." Pointing to the bar, Margot said, "She was in there, talking shit about you, and all you do is stand there. Tell her to fuck off!"

Margot shocked herself with the force of her rant. Where was all this coming from? Was it the scotch? She bent unsteadily to grab her purse from the sidewalk where it had fallen, then she straightened up and started to walk away. She needed to go home. To clear her head. To sleep it off.

"At least come in so I can clean you up or get you some ice or something," the man said, his voice full of concern.

"Thanks, I'm good," Margot said, through the iron tang of blood in her mouth. The throbbing pain of the cut was exhilarating, although the sight of blood was making her a little woozy.

Margot took a couple more steps away, trying to hide the wobble in her ankles, when she heard the man say softly, "Thanks for trying to help. Cassidy is unstable, you know. I only realized it after we went out a couple of times. I ended things a few weeks ago, but she's still furious."

Margot hesitated and turned to him, ready to scold him again. Instead, she stood frozen, scrutinizing his lost expression. It was so unexpected. Tall and broad-chested, he was certainly over six feet tall, but his dark, expressive eyes held a deep sadness, as though this was only the latest in a long line of troubles.

He was so handsome, so magnetic, Margot knew he wouldn't have much trouble finding another woman. She was glad Cassidy was gone and hoped he'd find someone nice next time. After this long moment, Margot felt awkward for staring at him, so she turned away quietly, and resumed her pace.

"Please, let me give you some ice," the guy reiterated, catching up to her easily and taking her by the elbow.

"I'm fine." Margot shook her arm loose. Then, noting his pained look at her rebuff she said, "You're bleeding too, you know."

He looked unsure whether or not to laugh. "Listen," he began once more. "Come in for a minute. I don't even know your name."

Margot looked him dead in the eyes, her gaze unwavering despite being utterly unsettled. "Fine," she said and followed the man into the tattoo shop. She gazed around in wonder as he rifled through the contents of a messy drawer in an antique, green metal desk. There were pictures everywhere and ink bottles lining shelves and equipment she didn't recognize but could guess the purpose of. The place was cluttered but somehow immaculate at the same time. It was comfortable. Margot was glad there were no customers.

A moment later, the guy walked over to her. He was wearing black nitrile tattoo gloves and holding sterile packaged gauze in one hand and a plastic baggie in the other.

"Here," he said, offering the gauze to Margot. She unwrapped it absently, her gaze gravitating back to the surrounding space. Images of tattoos festooned every wall and covered most of the ceiling. Color photographs of arms, legs, backs, breasts, and buttocks plastered all available surfaces. Some of the tattoos were colorfully decorated, some lay in stark, contrasting designs. Every conceivable combination of colors and patterns had been rendered.

The man returned once more with the plastic baggie, which was now filled with ice, and reached it out towards her.

"May I?" he asked politely.

Margot hesitated. Her heartrate increased. She was ready to bolt. Instead, she fought the urge to run and accepted his offer of ice. "Okay."

Gently, the man put one hand behind her head while with the other he held the ice against her split lip. Despite his imposing presence and rather enormous size, especially up close, he was tender and thoughtful. Margot knew he would be.

Margot's lip stopped bleeding, but the throbbing had increased in intensity. It was like being alive for the first time in recent memory. The sensation terrified her.

As she was about to pull away from him, the man asked, "What's your name?"

"Margot."

"I'm Chase Goodwin. It's a pleasure to meet you, Margot. I'm sorry for Cassidy's behavior."

"Why are you sorry? She's not a marionette. It's not your fault she hit me." Margot shifted uncomfortably, her head still in his confident hands.

"I'm sorry you got hurt." He looked sorry.

"It's not that big a deal," Margot muttered. "Is this your shop?"

"Yeah. I bought the whole building about fifteen years ago and I live right upstairs."

"This real estate is worth something now. Ever think of selling?"

"Why, are you a real estate agent?" he asked, chuckling.

"Nope," Margot said. "Just curious."

"Saving for retirement has never been a big part of the tattoo industry, so this building is my retirement plan. I'll sit on it for another twenty years then sell it and retire. That is if I don't get tendonitis first."

"Are these all your designs?" Margot asked, gesturing to the ceiling and walls.

"A lot of them are." Chase sat up a little straighter. "I rent space to other tattooers too. I've got two part-time guys and a gal in here a few days a week. Helps pay the bills."

"Oh."

Chase's breath feathered against her chest and neck as he talked, still holding her, still pressing the ice to her lip. His muscles were taut beneath his form-fitting black t-shirt, his forearms were full of colorful stories. The dark stubble on his cheeks highlighted his features. His eyes were large, almond-shaped, and a deep, warm brown. He was close enough for her to smell him. Too close. She tried her hardest not to think about it.

Chase was indeed very good looking. A thin line of blood had dried along his cheekbone where Cassidy had caught his skin with her ring in one of her flailing punches. Seeing his blood was worse than seeing her own. Light headed again, she breathed in and out with intention, trying desperately to steady herself. She shifted and forced herself to look away. She never should have accepted his offer of kindness.

"I'm sorry, Margot," he said, releasing her. "I don't mean to make you so uncomfortable."

"It's okay. I'm fine. I should go."

"Husband's probably worried," Chase stated, glancing at her hand, where the enormous diamond in her engagement ring glittered anemically in the neon light.

Unsure whether to correct him or avoid his assumption all together, Margot said, "That would be impossible."

Standing up to leave, Margot caught the bewildered expression on Chase's fine features, but she wasn't about to clarify. This had gone on quite long enough.

From the door she gazed back. "Good luck."

"You too. See you around. I'll buy you a drink next time."

Margot didn't answer and she didn't look back. For one moment she paused before she pushed open the glass and metal shop door and walked out into the night air, accompanied by a tinkling of bells. Confronting Cassidy had been a momentary resurgence of her pre-Kevin feistiness. It had felt powerful. She'd been a little punk rocker, after all, in what now seemed like someone else's life. The few fights she'd been in over the years, mostly with idiots who'd groped her or Ginny, played like scratchy films of someone else, someone stronger, in her mind. But the memories were hers.

Cassidy's fist connecting with her lip had reminded Margot that she hadn't always been this reserved, classy accountant. She had been young and wild and creative. What a refreshing thought. With her lip still pulsing painfully, and the taste of blood lingering between her teeth, Margot smiled all the way home.

———

Margot's tiny frame was instantly absorbed by the darkness outside as she left. Chase's stomach tightened. She was an enigma. What could have possessed her to rush from the bar to intervene in a fight between strangers? Why had she flinched when he'd touched her? Her eyes, the richest shade of blue he'd ever seen, were haunted. Who was she?

Margot's pearls had glowed luminous against her slender throat. Her fine-boned hands had fidgeted uncomfortably as he'd tended to her lip. Her high cheekbones and flawless swan-soft skin, combined with her pale gold hair, were ethereal. She was dressed elegantly, as though her clothes were an extension of her physical charms.

Chase couldn't help but notice her extraordinary beauty, but there was so much more to her than the elegant, reserved façade.

An unexpected undercurrent of intensity had erupted from her like hot lava as she'd dove between him and Cassidy. It had shocked him into silence for a second, as he'd observed the instant transformation. She'd sworn. She'd chastised him vehemently for putting up with Cassidy's bullshit. She was right, too. He shouldn't be so patient with Cassidy's outbursts. They needed to stop. Maybe this would do the trick.

Livid crimson blood had spattered from Margot's lip onto her fine blouse. It had caused Chase serious physical discomfort and he couldn't figure out why it had tied him in knots. As a tattooer, he was used to handling blood. He blotted people's blood all day long as he drove tiny needles into their skin. Somehow, Margot's blood seemed different. It had been akin to watching a child bleed. His stomach had dropped, and his heart had twisted at the sight. The effect she had on him was surprisingly physical and intense.

Chase turned his attention back to the shop. He hadn't fully finished cleaning up after his last customer yet. He'd stepped outside to get some air when Cassidy had confronted him, drunken accusations flying like bullets. He'd known she had a wild streak from the first moment they met, but the way it had manifested into full-blown insanity over the short course of their relationship had honestly shocked him. She was so much more volatile than he'd expected. In retrospect, he wished he'd steered clear, but wishing wouldn't alter the past. If only.

Cassidy had watched her friend get a tattoo one afternoon and had flirted with him mercilessly the whole time. She was witty and good looking and he'd been drawn in. Then, she came to him a week later and said, "Have your way with me."

"What do you mean?" he'd asked, in shock.

"Draw whatever tattoo you like. Whatever you think suits me."

What a turn-on. Chase couldn't resist.

"Where do you want it?" he asked, going with the double entendre.

Seductively, Cassidy had pulled down the loose collar of her t-shirt over her arm, pointed to her shoulder, and said, "Right here."

Chase knew exactly what to draw. He did a quick sketch, showed it to her, and waited for her response. The drawing was a prowling tigress with a rose in her teeth.

"Prrr-fect," Cassidy growled.

The full color design took two visits to finish. By the end of the second session, Cassidy had sunk her claws in. Chase took her out for drinks afterwards and they made out in the booth. After that, he'd been out with her twice more. Once for dinner and a rock show, the other time at a mutual friend's birthday party. That night, when Cassidy got drunk, she turned on him when she saw him talking to his friend Sheila, the bartender from the bar next door to his shop. Sheila was a stunner, and while Chase knew she was a lesbian and married, Cassidy didn't.

"You fucker," she yelled, wedging herself between him and Sheila.

"Woah, Cassidy. What's up?" he said, mystified.

"You're flirting with her, but you're here with me." Cassidy's eyes looked unfocused but furious and she was swaying slightly. "You're a bastard like all the rest."

"Don't get nasty," he said, trying to stay calm. "I'm only talking to my friend Sheila. Sheila, this is Cassidy. Cassidy, this is Sheila."

"You slut," Cassidy yelled at Sheila. "You're trying to steal him from me."

Sheila's laugh, genuine, clear, and bright, rang out. Her dark curls and mahogany skin were radiant in the candlelight of the party. "You're crazy. Go home, honey. Chase is all mine tonight." She draped her long, athletic arm over his shoulders and when Chase turned to see what she was doing, Sheila kissed him fully on the lips.

If Sheila had kept her razor sharp sense of humor under wraps, maybe Cassidy would have let it go. Instead, it was napalm on the flames. She went wild. The disaster ended with Cassidy being dragged away by friends and escorted home. Chase was mortified.

Sheila laughed endlessly. "You really know how to pick 'em, buddy," she said, patting him on the back. "She's a true nut job."

"Looks like it. I've only been out with her a couple of times. What a disaster. You didn't help, by the way."

"Are you kidding? I did you a huge favor and you know it." Sheila winked at him. "Thank me later with a free session."

When the shop was finally clean, Chase headed next door to see if Sheila was working. She'd want to hear the latest installment in the Cassidy saga. He turned off the lights to the shop and headed next door to the bar.

Sheila looked tired. She mustered a smile when she noticed him at the bar, and she brought him a beer. "Keep it local," she said, setting down a Battery Steele Flume. It was a double IPA, and it would do the trick.

"Thanks, Sheila. Long night?"

"The longest. You look roughed up. What the hell happened? Tiger get you?" Sheila's eyes danced with mirth.

"You heard."

"Chase, everyone has heard by now. Man, Cassidy is something else. I heard some prissy gal came out and broke it up between you guys."

"Yeah. Then Cassidy punched her in the face," Chase said, slumping a bit, leaning his elbow on the bar. "What a fucking nightmare."

"I know. Cassidy had been in here fueling up before she headed next door. I would have warned you, but I didn't know she'd go that far." Sheila might have felt a touch of remorse, for her gaze met his. For a moment, her humorous façade slipped away. They shared something honest and sad before another customer interrupted by ordering a beer.

"If you see Cassidy in here again, text me, please. I can't have her bursting into my shop and fucking with me while I work."

"Will do," said Sheila. She nodded her head as she poured the beer. "What else is going on?"

"Nada. Just drawing, playing guitar. You know. Wasting my time."

"Your art and music are anything but a waste of time."

"Thanks, but things are falling apart with the band." Chase shook his head.

"Bryce looked like shit last time I saw him," Sheila added, shaking her head sadly.

"Yeah. He's out of control. None of us can get through. He needs a long stint in rehab, otherwise he's going to end up on the street or dead. What a waste."

"You need a new band. Some fresh people to play with." Sheila idly polished the bar.

"I know, but everyone's so young. They think the dawn of punk was Cake."

"Jesus." Sheila rolled her eyes. "They'd best spend some time in here. I'll school 'em."

"Great. I'll send the whippersnappers your way." Chase finished his beer, lay a ten on the counter, and said, "See you soon."

"Later, Chase. Stay out of trouble, would you?"

"Never."

FOUR

What was pain but an electrochemical response to stimulus? The memory of her lip being split wide open in a brawl still elicited a swoop of excitement in her stomach a week later, leading Margot inevitably to wonder what a more sustained kind of pain would do. Would it bring her back to life like a defibrillator? Would it be aberrant behavior for her some-day therapist to analyze? Did she even remotely care? Only masochists wanted other people to hurt them. Was she a masochist? That didn't seem right either. She wasn't sure what she wanted, but the pain, the glorious pain of having her face punched, had lit a fuse inside her. She needed to feel something again. She needed to feel alive.

During every moment she wasn't working, Margot mused on pain, emotional and physical. She'd experienced enough emotional and physical pain for ten lifetimes, but this new kind of pain was different. The physical agony of the car accident had been so linked to the emotional anguish of loss that it was debilitating. Combined, those twin pains had overloaded Margot's circuitry, resulting in a total shutdown. It had been eleven months, one week and two days since her life, as she'd known it, ended. Now, approaching a year later, Margot could sense a shift. The crushing tsunami of anguish she'd been decimated by was receding back into the unpredictable sea of life's experiences, an anomaly of timing. A tragedy.

The devastation of her entire world, as surveyed from the survivor's perspective, had left her with a jaded vision of all she'd been foolish enough to take for granted. The solidity, the permanence, the expectations were all ephemeral and so dubious she wondered how she'd gone over thirty years without noticing. It was all a sham.

But now what?

That question haunted her. *Now what?* What was she supposed to do, now that she saw the darkness below life's beautiful façade? What was she supposed to do with her own survival? Nothing had pierced the thick layer of ice covering her heart. Nothing, that is, until Cassidy's fist had flown, unhindered, through the molecules of air between them, landing with a solid, physical blow, and shattering the frozen woman before her. What was left now that the ice had finally cracked?

The tattoo shop haunted Margot as much as the swollen lip, which she'd explained at work with complete and utter honesty, eliciting obvious shock from her few colleagues. She could have said she'd fallen. She could have said her heel had caught in the brick sidewalk and she'd landed on her face. It was plausible, no one would have questioned her, given the state of the bricks in Portland.

But why lie?

The truth was so much better. It gave purchase to the idea of pain as a way forward when no other had presented itself in a year. Each time she described Chase, the photographs in his shop surrounding her like a gallery of possibilities, the ice he'd pressed to her wound, each time she relived that moment, the first moment of *life* in a year, she could feel his breath on her chest and the cold on her mouth and the raw sting of the cut like it was happening now. The same way Margot had relived the accident for months afterwards in an endless loop of horror, she now fixed her mind on the tattoo shop, longing once more for a glimpse into its unfamiliar depths. But it was not her world.

From the window booth at the bar, Margot watched the street, night after night. Nothing interesting had happened since and Margot almost wished for another incident. She wanted another fight. Maybe it was an addiction, this longing for pain, for some kind of brutal contact, and she was in withdrawal. As the days passed, the frost encroached once more upon newly thawed territory. Terror that she would be sucked into lassitude once more shook her deeply.

Forlorn, she sipped her single drink, paid her small tab, and left. As she stepped out from the bar, Chase appeared at the door of his shop, his timing uncanny. Margot tried not to show her surprise.

"Margot," he said, his voice gentle and deep, his eyes unfathomable. "Your lip looks better."

"It was better almost immediately. You don't seem permanently scarred either."

"Not this time," he quipped.

Margot grasped her purse tightly and her pulse raced. She wanted to ask Chase a question, but she hadn't thought it through and wasn't sure what she even wanted for an answer. She steeled her nerve anyway. "May I talk to you about something?" Her gaze was intense, her eyes wide.

"Sure. Wanna come in?" Chase gestured behind him into the well-lit shop. There were people inside, a tattoo artist and a patron, both nearly covered with ink, laughing and talking easily.

Margot glanced in, already feeling out of place in her crisp white oxford and flared linen chinos. Her expensive heels and matching handbag could not have been more incongruous to the chaotic, vibrant space behind Chase. Expectantly, he waited for her answer.

"You know what? It's okay. Never mind."

Margot walked away from him, having lost her nerve all together.

"Good night, Margot," he called after her.

She kept walking, berating herself for her extreme lack of daring, as her inner frost encroached ever further, threatening to turn her heart once more to ice.

What did she want from him, exactly? Was she going to ask about getting a tattoo? What would she even put on her body, were she to acquire a tattoo? A gaudy heart and dagger or flashy stylized flowers were too absurd to entertain. She was an accountant. She'd had a hard time putting color into her home décor, let alone permanently onto her flesh. Besides, her skin was so pale it would look ridiculous to have this one bright image standing out against the rest of her starkly white body. No illustration could represent her identity, her love, or her history well enough to engrave it into her skin.

And yet, the gravitational draw of a tattoo began to consume her. Pain manifested into art, scars into beauty. Margot couldn't deny the appeal. But what? Could Chase tattoo invisible designs on her skin? A matrix of interwoven marks only she could sense? Only she could feel? He would think she was crazy.

As she walked home, the few stars she could see through the city's ambient light appeared, making her feel more alone than she had since Cassidy's assault. Understanding that humans are meaningless in the grand design of the universe, a thought she'd come back to again and again this past year, echoed in her mind. *You don't matter at all*, it mocked her, night after endless night.

Kevin hadn't possessed her inclination toward speculative thinking. Black and white, his philosophy had left little room for conjecture. He looked for answers, definitively, and was willing to work hard for them. This was part of what made him such a gifted heart surgeon.

"What about the patterns in nature? The Fibonacci Sequence, for instance?" Margot had asked one evening as they sat on their terrace, basking in the glory of the deepening night sky.

"Is that the spiral one?" Kevin took a sip of his wine.

"Yes. The mathematical pattern of the spiral. 1, 1, 2, 3, 5, 8, 13, 21, and so on. Take the last addend and add it to the sum to find the next number in the sequence. One plus two is three, two plus three is five... Mapped out on paper the numbers create a perfect spiral." She traced a spiral against the sky with her finger.

"Right. You know I never had a mind for math like you do, sweetie."

"It's not from my math mind, Kevin. It's one of the greatest discoveries in history. The pattern is extrapolated out from the minutest of electron trails to the widest of galaxies. The spirals are all represented by the same formula."

"It's pretty cool." Kevin leaned back against the cushion and stretched out his legs.

"Yes it's *cool*, but what do you think it *means* that nature can have these grand patterns repeating themselves?" she had pressed, leaning forward and staring at him.

"It doesn't mean anything," Kevin said, suppressing a yawn. "It's a given, is all."

"All right, what about the mind? How do you explain consciousness, Mr. Fancy Doctorpants? There's no physical explanation for that." Her tone was playful, but she was annoyed at the same time, taking his disinterest as flippancy, rather than what she now suspected it was: a void of creative thought, of philosophical spirit, of imagination.

"Mr. Fancy Doctorpants has had a long day. Come on over here." Pouting, she'd abandoned her unanswered question, supplanted too easily by the prospect of intimacy. Kevin was an attentive lover. He fed her body and her heart, if not her curiosity, and it had always been enough. Their lovemaking was playful and tender and frequent. It had kept them close and sustained their connection. Kevin may not have nurtured her inner philosopher, but her body never once complained.

Now, reconsidering her initial question about the meaning behind patterns in nature, Margot walked alone beneath the meager offering of stars. Kevin was probably right after all. What divine plan could have devised such a miserable, devastating end to life as the one she'd lost all hope of love to? Patterns weren't proof of anything other than the math they represented. At least numbers couldn't lie. Maybe she'd tattoo Phi on her wrist and be done with it.

FIVE

As she awoke to a thin morning glow, Margot ran her hands up and down her chilly arms. The pale light streaming softly through the lace bedroom curtains produced a noticeable design on Margot's skin. The image jarred her sleep-dulled mind into full consciousness and nagged her until the full memory presented itself. The light patterns on her body reminded her of draping her bridal veil over her arm. Sadness crept into her heart as she pictured it, ivory lace on ivory skin, glowing together as one. The designs of the lace were so elemental to her psyche, so central to her history, they already felt like a part of her body. Putting the veil away had been necessary, for she'd been obsessing over it, but now Margot reconsidered.

As Margot moved her hand once more through the shaft of broken sunlight, the patterns on her skin shifted. They were the comparatively boring designs of mass-market, machine-made fabric, but as she watched them intensify with the strength of the rising sun, they brought to the surface of Margot's mind an idea that had been buried there all along. Margot sprang from her bed and cursed herself for consigning the veil nine feet above her head, on the top shelf of her closet.

After retrieving a broom from the bathroom closet, she stood on her vanity chair and held the broom aloft, poking at the edge of the box, jimmying it free from its high perch, watching it teeter precariously on the edge of the shelf before freefalling onto her head. Margot laughed aloud, and the sound of this foreign ejaculation was as jarring as the impact of the box.

The veil would be perfect. The delicate flowers, vines, and swirls, the spirals eddying into smaller spirals, the elegance of the netting beneath the design, and the way the decorations seemed to float above, the designs were so much a part of her already she could see them in all their detail in her mind's eye. Margot had found a clear trajectory and it was a beacon in dark waters. She finally had a plan.

It was Friday, and although she had never taken much advantage of the casual Friday dress code at her office, she would today. The slim jeans she dug out of her closet hung too loosely but paired with a shell pink top and rose gold chain, Margot had achieved a look she could pull off at work without attracting too much notice, while not feeling absurd on her after-work mission.

Fully dressed, Margot took the box containing the veil from her bed. Without opening it, she carried it downstairs, set it on the foyer table, poured her coffee, and prepared to leave.

No one questioned Margot about her unusual parcel, nor about her sudden inclination towards casual clothing. Even in jeans, she looked elegant. That she couldn't help. The day stretched on and on, numbers became a drudgery rather than the usual numbing agent. Her boss caught her looking distractedly out the window a bit after four.

"You all right today?" he asked. Jim Carter was a robust man, his natural demeanor with his staff ensured him both love and respect. His ruddy cheeks and rugby player's bearing were incongruous to his desk job, so he welcomed any excuse to wander the office.

"I'm fine. A little distracted." Margot smiled in a vain attempt to diffuse any further questioning.

Jim leaned against the doorframe, nearly filling it. "You know we're all here for you, Margot. Any time you need anything. It's been a horrible year for you, but it's never once showed in your work. Have you thought about taking your vacation soon? Lord knows, you've earned it."

"Vacation always sounds better than it is in reality," Margot said, fidgeting with a pen. "Besides, I like the work, Jim. You know that."

"Just an idea, kid. Why don't you cut out early?"

"Only if you do," she replied cheekily, knowing he rarely left before six.

"Touché. See you Monday."

As he left her office, Margot glanced at the clock. Maybe she would leave early. Maybe she should. As she was steeling herself for a departure from routine, her phone rang. On the other line was a client with whom Margot had spent hours trying to unravel the mysteries of the woman's late husband's accounting methodology. "Good afternoon, Mrs. Paulus. How are you?" Margot settled back into her desk chair once more, ready for a long conversation.

At five after five, Margot gathered her things, including the box, and she walked past Jim's office.

"Go home," she called, waving behind her.

"Never," he shouted after her, laughing.

The spring air was welcome after the stale fug of the office all day and Margot breathed in deeply. A smile spread across her lips as she considered her next stop. As she walked down the block, however, fear gripped her once more. What was she thinking? This was a terrible idea and she had finally lost her mind. Her pace slowed, her resolve wavered. Feeling like a defeated child, she aborted her mission and headed to the bar instead.

From the window booth, she watched the street, as she did

each night. Melancholy settled in as waves of people sloshed about like flotsam. She was about to leave when a familiar person pierced the monotony. Chase looked up at her from the sidewalk below, an uncertain smile playing at his lips. Margot looked behind her in an embarrassingly comedic move, and then met his gaze once more. She nodded her head in greeting.

This was all the invitation Chase needed. He entered the bar, chatted with the bartender as she poured his beer, and finally approached her table. Dread overrode Margot's ability to think. She shrank into herself as her remaining shreds of resolve vanished.

"My savior," Chase said with a genuine smile. He held up his glass in a toast to Margot. His dark eyes glittered in the neon light cast from the sign above.

"Hardly," Margot replied, feeling silly. She tilted her nearly empty glass towards his and they met with a clink.

"How was your week?" he asked her, leaning back in the booth. It protested beneath his mass with a squeak.

"What, are we old friends now?" Margot said, piqued.

Chase frowned, but continued. "If you'll allow me the liberty. You took my ex to task and she hasn't bothered me since. I wanted to thank you."

"You already did that," Margot replied, wishing she could be friendly instead of confrontational.

"Right. Well, you wanted to ask me something yesterday. What was it?"

Margot's composure crumbled like a Roman ruin. She wanted to run. She wanted to disperse into light. She couldn't abide the unsettling sensation of learning to trust someone new, of asking this stranger to do to her body what she longed for. Her breathing was hard, her heart fluttered frantically against her chest, and her eyes started to mist up.

Chase's expression changed. He reached forward and took her hand which lay impotently on the table. "Take your time."

Steadying her breathing, Margot took her hand back, turned

away from him, and gazed out the window. She folded her hands tightly in her lap. For a long moment she sat still, silent, considering how to proceed and coming up with nothing.

She wanted this, she reminded herself. The only reason she and Chase hadn't been talking for the last hour was that she'd chickened out and come here instead. Now, he sat before her like a gift, patiently awaiting her next move.

"I want you to tattoo me." She turned to him, her eyes wide and lost, her voice more intense, more vehement than she had intended.

"Were you nervous about asking?" he said, looking genuinely surprised.

"I've never gotten a tattoo before." Margot shifted in her seat. "I feel stupid."

"Why would you feel stupid? I tattoo people all day. It's my job. There's nothing to feel stupid about."

"Right." Margot didn't know what to say next.

"Do you have an idea of what you want?" Chase asked.

"Yes. But I can only come in the evenings after work. Are you there late?"

"It won't take more than an hour or two," Chase said, taking a sip of his beer. "Most tattoos are quicker than people think."

"Not this one," she answered softly. "Can we go next door and talk? I want to show you something."

"Sure," Chase replied. If he was perplexed, he wasn't showing it. He tipped back his glass with an ease of movement Margot envied and drank down the remainder of his beer. "Let's go."

Margot slipped out of her seat in the booth, taking her purse and the box with her. She glanced around the bar as they left together, wondering what people would think of her leaving with a man tonight. No one, absolutely no one, even looked up, let alone cared. Margot shook her head bemusedly and followed Chase out the door.

The tattoo shop hadn't changed since she'd been there.

Mercifully, it was empty of people at the moment, so Margot relaxed a little. Chase led her to a desk covered with artwork, pens, paper, pencils, and photographs of tattoos, all of which obscured an antique laptop and a forgotten cup of coffee. Chase surveyed the debris and swept some of it aside, smiling easily.

"So. What did you want to talk about?" The springs of his ancient desk chair, the polar opposite of her ergonomically correct Aeron chair, creaked and moaned as he sat down and leaned back. Margot feared the mechanism would give way beneath his brawn, landing him on his ass, but her fears proved unfounded. His smile was disarming. His teeth were white and perfectly straight.

"Like I said, I want you to tattoo me."

"Okay. You have an idea? I'm also happy to design something together. I've got like a million books. You don't seem like the flaming heart type, but correct me if I'm wrong."

"No flaming hearts, thanks," she answered, trying not to sound peevish. "I want this."

———

Margot proffered forth the box she'd clutched tightly to her chest. Laying it on the desk between them, Margot gently pulled the top off, lay it beside her on the ample chair, and drew back the layers of tissue paper. Revealed in all its antique glory was a piece of lace, folded up, looking like a museum piece.

Margot lifted it gingerly from its shroud and stretched some of the fabric over her skin. "I want you to tattoo these designs on my body."

Chase inhaled sharply, eyeing the complexity of the design. Leaning in closer, he reached forward but before he touched the lace he met Margot's haunted eyes.

"May I?" he asked reverently.

Wavering slightly, she nodded in the affirmative.

The lace looked incongruous in his masculine hands, yet he handled the fabric with the utmost care. It was soft and light, barely there, yet complex in the extreme. In its delicacy, the lace seemed too personal, almost as though he was handling her undergarment. "This is very beautiful. It's antique, right?"

"Yes," she answered in a barely audible voice.

"Where is it from?"

"Belgium. My grandmother came to America from Belgium right before the war. It was one of the only things she had from her old life."

"Belgium. I've never been there." He stood and carefully pulled the full length of the lace from the box, examining its edges and details. Thoughtful not to let the lace touch his unkempt desk, he eventually returned it to the box and sat back down.

He hesitated to say it, but he needed to be honest with her. Softly, Chase said, "Margot, I'm not sure I'm the right person for the job. This is like filigree, it's really complex and perfectly symmetrical. I mean, I'm more of a graphic designer than a fine artist."

"Oh," she said, looking crestfallen. Her disappointment just about killed him. "Sorry to bother you then." She stood abruptly and placed the lid back onto the box. Her slender hands trembled as she tucked a loose edge of the fine material back under the lid. She seemed so fragile and incredibly sad.

"You're not bothering me," Chase said, not wanting her to leave. "But I wouldn't want to mess up."

"I understand," she said softly. Her hands rested on the box lid and she met his gaze.

"I'll give you some names of tattooers who might be a better fit."

"No. I wouldn't want anyone else."

Chase was touched. He was hardly the only tattoo artist in Portland, but for some reason, Margot wanted him. "I'm flattered," he said earnestly.

"Don't be," she said, with a sharp tone, but her expression betrayed her.

Rather than let himself be hurt by her rebuff, Chase walked around the desk and looked down at her. "Hey, is everything okay?"

"I'm fine." Anger flashed in her eyes. "If you can't do the job, I won't have it done. It was a stupid idea anyway."

"It's actually a beautiful idea," he said, uncertain how best to proceed. Plagued with insecurity about his level of skill, he wondered if he could do her idea justice. He batted back his fear and said, "How about this. If you leave the lace with me, I can practice drawing it and do some designs. Then, you can make an informed decision. What do you think?"

Margot hesitated, looking down at the box. Her glance darted to the mess on his desk, the undrunk coffee, the piles of papers.

Chase intuited her inner conflict and stated, "I will treat it with the utmost care, Margot. I won't let anything happen to it."

With a deep intake of breath, she met his earnest gaze. The sensation of standing on the edge of a cliff, ready to jump, turned his stomach to jelly. Her expression softened. Something between them subtly shifted. The conversation became more intimate.

"Nothing can happen to this," she whispered. "Nothing. It's all I have left."

"You have my word."

Margot hesitantly removed her hands from the box where they had lay frozen. "Okay."

"Did you want the tattoo on your arm or your back? And what color were you thinking?"

"White. I want it to be white."

"Your skin is so fair, though. It won't show up very well."

"I know. I don't want it to show at all." Pointing to a sketch pad on his desk, she asked, "May I?"

"Sure."

She took up a pencil, flipped to a new page, and sketched the stylized outline of a torso. Upon it, she drew a deep, curved, graceful line from the clavicle down the front, between where the breasts would be, and back up the other side. Then, sketching another torso, she drew a line from mid-shoulder, dipping slightly, and back up to the other shoulder. Along the arms of both drawings, she drew a cap sleeve, dipping over the rounded part of the shoulder. The back plunged deeply. "This is what I want."

"Over your front, shoulders, and back like a shawl?"

"Yes."

"In white," he stated. It wasn't a question.

"In white."

"This is intricate." Chase drew his finger along the line she'd drawn. "It's going to take at least four longer sessions, maybe more. It might get pretty expensive."

"I don't care."

Chase looked at her intently and said, "I'm talking possibly over a thousand."

"Money is not an issue."

Chase breathed in and studied her for a moment. "Okay, Margot. I'll try."

"Thank you," she stated. In an uncharacteristically intimate gesture, Margot patted his hand which now lay protectively over the box. His eyes widened slightly as a thrill of energy pulsed through him. Unable to speak, he nodded.

As she stood up, she dug into her purse and retrieved a business card. She handed it to him and said, "Email me when you're ready."

Margot didn't look back as she left the store without the lace.

Dumbfounded, he looked after her. Who was this petite beauty who had blown into his life like a stray golden leaf? She was clearly a tortured soul, for if Chase could recognize one thing in other people, it was the sorrow they carried in their hearts. He felt for her. She was struggling with something serious, and she didn't trust him at all.

Yet *she* had come to *him* with the idea for a tattoo. Certainly, she didn't seem like the type, although he knew that was a generalization. Looking down at the lace, he wondered why it was so important to her. It had been her grandmother's. It was a family heirloom. That much was obvious, but he suspected her attachment ran deeper. The long lace rectangle was too small to be a tablecloth, but it could have been a shawl or a dresser runner. He opened the box again and passed his coarse, strong hands over the fragile designs. Their complexity was striking. Someone, long ago, had designed this lace, someone who understood symmetry and art, proportion and mathematics. It was a beautiful object in its own right, and when combined with whatever personal meaning it held for Margot, it would make a lovely tattoo. Unfortunately, he still wasn't sure he was the right guy for the job.

Before he placed the lace back in the box, he brought it closer and smelled it. The faint scent of beach roses came to him, telling of another time, long ago. The fragrance clung to the lace tenuously, and time would win out in the end, obliterating its presence entirely. Was the scent Margot's? It made him miserable to think of all the reasons she clung to this lace as desperately as the scent of roses clung to it.

Chase closed up the shop and brought the box of lace upstairs to his loft. The holophane lights hanging from the high beams above sparked to life as he flicked the switch. Margot was right, he could sell this building for a mint. All in good time.

Chase set the box down on the stainless steel kitchen island he'd reclaimed from a restaurant that had closed years before. The head chef there was a client. During a tattoo, he informed Chase the owner wanted everything that wasn't brick walls and wooden floors taken out of the restaurant the day before their lease was up. The landlord had been a tyrant and the owner wanted nothing left in the space that might be of value to him.

Chase had always been handy, so he'd built the kitchen himself from scavenged cabinetry and stainless steel, lending it a rough, industrial look that was at home in the loft.

The sun was setting, lighting up the sky behind the buildings across the street. His enormous front windows lent a perfect view of the sky each evening. Chase grabbed a beer from the fridge and sat in an old armchair near the windows. He took his guitar from its stand and played as he watched the sky change, but all he could think of was Margot's haunted eyes.

Eventually, he gave up on the song he'd been practicing and went to his drafting table. He cleaned it off with spray cleaner and retrieved a sketchbook and a fine mechanical pencil. He spread the lace out and started to draw. Rendering the complex design was every bit as challenging as he'd thought it would be. This would take some serious work to get right, but the very last thing he wished to do was disappoint the mercurial, mysterious Margot. And if there was one thing Chase could do well, it was work hard.

———

At home, Margot locked the door behind her, kicked off her heels, and headed for the kitchen where she poured herself a deep glass of Pinot Noir. The fridge was barren but for a block of cheddar. This she removed to a wooden cutting board. She cut a few slices of cheese, put them on a plate, and headed with her spoils to the terrace. The French door was swollen firmly shut. Realizing she hadn't opened it once in eleven and a half months, she set the cheese plate and wine down on the floor, grasped the door handle with both hands, and pulled with her entire body weight. After her third tug, the recalcitrant door opened, nearly knocking her off balance.

The patio furniture had not been put away last fall, but it looked nearly the same as it always had, stark black iron against the bluestone pavers, with the white of the house's antique clapboard behind. The cushions, too, had been left out, but perhaps they were meant to withstand the elements, for their muted teal also looked unaffected. Margot set her wine glass and cheese plate on the dirty, glass-topped table, leaned back against the cushion of the glider, and watched a girlish blush spread across the sky's great visage.

Sipping the wine, Margot allowed herself a rare moment of peace, daring to wonder what Chase would come up with for a design.

Margot had not wanted to wear the wedding veil. Her mother had gently reminded Margot of the veil's deep connection to her family, to her roots.

"It's so old fashioned," Margot said at her first dress fitting. Her mother had brought the veil along, despite Margot's unenthusiastic sentiment.

"It will complement your natural beauty, darling," her mom returned with a knowing smile. "Just try it on. For me."

Margot humored her mother, believing perhaps once she tried it on, her mother would see how silly it looked and leave her alone. Something unexpected and rather magical happened, however, as Margot's mother gently pinned the veil to Margot's elegant chignon. The simplicity of her pearly silk dress, contrasted with the complexity of the lace, looked nothing short of chic.

Trying to hide her widening smile, her mom turned Margot toward the mirror, tears in her eyes. Together, their twin reflections smiled back, her mother's faded, greying blonde hair nestled into Margot's spun gold, but their sparkling sapphire eyes were identical. Her mother held Margot's narrow shoulders and pressed a kiss to her cheek. All her life, Margot had loved her mother deeply and in that moment, before she too was lost, their love seemed beyond physical measure. It was too strong to classify. Like the lace, it had transcended time and had become an intricate thing of beauty all its own.

The memory of her mother was agonizing. Margot tipped

the wine glass to her lips until it was empty. The last, inert ruby droplet nestling at the bottom of the crystal globe was too depressing to contemplate. Margot lifted herself from the cushions, which had proven a little damp and musty after all, and walked back inside, turning her back once more on the ever-changing glories of the evening sky.

SIX

Chase didn't email her. Instead, he interrupted her workday with a most unexpected call.

"Margot?"

"Yes," she answered hesitantly, unsure who was on the other line.

"It's Chase. I have some designs ready for you to see. Do you have time to stop by after work?"

"I told you to email me," Margot replied sharply.

In the ensuing pause, Margot felt like an asshole for saying anything. She leaned forward, closed her eyes, and rubbed them.

"Sorry," Chase said. "You're right."

"No, I apologize. That was rude of me. It's been a long day. I can stop by after work if you're going to be around."

"Okay. See you then." Chase hung up and Margot wasn't sure how offended he was. She felt terrible.

Expectation nagged at Margot for the remaining four hours of the afternoon. Unsure how something as incongruous as a tattoo could preoccupy her so deeply, she stared out the window for the hundredth time. It seemed like a day for a walk by the ocean, rather than sitting in an office. Couldn't she walk out? Remembering Jim's remonstration, Margot boldly turned off her computer, locked away the confidential files she'd been working on, tidied her desk, and grabbed her purse.

Moments later, Margot walked into the tattoo shop. Chase looked up from the hairy leg of the large man he was tattooing and smiled at her warmly.

"Sorry," Margot said, hesitating on the threshold. "I'll come back."

"No, stay," Chase said eagerly. "I won't be long. Make yourself comfortable."

"People hang out here all the time," the other man added. "Wanna see?"

Margot had never watched someone get a tattoo before. Timidly, she approached the two men and looked down. "Oh!" she exclaimed with surprise. "That's, um, that's really..."

"Cool, right?" the man interjected.

"Yes. Cool. It's very cool."

Margot's breathing grew shallow as she watched the needle piercing the man's skin. The tattoo was of a muscle, the exact muscle beneath that portion of his leg, finely wrought with extraordinary detail. It reminded Margot of one of Kevin's illustrated medical textbooks. *Gastrocnemius, soleus, flexor hallucis longus, popliteus...* Reciting the names of muscles together had been like a bizarre form of foreplay while studying for his medical boards, so long ago.

Kevin had needed to know the Latin names of every body part. Margot had quizzed him seductively, removing an article of clothing for every name he got correct. It wasn't a long game, usually, and resulted in a welcome distraction from his studies. Margot always joked that she could have taken the medical boards right alongside him, she'd helped him study so much.

As Chase worked, the buzz of the needle mesmerized Margot. Time betrayed her. Kevin's presence in the muscle, her body nude against his, their soft giggles in the tiny apartment, the buzz of the needle, the feel of Chase's breath against her cheek, Cassidy's fist crashing into her lip... The jolt back to reality was sharp. The buzzing had stopped. Margot looked up to find both men looking at her with concern.

"What?" she asked, startled from her strange reverie.

"Are you okay?" Chase asked.

"Yes," she replied, pulling in a deep breath. "I'm tired. I think I'll sit down."

Walking unsteadily over to the chair she had sat in the week before, Margot removed an aluminum water bottle from her oversized purse and took a drink. She had been lost in that moment, in that memory. It was utterly disconcerting. Breathe in, breathe out, she commanded herself. *You've already lost everything. There's nothing left to lose.*

Half an hour later, Chase and the man settled up in cash. On his way out, the guy called over to Margot, "Your turn." He waved goodbye genially.

"Bye," Margot called back weakly, mustering what she knew was an unconvincing smile.

Chase saw the guy out and turned back to Margot. "You all right?"

"Yep."

Crossing back towards her, he straightened up his tools, disposed of some things, and disinfected the space. Margot waited patiently, wishing she'd stayed at work until five. That would teach her to leave early.

"Are you nervous?" Chase's voice was kind as he cleaned. "Did seeing me work on Brandon's tattoo get to you? There's always a little blood."

There's always a little blood, Margot repeated in her mind. Wasn't that the truth. Chase stopped his work and looked at her expectantly.

"I'm fine," she said. "I skipped lunch."

"You shouldn't skip meals. You're so slight."

His comment, although meant to be helpful, was like a blow. "I realize I'm too thin. Trust me, I live in my skin. I'm aware of how I look."

"I wasn't implying you're too thin. That's not what I said." Chase frowned; the crease between his eyebrows grew more pronounced. He lowered his arms, still holding the spray cleaner and towels. "Did you change your mind about this or something? You don't seem the same today."

"For the last time, I told you, I am fine. Did you want to show me the designs you came up with?"

Hesitating for a moment, still looking confused and kind of annoyed, Chase finally replied, "Sure." He put his cleaning supplies away on a shelf. Then, he opened a closet, removed the box containing her veil, along with a sketchbook, and returned. His desk was neater today. Instinctively, Margot understood it was his gift to her. Chase lay the box reverently before Margot. It was like having a piece of herself restored to its proper place, although she hadn't realized how hard it was to have it missing until it was back. She stood and opened the box.

Chase had meticulously folded the lace and carefully wrapped it in the tissue paper. It was touching.

"Thank you for taking care of it," Margot said softly.

"I can see how valuable it is. To you."

Slowly, Margot replaced the top of the box, rested both of her slender hands on top, and met Chase's gaze. "It is."

"Well, here's what I came up with. I did a lot of sketching from the lace. It was actually a very Zen activity, if you know what I mean. I kept losing track of time, lost in the patterns. The person who designed it was a genius."

As Margot looked through the sketchbook, Chase kept talking. "The symmetry is remarkable. It's handmade, right?"

"It is. My great-great-grandmother made it for my great-grandmother's wedding."

"It's beautiful. She was a real artist. Do you make lace?"

The question caught Margot so off guard she let out a little laugh. "Me? No. Much to my grandmother's chagrin. Unfortunately, her craft died with her."

"It's too bad. What an incredible thing to be able to do. I can knit, but this is something else entirely."

"You knit?"

Chase grinned and said, "Yeah. I make hats."

"I don't know why that surprises me. Nothing should surprise me anymore." Margot turned her attention to the sketchbook. Each of Chase's designs, as he had learned the lace, became more and more intricate, as though the fabric had started speaking to him. He had begun to understand its language, and with his increased understanding, his work had become finer and more nuanced.

"These are lovely. Do you feel confident you can apply this to my body?"

"That's a weird way to phrase it, but yes. I know I can do these designs justice. I was intimidated at first, but it's like anything. The longer you study it, the clearer it becomes." He pointed to the page and said, "I would put this center panel in the middle of your back, working out radially from there. The edges along your neckline and arms would be more like the edges of the lace itself. I would work from center out to maintain the symmetry."

"When can you start?"

"You like them?" he asked, sounding genuinely astonished.

"You did exactly what I'd hoped you could do. You took the designs of the lace and translated them into a shape that will fit over my body. It's perfect."

"Okay, then. Um, I guess we can start whenever you like."

"Would now be okay?"

"Now?" His eyes were wide with the implication of the question.

"Or sometime soon," Margot capitulated.

"Let's look at my schedule." Chase unearthed an actual calendar from his desk drawer. Flipping through the pages, he said, "Would you want to come once a month?"

"Can't I come more often than that?" Margot asked, trying not to sound desperate.

"Once every two weeks?"

"I was hoping to come twice a week."

"Oh. If people want to hustle through the process, I see them more often, but twice a week is a lot. Your skin needs enough time to heal between sessions. It's a lot more painful going that often since the swelling hasn't had a chance to go down. Two weeks is standard."

"I'd like to come twice a week, please," Margot interrupted, emphatically.

Chase regarded her curiously, looked back down at his planner and said, "Okay, I guess I can move from one side of your body to the other so we give your skin a chance to heal. How about Tuesday and Friday evenings at six?"

"That works. Is credit card payment all right or do you prefer cash?"

"I don't have a card reader but check or cash will do."

"Fine. See you Tuesday." Margot started to take the box from the desk between them. "Do you need this or should I take it home?"

"If you don't mind, I'd like to keep sketching from it. That is, if you don't need it."

"Need it?" Margot repeated softly, looking up at Chase's dark, warm eyes bemusedly. "No. I don't need it."

———

As Margot trailed away, a disoriented moth abandoning the light, Chase was more puzzled than ever. While he'd been tattooing Brandon, he swore there were tears in Margot's eyes. She'd glazed over, like she wasn't really there. It was so strange. What had she been thinking?

When she snapped at him for advising her not to skip meals, it had been personal, like a slap across the face. She was so defensive. She vacillated between an aloof interest in him and his work to complete disdain a moment later. Her flares of temper were stunning. It shouldn't surprise him, though, considering their first real encounter had been just that. A flare of extreme temper.

There was more to her than he could see. The elegant accountant she presented as was a façade, hiding something else, something edgy and raw, something he hadn't noticed at first glance. Now it was all he could see.

As she'd perused his designs, her countenance had softened. Her smile, although sad, seemed genuine and was the loveliest thing he'd ever seen. She liked his work and it thrilled him. It made him want to please her. Was it evident in the sketches how much he'd enjoyed drawing the lace? His skill had increased exponentially with practice. Although it was unlike anything he'd ever done, he was proud of the work. He was determined to do the lace justice and the tattoo would be exquisite.

Why did Margot want to rush the process, though? Maybe she would change her mind after the first session. She was a tattoo virgin, after all, and people seldom considered the physical reality of the process. It is painful. As Chase's mind spun, he finished cleaning up, grabbed his sketchbook and the lace, and headed upstairs. After a quick dinner, he plugged in his guitar and played a few songs.

The guys would be there soon for an early practice and he was itching to make some real noise. Chase tried to ignore the deepening pit of fear in his stomach over what condition Bryce would be in this time. He'd find out soon enough. At seven, Chase headed down the back stairs to unlock the door. Bryce was standing outside waiting, his eyes looked red-rimmed, but he met Chase's inquisitive gaze with a tired half-smile.

"Hey, man," Chase said, unable to hide his burgeoning sense of relief.

"Hey," Bryce said, stubbing out his cigarette on the ground with the toe of his shredded black boot.

Jake pulled up and parked. He got out and Chase went over to help him carry his amp up the stairs. "What's up?" Jake asked apprehensively, as Chase approached.

"Nada. All clear," Chase said, nodding his head towards the doorway where Bryce had just gone up.

"Good. I didn't want a repeat of last week's shit show."

"Me neither," Chase said. Although he agreed with Jake, and they both knew Bryce's addiction was unpredictable, Chase bristled a little at Jake's harsh tone. Something else was going on. "How's Anna?" he asked, hoping to brighten the mood.

"Good. She's glad the weather's finally nice. She hates Portland winters."

"Everyone hates Portland winters," Chase said, laughing.

Upstairs, Bryce was tuning his drums, trying to find the right sound. He looked up at them when they came in and he nodded to Jake who nodded back. In the brighter light, Chase could now see the dark circles under Bryce's eyes, the clammy pallor of his skin, the hollowness of his cheekbones. He wasn't high right now, but he'd need to get high again soon. Chase's heart twisted. How had this happened to his friend?

"You look like shit, dude," Jake said to Bryce as he plugged in. "Just sayin'."

"Coming down with something," Bryce said, looking away.

"Let's play through our set to get going," Chase said, trying to keep the guys from talking too much. Otherwise, he feared, it wouldn't end well.

"Sure," Jake said.

They played for a while, but Bryce's chops were off a shade and his usual energy was missing. Chase couldn't imagine him making it through more than an hour in this state. Unfortunately, Chase was right. About seventy minutes in, Bryce got up to use the bathroom.

He took forever. Chase was slow on the realization, and Jake beat him to it.

"You know what he's fucking doing in there, don't you?"

"What?" Chase asked, but even as the word left his mouth, he knew. "Fuck." His heart sank.

"I can't do this, you know," Jake said. "I need a real band and so do you. We need to find a new drummer."

The idea of kicking Bryce out of the band was tough to take. Chase hated confrontation. He wanted to keep the peace, make everyone happy, be the backbone. This time he knew it wasn't going to work. Jake was absolutely right.

When Bryce came out of the bathroom looking bright eyed and languid, Jake lost his shit. "Let me see your arm, asshole."

"Fuck you," Bryce said, trying to edge his way around the bassist and back to his kit.

"No, fuck you! You're in there shooting up and you want us to just ignore it? No way. I'm out of here."

"Jake, hold on," Chase said.

"No, dude. I'm done waiting for this asshole to get his shit together. I'm done." Jake unplugged his bass and grabbed everything. Chase went to help him with his amp, but Jake said, "I got it."

Bryce, standing still in the center of the room, seemed to have lost the capacity for speech. Chase said, "Go home, Bryce. We'll talk this week. We need to figure this out. But you can't get high in the middle of practice, in the middle of my home. It's not okay. I'm not fucking around, man. This is your last chance."

After everyone left, Chase stared forlornly at the silent drum kit. "God damn it," he said, kicking the kick drum. He stormed towards the door, put on his coat, and headed downstairs to the bar. It was crazy crowded, so he took a long walk instead, all the way down Congress Street to East End Beach, where he stared at the moonlight glinting on the water. He had never felt more alone.

———

Unable to settle to anything, the days passed strangely for Margot. Anticipating her appointment with Chase was like a countdown to some major life event. It's only a tattoo, she kept reminding herself. The closer Tuesday came, though, the more restless Margot grew. If the weekend had been interminable, then Monday was a life-sentence. Her phone rang in slow motion. Emails were like splinters driven beneath her fingernails. Each moment was agonizingly slow, the nuances of her work, usually a net of solace, were instead transformed into tiny devices of torture.

Monday afternoon, Margot couldn't handle the tedium any longer. She picked up her phone to text Ginny.

Let's do something.

Who is this? was Ginny's snarky reply.

You're such a child. Aren't you always complaining how we never do anything anymore? Let's go for a walk after work.

A walk? How about drinks and live music?

Fine. Whatever. Just tell me where to meet you.

Ginny knew the best places to hang out anyway, so putting their social events in her hands had always been a safe bet. As soon as the clock said six, Margot turned off her computer, locked her door, and headed down the hall. As she passed Jim's office, Margot called out, "Go home."

"Never," he answered. Margot smiled and got in the elevator.

Within the hour, Margot had made it across town to one of the Bayside breweries. Ginny was already comfortably lounging on a rough-hewn bench, entranced by the antics of the band. Margot grabbed a beer and took up the small space next to her friend. Ginny smiled and squeezed Margot's knee affably before returning her attention to the band.

Unfortunately, the music was not Margot's style. Bluegrass was so campy. It was reminiscent of days spent foraging in the woods or of farmhouse wedding receptions, not that Margot had much experience with either. As the band played their joyful songs, Margot regretted the spontaneous text she had sent to Ginny earlier.

"Why are we here?" Margot asked miserably, leaning over to her friend, their shoulders touching.

"I met the fiddle player a few weeks ago. We've been texting back and forth, and he asked me to come." Ginny shot Margot a naughty look.

"I knew it. You know I hate bluegrass. This is painful."

"Sorry. I should have warned you."

"Yeah. You should have. Buy me another beer and all is forgiven." Margot feigned a smile and her friend complied.

Returning with their second round, Ginny sat down and said, "Cheers. Thanks for texting me."

"Cheers," Margot replied, trying to make herself heard over the screeching of the instruments in their gleeful careening crescendo.

"He's cute, isn't he?" Ginny said, her eyes dopey.

"Who?"

"The fiddle player, Margot. The reason I'm making my punk rock friend sit through a set of bluegrass music. He's got a great…" Hesitating, she blushed. "Profile," Ginny blurted, as the two women looked at each other and giggled.

"Yeah. What a profile. His biceps are pretty nice too, but I'm sure you hadn't noticed."

When the set was over, the handsomely profiled fiddle player strolled languidly to their table. "Hi, Henry," Ginny said, her voice low and sexy. "This is my old friend Margot. Margot, this is Henry."

"Who are you calling old?" Margot quipped, forcing herself to smile and taking the fiddler's proffered hand.

"It's a pleasure," he said warmly. "Thank you for coming, ladies." Although he addressed them both, his gaze was locked on Ginny. Margot's stomach twisted uncomfortably.

"I actually need to go, so you guys have fun," she stated quickly. Before Ginny could try to persuade her to stay, Margot drained her beer, stood up to leave, and waved goodbye. Henry *was* cute in an earthy, bearded sort of way, and Margot wanted to give them space. Knowing Ginny, though, she'd give him a whirl and then ask to see his tax returns.

On her way home, Margot's thoughts flashed once more to her looming appointment with Chase. By this time tomorrow, she would be irrevocably changed. The notion was exhilarating.

SEVEN

A garrulous bird lifted Margot from sleep on Tuesday morning. At first, the bird's odd call tangled with the dream she was in. The reality of her surroundings slowly supplanted the dreamscape, giving way to a sense of exuberance about the day ahead, something so unfamiliar Margot didn't know how to handle it. She lifted herself from the bed without the usual sense of dull necessity. The daylight seemed brighter, as though curtains had been drawn aside.

Reality prickled uncomfortably from beneath this serene façade and Margot berated herself for such fanciful thinking. It was complete foolishness. Nothing had changed, nothing would change. Yet even sobered, Margot's step was lighter than usual.

Once she made it to work, the day wore on. A meeting with a new client surprised her somewhat, being out of the ordinary, a welcome distraction. By the time it was over she was almost done for the day. She had a cup of coffee in the break room, made a few more phone calls, and packed up. At ten minutes of six, she walked briskly out the office doors, took the elevator down to the lobby, and headed out into the vivid late afternoon light.

Chase was waiting for her at the shop door. His hands still

had the distracted air of a former smoker, every so often patting his breast pocket. Shifting his weight absently, he looked out over the busy sidewalk. Margot spotted him before he saw her, and her heart did a backflip. She hoped he hadn't noticed her faltering step as she approached.

As soon as he spotted her, Chase unleashed his charming smile. "Hi, Margot. Are you ready?"

Looking around embarrassedly, Margot quietly replied, "I am."

"Come on in." Then Chase asked, "Do you mind if I lock the door? I don't want any crazies coming in off the street interrupting us."

"What?" Margot replied alarmed.

"It has happened before, especially in the evening."

"Well, then please do lock it."

Chase locked the door and walked towards her, maintaining eye contact. "Did you want me to start with the front or the back?"

"Of what?" Margot asked. She was disconcerted and flustered, her was heartrate increasing wildly.

"Of your body," Chase replied, looking amused. He paused a few feet from her and leaned against a counter.

"Oh. I don't know. Front, I guess?"

"Okay. You can take off your top in there." He pointed to a curtained off area of the room. From a cupboard, he removed a soft, plum-colored shawl. It looked hand-knit.

Rising panic surged through Margot's limbs and down into her fingertips, as she took the shawl from Chase's steady hand. Only in contrast to his did she noticed her own hands were trembling. Her breathing had grown shallow, like she was running out of air. How had she not once considered the fact she would have to undress? This was a terrible idea. She wanted to bolt. But then what? She had made it this far, hadn't she?

"You okay? Having second thoughts?" Chase asked, watching her with concern.

"I'm fine," Margot snapped, embarrassment vying with panic for full control. "I'll be right back."

In the dressing room mirror, Margot was confronted with her own pale face and horrified eyes. What a sight. Chase must have thought she was insane. Maybe she was.

Shakily, she unbuttoned her blouse. Fumbling with the delicate mother-of-pearl buttons, her fingers were leaden. When she had finished unbuttoning, she slid her shirt off her shoulders, revealing her avian frame, her clavicles protruding sharply, as though her skeleton was trying to escape. Should she keep her bra on? Would Chase ask about her scars? Fuck. Of course he would. This was a terrible idea.

"Are you okay in there?" His voice was gentle and kind. It made her even angrier at herself.

The people in the pictures plastering the walls looked down from various heights, mocking her fragility, mocking her pain, her inexperience. She glared back fiercely and mustering all her nerve answered, "Yes." In one deft movement, Margot unhooked her bra and hung it up with her shirt, white lace against white silk. Draping the shawl around her shoulders and tucking it over her arms for security, Margot brushed the curtain aside and confronted Chase.

Smiling, he gestured to the reclining barber-style chair beside him. A variety of colorful duct tape strips crisscrossed the seat of the chair. Margot absently wondered whether the adhesive from the peeling tape would ruin her pants. An array of tools was arranged on a tray on a table. They looked intimidating. Margot walked to him and slid onto the chair, desperate to get her trembling limbs under control.

"Are you ready?"

Margot clasped her hands together tightly and answered, "Yep."

"Do you need a drink of water or anything?"

"Nope."

"Okay. I did some research on white and found the most highly pigmented color on the market. It should look fantastic."

"Okay."

"Okay," Chase said. "Lean back, Margot."

Breathing hard, she did as she was told. Chase rearranged his tools, put on some black nitrile gloves, and reached for her shawl. Instinctively, Margot clasped it tighter and looked him in the eyes.

His hands fell to his sides. "It's okay if you don't want to do this," he said gently. "You wouldn't be the first. Please, tell me now before I go any further."

Releasing the shawl, Margot whispered, "Sorry. Reflex." Pulling the shoulders and front of it down so that it covered her cleavage but little else, she asked, "Is this right?"

"Perfect. First, I have to clean your skin with green soap, and before you ask, that's just what it's called, no clue why. Then I'll shave the area."

"What?" Margot pulled away from him again, horrified.

"It's part of the process. Shaving gets the area totally smooth. If the needle hits a hair, it's not good."

"Won't my chest grow back hairy?" Even as the words came out of her mouth, Margot knew they were absurd, and she let out a little laugh.

"No," Chase answered, failing to conceal a smile. "Your chest will be as pristine as ever. Are you still okay with this?"

"I guess so. It's weird though."

"It is weird. After I shave you, I wash you again. Ready?"

"Yes."

The intimacy of Chase washing her body was startling. His gloved hands felt peculiar against her, as he wiped away the soap with paper towels. The sensation of the razor gliding against the taut skin of her chest was foreign, dangerous, incredibly bizarre. He washed her again and wiped her down with more paper towels.

"Now, I need to disinfect the skin with alcohol."

"Okay."

Chase gently drew alcohol pads along the alabaster surface of her skin, leaving a chilled, moist trail that was incredibly sensitized, even to the slightest breath. The potent smell of the alcohol mixed with Chase's spicy, sweet scent. He was so close, his breath tingling in the alcohol trail, his gloved fingers pressing against her. Margot forced herself not to look at his handsome, stubbled face and his muscular arms, so close to hers. He was doing a job and she was a client. She was safe. She took some deep breaths and focused instead on the ceiling.

Gingerly, Chase ran another alcohol wipe along the slight rise of her body above the shawl, then into the recess between her breasts and back up the other. It was so cold, and so unfamiliar to be touched by a man who was not Kevin, even if it wasn't an intimate touch. Margot shuddered involuntarily at the sensation, drawing her breath in sharply.

Chase's concerned glance darted to meet hers and she smiled wanly to cover up her discomfort.

"It's cold," she said, shivering again.

"Yeah. I don't know why alcohol feels colder than having water on your skin. It's weird."

Muscles clenched in tension, Margot waited for Chase's next step. "This is a stencil of the basic outline of where I'm working so the lines are perfect. This liquid moisturizes the skin and wets it so I can apply the stencil paper. I've made these in sections. Since it's your first time, I'm going to start small, right in the center. It might also be a little more painful since you don't have any fat on your body. Tattooing over boney areas can hurt a little more and your sternum is thin skinned to begin with."

Margot's cheeks grew hot. This was the second time he'd mentioned she was too thin. She hadn't been able to eat in a year, and she'd always been slight to begin with. "I am not a fragile flower, Chase. Don't worry about me."

"With respect, Margot, I wasn't trying to insinuate anything. I've seen the burliest men cry over an ankle tattoo. I want to be sensitive to your needs. Communicate your level of discomfort with me, please. I don't want you to be miserable."

Nodding, all Margot could think was that she couldn't wait for the pain. Pain was the entire reason she was there. "Trust me, I'll be fine."

———

Nervously, Chase applied the stencil to her breastbone, carefully pressing it flat from the center outwards. As he lifted the paper, a ghost of the design remained on her skin. It looked surreal and utterly beautiful. Margot tilted her head down to look at it and smiled.

Chase's heart beat furiously. He'd done countless tattoos on men and women alike. Some of the women had been knockouts and yet he'd never reacted like this. Why was this tiny woman disconcerting him so deeply? As he'd cleaned her skin and shaved her, her energy seemed to rise up through his fingers, through the gloves, into his very muscular system. He could feel part of her pulsing through him, compounding the tension. She was terribly nervous, that much was clear, but it was more than that. It made no sense to him. Even when he'd tattooed Cassidy, with her extreme flirtations and the sexual tension between them, it hadn't been like this. This was something else entirely and it bothered him not to be able to name it.

"So, that's the tattoo gun?" Margot asked as he opened the ink.

Chase cleared his throat as he reigned in his thoughts and said, "Yep, but it's not actually a gun. We call it the machine. Here's the needle, here's the ink, and I balance it like so." Chase demonstrated, hovering the needle above Margot's heart. It gave him pause. "Are you certain you want me to do this?" he asked. She nodded with conviction. "Okay, then. Relax, Margot."

With the buzzing of the machine energizing the space between them, Chase combatted his anxiety by humming a tune he'd been working on. His brawny body felt ungainly beside Margot's fine-boned elegance. Her body was tense as a spring beneath his hand, which rested as gently as he could manage, on the edge of her clavicle. Margot's eyes closed in anticipation and Chase studied her features. She was totally exquisite. Her skin was clear and milky, her hair was the kind of gold people paid big money for, but hers was natural. He could tell. Even beneath his harsh neon lighting, she was luminous. Incredibly beautiful.

Chase steadied himself and focused on the task ahead. As the needle pulsed into her skin, breaking through its surface, piercing her a thousand times per minute, Margot gasped. Chase froze and stared at her in alarm. The buzzing ceased, the machine lay inert in his hand, and Margot opened her bright eyes. While Chase expected her to cry or to run away, she astounded him by saying, "Sorry, I'm all right." Looking embarrassed, she confessed, "It surprised me, even though I knew it would hurt. It stings like a thousand tiny bees, doesn't it."

"Yes. Are you sure you're okay?"

"I am," she said, smiling more genuinely than he'd ever seen her smile before. "This is exactly what I needed."

Chase examined her for a moment more, making sure she was all right. Her comment was strange, but people often said or did odd things in moments of stress. Satisfied she was indeed okay, he nodded once, looked back down at the design on her chest, and resumed his work.

———

Margot lay on the chair, staring into the void. Her mind went blank as she let herself absorb the sensations, completely abandoned to the moment. Chase pulled her skin taut as he worked, pressing against her body, lubricating her skin, dabbing her blood every so often with paper towels, and rinsing his needles to keep the white ink clean. Entranced by the rhythm of his process, Margot focused in on the pain. It was exactly what she'd hoped it would be. She forgot everything else, grounded in the moment, beneath Chase's deft hands.

As Chase worked, Margot's body relaxed into the experience. She let go, as the past melted away. She focused only on the sound and the feel of the needle on her skin, in her skin. The pressure of Chase's hands on her. The drone, the sting, the intentionality of the act.

When Chase set down the machine and stretched his back, Margot snapped out of her reverie. Had any time passed? Confused, she glared at him and asked, "Is that it?"

"That's all I was planning on doing today. It's your first time and I didn't want to go too far. Do you want to see it?"

"See what?"

"The tattoo. Do you want to see it?" He held up a mirror, his expression one of suppressed concern.

"Oh. Yes. Thank you." Margot accepted the mirror, held it out from her body, and angled it down. In the reflection, her chest was red and swollen, but beneath the swelling there glowed an intricate pattern of crystal-white lines, a network of interwoven threads, all drawn from the patterns in her veil. She gasped. In all her imaginings, she'd never wondered what it would actually look like on her skin. She was surprised by the effect it had on her. Her throat was tight, her heart swelled with unexpected emotion. It took her a moment before she could whisper, "It's...it's beautiful. Thank you."

"You have to take good care of the site. You don't want an infection. It's also important not to wash with hot water too soon or the ink can come out." As he washed her once more, applied antibacterial cream, and taped clear plastic film over the design, Chase explained everything she would need to do to care for her throbbing chest. He even gave her an informational sheet reiterating his verbal instructions. "Not everybody gives out an instruction list, but I don't want anything to happen to you."

Margot's glance darted up in time to see a slightly pained

look on Chase's face as he spoke. He managed a smile, and Margot wondered exactly what he was thinking. Could he have some idea why she was here or was it something else?

Margot slid off the chair. Her legs were stiff. Awkwardly, she gathered the loose plum shawl around her, trying not to disturb the plastic wrap Chase had lay over the tattoo.

"Thank you, Chase. It's exactly what I'd hoped for. How much do I owe you?"

"It's three-hundred dollars."

"I'll be right back." Margot went to the dressing room to put on her clothes. Her body was such a strange sight, reflected in the mirror. Having this addition, a network of new scars, reminded her painfully of her time after the accident. It was like a stranger's image was being reflected back instead of her own.

Margot dressed quickly, gathered her purse and the shawl, and returned to Chase.

He was cleaning the tools and work area, so Margot went to his desk and took out the cash. She was drained, spent, exhausted, but somehow, strangely content. The pain of the experience had been enough, as she had hoped, to distract her from her preoccupations. She was thankful. She counted out three-hundred-fifty and left it on Chase's desk, under a very out-of-place Murano glass paperweight.

"Thank you. See you Friday."

"Goodbye, Margot," Chase replied, his expression remained clouded. "Until next time."

EIGHT

Margot left the shop swiftly without turning back. What the hell? She'd barely spoken, and she'd barely glanced at the tattoo. Her demeanor had been odd since they'd met, vacillating between apprehension and belligerence. Something was off, but he had no idea what. As he'd tattooed her, the energy emanating from her had changed from trepidation to something else. Something akin to euphoria. He'd never seen anything like it. It was disconcerting. Chase didn't know what to make of her at all.

Then, there was the matter of her scars. They were literally everywhere, scattered across her body. Not wanting to hurt her feelings or set off her hair-trigger flight response, he hadn't mentioned them, but they were certainly part of the story. They must be from an accident, and judging from their color, a recent one. Maybe she wanted to cover them up. Maybe that's why she was here. Such superficial reasoning didn't fit with the picture of Margot he was piecing together, though.

Some of her scars were short and deep, others were longer, tapering off like lines drawn by a distracted toddler. Her face was stunningly beautiful and had somehow been mostly spared the spray of glass or shrapnel or whatever had marked the rest of her body. He thought of his parents, what their bodies had looked like in the end, and understood. Margot was a survivor. Of what, he wasn't sure.

Her marine-blue eyes had haunted him since the first moment he'd seen her, sitting up in the booth at the bar. Her sadness still pierced him, and since that first glance, it was as though she understood everything about him. Strangers couldn't know so much, he'd told himself, and shrugged it off. He'd gone back into his lair and put her firmly out of his mind. But now, he saw that sadness anew. It was yet another scar. A much deeper one.

When she'd bounded into his argument with Cassidy, throwing herself bodily between them, her ferocity, her willingness to take a blow for the sake of a stranger, had baffled him. How did that piece fit into the puzzle of Margot? Everything she said and did added to the complexity of the woman.

After he'd cleaned the shop up and disinfected, he turned off the lights and headed upstairs. His apartment was a study in spartan living. The loft space dwarfed his simple couch, armchairs, and coffee table, all second-hand oddities. Chase hated the claustrophobic feeling most kitchens had, so when he'd designed his, he'd made it open to the rest of the apartment. The only space he'd walled off was the bathroom at the back.

The loft itself had been unused for many years, and when he'd bought the building he'd realized its potential immediately. The windows at the front and back soared to the full height of fifteen feet, bringing in so much light he barely ever turned on the overhead lights during the day. At night, he lived his life in this fishbowl, caring very little that if anyone wanted to, they could see everything he did. No one, however, seemed to care.

The raw brick walls were interspersed with punk album covers by way of art, and a kitschy Elvis clock ticked away whenever he remembered to put batteries in it. He hadn't lately, so Elvis's hips were frozen in mid-gyration, his arms pointing to random numbers, meaningless.

The high pressed-tin ceiling was painted white, although it was peeling a bit now. Chase loved this space. It was his own. He'd bought it with the money his parents had left him. Thank heavens they'd had insurance, or he would have ended up a penniless waif. They had loved him, and that love was present in every choice he'd made for himself. He had tried very hard to honor them more in death than he had in life.

Teenagers are naturally quarrelsome, his older sister Caroline had told him after the funeral. It wasn't his fault he hadn't had a better relationship with his parents. But whose fault was it, if not his? Not his dad's, certainly. The man had only ever been kind and endlessly patient, albeit dorky. Not his mother's, Lord rest her soul. She had loved Chase infinitely. And if the damage to their relationship hadn't been on his parents' part, that left Chase as the culprit. Caroline said that given time, their relationship would have mended on its own, that Chase would have grown up and grown to love them again. The tragedy was, he'd never have that chance.

The guilt had eaten away at him for nearly two decades. Losing someone you love is hard enough. Losing someone you love after you've been an asshole to them and never getting to apologize? That was something else entirely, and it had turned Chase into the man he was, desperate to make things right, to be a good person, to make them proud.

Tattooing Margot must have taken more energy than average, because Chase was hungrier than usual. The quinoa and veggie casserole he'd made on Sunday and frozen would have to suffice, so he defrosted it and took a beer from the fridge. Back at the couch, Chase looked out the windows at the slice of city beyond. Lights from the theater across the street cast a warm, wide glow. It was never completely dark. Somehow, for years it had helped keep his loneliness at bay. The city was an ever-present companion, the ambient light a comfort. Tonight, though, his loneliness had been amplified. It was deafening. He called his sister, but there was no answer.

Chase finished dinner and his thoughts meandered back to Margot. Whatever trauma she'd been through, it was fresh. She was barely holding it together, and as he well remembered, she'd have to hit bottom a few times before she could rise above it. With all his broken heart, Chase wished her well.

―――――

For days after the tattoo, Margot reveled in the lingering ache of her sternum. Whenever her thoughts strayed too close to Kevin, she focused back on her throbbing chest, breathing the sensation into her emotional state, thankful for the distraction. Nothing in a year had worked so well.

The new assignment she had at work was almost as effective, however, and Margot followed all the numbers with aplomb. By Friday, the swelling on her chest had gone down substantially and the tattoo site didn't hurt anymore. She couldn't wait to see Chase.

He was waiting for her at the door once more, this time with a guarded expression. Margot's heart sank. Instinctively she knew his manner related to her odd behavior during the last session. Steeling herself, she greeted him and put out her hand. His eyes widened in curiosity as he took her hand and shook it.

"I'm sorry for my demeanor last time I was here," she said. "I was unbelievably nervous. I'm not anymore."

"I only half expected to see you again," Chase admitted.

"Yeah, I figured I'd freaked you out. Sorry."

"Don't apologize, Margot. It's all a leap of faith."

Chase's words percolated in her mind a moment before she nodded her head and said, "It really is. Shall we?"

Smiling, Chase put his hand before him and bowed his head, ushering her chivalrously into the tattoo shop. Without being asked, Margot took the shawl from the chair and brought it into the dressing room. Chase had washed it for her, its fresh clean scent made her almost giddy. She returned to him with the shawl draped down her back and shoulders, and loosely gathered in front to hide her cleavage. The tattoo seemed to hover above her healing skin, ghostly white.

"Wow. I didn't know exactly what to expect, but that looks amazing," Chase said, staring unabashedly at her chest.

Margot suppressed her natural reaction to cover up. It was his artwork, after all, alive on her body. "I love it. It's exactly what I wanted."

"Let's keep going. I refined the next design. Oh, and I owe you change from last time. You overpaid."

"You owe me nothing. You're undercharging. I looked it up." She smiled directly at Chase's surprised expression. He smiled back.

"Thank you, Margot."

Chase repeated his purifying ritual, cleansing her skin, shaving her, disinfecting, applying the stencil, and asking her if she was ready. Trying to quell her nervous excitement, Margot replied, "Absolutely."

For the next few hours, Chase traced the designs of her family's history upon Margot's skin. As he worked, she could extrapolate the path of the machine in her mind. The swirls came to life, the netting enveloped her skin, the floral motifs were etched into her very body. The sting grounded her into the present, into the moment, allowing her to reconnect with the reality of the world before her.

It was over too soon. When Chase told her that was all for today, she almost cried. "Really?"

He caught sight of her transition from near ecstasy to sadness and renewed concern blossomed in his expression. "Margot, why are you doing this?"

"Doing what?" she asked, alarmed he would ask her such a personal question.

"The tattoo. What's going on here?"

"That's my business," she said softly, held captive by Chase's unfinished work. He still hadn't disinfected or wrapped her.

"People come in here for all sorts of reasons, from personal memorials to drunken bravado. I try to make sure they're good choices. For everyone. I get a different feeling from you."

Maybe he would stop asking questions if she simply didn't answer. Desperately, she looked down at her thin hands, her loose wedding ring, her swollen skin raw beneath new ink, and willed Chase to look away. After a moment he did. He disinfected her, applied the ointment as gently as he could, and then wrapped her chest in clear plastic.

"All set," he said, quietly.

Margot slid off the chair and walked to the dressing room. She drew the curtain closed and leaned her forehead against the mirror glass. The sadness was overwhelming. Desperately, she wished for time to reverse and undo everything that had happened, to give back all that had been taken from her. She wished she could be whole once more and that she wasn't such a wreck. But a wreck was exactly what she was. It couldn't be changed, it could only be mitigated, held at bay, controlled, managed. Inside, however, the oppressive weight of grief weighed her down. She would never fully heal, never be a whole person again. Her loss was too complete.

When she finally gathered herself, Margot stepped back and looked in the mirror. The new lines traversed her chest in perfect reverse symmetry, flanking the previous session's work. The scrollwork flew out in a wild, ecstatic swirl, pulling against the gravity of the center design. The tattoo closely referenced the lace of her veil, but it was Chase's interpretation, his artistic vision of the veil, as though he'd been drawing from a living thing.

After she dressed and sheepishly exited the dressing room, Margot stood quietly for a moment. After returning the shawl to Chase's desk, she said, "I was in a serious car accident last year and I haven't quite gotten over it yet."

He abruptly stopped what he was doing and walked over to her. He snapped off his gloves and threw them in the trash. When he stopped, he was close enough that she could feel the heat of him, the size of him, his actual gravity exerting itself upon her sphere. Margot stood her ground and looked into his deep, dark eyes.

He hesitated for a moment, then put one hand on her arm gently. "I'm so sorry. I had a feeling something had happened. Thank you for telling me. You're going to be okay. You're a good person, Margot. You simply need time to heal."

"Oh, is that all? Is it that simple?" Her voice was more acerbic than intended.

"What do you mean?" he asked, removing his warm hand from her arm and leaning up against the desk next to her.

"I simply need to heal?" She couldn't help the simmering annoyance in her tone.

"Yes. And you will. And before you ask me how I could possibly know, I lost my parents to a car wreck when I was seventeen."

She swallowed back the lump in her throat. Her heart filled with remorse for acting like she was the only one in the world who had experienced loss and pain. How selfish could one person be? She said, "I'm sorry for your loss, Chase."

"Don't be. This world doesn't give out special favors. We make what we can out of what we have left."

Grief squeezed all the air from her lungs. It was like having a heart attack. Miserably, desperately fighting back her tears, Margot whispered, "What if there's nothing left?"

"There's always something left," he answered, softly. He reached out and stroked her cheek gently.

Margot struggled to find something else to say, as Chase's hand once more fell away. She gestured around the room and said, "You've made yourself into an artist. You have something beautiful to give others. I appreciate it. Your work is gorgeous. Thank you."

"I'm so glad you like it," he replied.

Margot couldn't take another moment of this man's kindness. It was stripping her down and she needed to leave. She reached into her purse and drew out a wad of cash.

"Here's for today," she said, handing it to him. "See you Tuesday."

"Listen, I don't want you to pay me extra."

"Don't people tip for a tattoo?"

"They do," he answered. He held the extra cash out to her. "But this is too much."

"Take it. Consider it compensation for dealing with an emotional disaster case bi-weekly." She smiled, trying to pass her comment off as a joke.

Chase dropped his arm back to his side, still holding the money. "Thank you, Margot. Have a good weekend."

Nodding her head, she turned and left Chase standing against the desk at the back of his shop.

On her walk home, Margot tried to focus on the burning sensation on her chest, rather than on the frustrating feeling that she had told Chase too much. She didn't want his pity; she didn't want him to know anything about her. He was not a therapist. Her past wasn't his business, whether or not there was a correlation with his own.

At home, the echo of her footsteps in the foyer was cold and empty. Carelessly, Margot kicked off her heels and left them akimbo on the marble floor. She headed for the kitchen where she poured herself a tall scotch and soda, ate a cup of yogurt and an apple, and took the scotch to the living room. Without turning on the lights, she sat in the evening's glow and drank.

What would Kevin think of her treating her body like this? Would he see it as a desecration? He certainly hadn't been fond of tattoos. He thought they were either slutty or trashy, depending. This was different, though, and she genuinely wondered what he would think. She took another long sip of her scotch. It didn't fucking matter what he would have thought. Kevin was dead.

The truck had come out of nowhere. Margot was driving them around in the country, the spring air warm enough for the windows to be down. Her hair had been loose, blowing in the wind, tangling itself into knots, glinting golden in the Sunday sun. They had been smiling and laughing and talking about family when a truck, which hadn't stopped at the cross-street's stop sign, barreled into them at fifty miles per hour. Kevin died instantly, as the entire passenger side of their car had been crushed, caved in, massacred. She had seen the pictures later, amazed that she had lived, shocked by the otherness of what once was a car and a human, now rendered scrap metal, scrap parts, blood and bone and muscle and metal twisting into a hideous sculpture.

Margot had blacked out instantly upon impact, but her concussion was the least of her injuries. Broken bones, internal bleeding, a thousand lacerations from where the safety glass of the windshield had embedded into her skin, where flying bits of metal had pierced deep into her flesh. She was a broken doll, airlifted to the very hospital where Kevin had saved so many lives.

Word of the accident spread quickly at the hospital. Margot received the best care. Doctors she'd never met visited her during her long convalescence to deliver their personal condolences. They regaled her with stories of Kevin's heroics in the operating room, his kind bedside manner, his love for his work. They shed tears for her loss, and for their own, as Margot sat mute in her hospital bed, immobilized, catatonic, nodding like a robot at their outpouring of feeling.

The physical recovery had taken months. All the while, her insurance company, working with her personal attorney, had sued the trucking company for the full amount of their insurance policy. When all was said and done, Margot had walked away with several million dollars. Everyone told her she was lucky to walk away at all.

Lucky, however, was not how she felt. Once the physical injuries had healed, once she was well enough to cremate what was left of her beloved, the true anguish settled in. The bodily pain had only been a veneer to what lay beneath, dulled for months by painkillers and shock, but the surface was all her friends could understand. Why wasn't she feeling better once she looked better? Loss is hard, they'd say. You'll get over it, they'd say. They had no fucking idea what they were talking about. She'd experienced a loss so deep, so complete, there was nothing left of her but a shell. One by one, she'd ignored her friends, berated the well-wishers, and flung back their platitudes. Ginny was the only one who'd stuck it out. Why, Margot had no idea.

Margot went to the kitchen, set her empty glass down, and grabbed the bottle of scotch instead. For hours, she wandered the house like a phantom, looking blearily at everything she had once loved, once valued. Their favorite wedding picture still perched on the mantle in a gilded frame. Their smiles, their youth, their magnificent beauty against that peerless blue sky rendered Margot immobile. Her veil was its own presence in the photo with them, lifted by the ocean breezes, fluttering out behind them like a ghost. Kevin looked so happy. He deserved to be happy. They both did. She couldn't understand why fate would take him from her and it filled her with rage.

Upstairs, she walked past the always-locked door and to their bedroom. In the massive closet, she used the broom handle to dislodge Kevin's favorite sweater from its shelf. She held it to her swollen chest, leaned against the doorframe, and sank to the floor. There she drank in the darkness.

Empty.

Alone.

Chase headed next door to the bar after Margot left. She'd been in an accident. It explained so much about her demeanor. It explained her scars. She was still recovering.

He wondered about her wedding ring. When Chase had mentioned her husband the night they met, Margot had waived him off the topic, although he couldn't remember exactly what she'd said. Maybe they were estranged. Maybe after the accident, Margot wasn't the same and her husband couldn't handle it. *Who knows.*

After ordering his beer and settling in at the bar, Chase took out his phone and Googled her name. *Margot DeWitt, Portland, Maine.* The first thing to appear was her profile at work. *The Carter Group, Accountants.* Her profile picture must have predated the accident, for before him was a smile that could launch a thousand ships. She was totally arresting. Happy. Confident. Whole. It seemed she specialized in investigative and forensic accounting. The accident had changed her from a perfect, happy woman into the fragile, mercurial wraith who now frequented his shop. It eviscerated him.

Going back to the search results, he scrolled down. A few entries below her firm's listing, an obituary caught his eye. The handsome young man in the picture smiled out from the past, meeting Chase's gaze with a challenge. *Doctor Kevin Morrison. Survived by his wife, Margot DeWitt, Dr. Kevin Morrison was killed in an accident in which their vehicle was hit by an out of control truck.* The obituary, obviously not written by Margot, impersonally listed the doctor's many accomplishments as a heart surgeon and a member of the Portland Medical Board.

The information settled in the pit of Chase's stomach like a stone. He put his phone away, wishing he hadn't looked her up. "Shit," he muttered under his breath and leaned his forehead on his hand, his elbow propped against the bar. Now it all made sense. Margot was a widow.

In the mirror behind the bar, Chase caught sight of his own eyes reflected back at him, those of a bewildered teen, an orphan, a man who had grown into his early loss. It had changed him too. How could it not? Loss changes everyone.

Sheila came over as he rubbed his weary eyes. "You okay, man?"

"Thanks, Sheila, I'm fine. Long day."

"Need another?" she asked, gesturing to his nearly empty beer. "It's on me."

"Sure. Thank you. You know that blonde woman who comes in here?" he asked as Sheila set his beer down and removed the empty glass.

"The one who dresses all chic and sits in the window alone?"

"That one."

Sheila narrowed her eyes and asked, "The one who got between you and Cassidy a while ago?"

"Yep."

"I've never talked with her. She keeps to herself. I try to keep track of her, though. She's very small."

"Yeah, she is," Chase agreed. He lifted the glass and looked at the amber liquid "You don't know anything about her?"

"Sorry. Can't help."

Sheila went and helped some other customers, but as soon as she was done she returned, leaned forward with both hands on the bar. "Something's bugging you, Chase. I can tell. Is Cassidy still driving you nuts?"

"Nah. She's moved on, I guess."

Sheila shook her head. "She was a mess last time I saw her."

"It's so depressing," Chase added.

"Did you ever figure out why the blonde girl got involved?"

"I still have no idea. This world is a mystery to me, Sheila. You're lucky to be married and done with all the craziness on this side of the bar."

"You're right. Now I get to sit back and watch you suckers fuck up *your* lives." She smiled, her dark brown eyes and wild curls lively and vigorous. Heading back down the bar to tend another customer, Chase watched her go. He was glad for this little community he had forged for himself, but Sheila was right. Dating was a nightmare.

Once upon a time, his own attempts at marriage had ended in disaster. Melanie had been beautiful, but her beauty had been a mirage, hiding the heartless creature who lay beneath. Chase had found her in bed with his associate, a veteran tattooer who worked in his shop. Granted the man had shown him a thing or two about their craft, but he had also shown him the real person his fiancée was. Chase had always been secretly thankful to the guy, for he'd saved him a lot of heartache and probable financial ruin. Melanie had only been with Chase for his money. That had been hard to take. Trust had not come easily for him to begin with, and Melanie drove the last nail into the casket, so to speak.

Then there was Sara. She was harder to think about, but that had ended too.

Since then, he'd kept it casual. Cassidy had been his most recent hiccup, and he wished he could exercise better judgement in the women he chose to be with.

In a maudlin mood, he finished his beer, said goodbye to Sheila, and headed up to his place. Ordinarily, he didn't let *aloneness* bother him, but tonight, again, he couldn't help but feel the loneliness of it.

He could still sense Margot. Her soft skin beneath his gloved hands, the way her striking eyes soft-focused on some distant thing as he drew upon her body, the faint scent of her as he worked. He was fond of her, for Margot, he now understood, was lonely too.

After he straightened up his meager possessions, Chase poured himself another beer, picked up his guitar, and plugged it in. He'd been working on a new song. It was full of minor chords and dissonance, reminiscent of stuff he'd liked in high school. This song had sounded ugly to him at first, but it had now been stuck in his head for weeks.

As thoughts of Margot tugged at his consciousness, he perceived the song's trajectory clearly for the first time. He'd been headed down the wrong path. A sweetness began to grow from the original idea as he altered a few chord progressions, adding a bridge that worked with what he'd developed. He played it a few times, tweaking some of the notes until they sounded right. Then, he recorded the new version on his phone so as not to forget what he'd come up with.

Playing it all the way through, words came to him as well. Soft words, comforting words, words that reminded him of his dad playing *Blackbird* for him on the guitar when Chase was a little kid, before everything had gone wrong. Lyrics that hadn't existed moments before now came from his lips fully formed, completing the song they were always meant to be. Thankful he'd recorded it all, he played it through once more, wrote down the words in his notebook, turned everything off, and headed to bed. At least something good had come from the day.

―――――

Margot awoke fully dressed in her closet with a massive headache and a stinging chest. All she wanted in the world was a long bath, but with the open wounds of her tattoos, she could barely take a shower. Settling on tea, she headed downstairs and made herself a large mug of chamomile and a piece of dry toast. With nowhere to go since it was Saturday, Margot settled in for the interminable weekend. Maybe she'd do some grocery shopping later or go to the water for a walk. She had to do something, or she would stay home, and drink scotch all day. That wouldn't be good for anyone.

After her tea, tattoo care, and an abbreviated shower, she set about cleaning her already clean house. From top to bottom, she dusted, swept, and mopped. The tile in the kitchen backsplash gleamed, the stainless-steel appliances shone. It took hours, so by the time she was done, it was noon. Still, she had nothing to do.

Kevin had loved coming home to their spotless house after his long days and nights at the hospital. Margot could read him instantly. His body language spoke volumes about how his work had gone. If he returned manic, energized, ready for intimacy, he'd been successful in surgery. He'd saved someone. He'd been praised for his work. If he was downtrodden or low energy, his surgeries had gone long, he'd lost a patient, he'd given a family tragic news. His work took a real toll on him when things didn't go well. He cared so much. Keeping their house immaculate was the least Margot could do to show her support. Kevin never took it for granted.

"We could get a maid, sweetheart. Why shouldn't we?" he'd asked one afternoon. Their bodies were bathed in patterned sunlight as they lay together on the white down comforter over their king-sized bed. Kevin's arm lay draped over Margot's body.

"I like cleaning the house," she'd protested.

"No one likes cleaning a house, Margot," he'd laughed. "Please, let's call an agency or something. I hate to see you put so much effort into this. The house is so big. It must take hours."

"I enjoy it. I listen to books or podcasts and the time goes by fast. I don't want a stranger in my house looking at my things," she returned.

"Do you think they'd judge you?" Kevin had asked playfully, tickling her stomach.

"No," she giggled, squirming. "I don't want to share this place with anyone. That's all."

Kevin had honored her choice, even if he hadn't understood it.

As she stood surveying the flawless space, devoid of the faintest trace of dirt or dust, grease or grime, she wasn't sure how to process the emptiness. Maybe her obsession with cleaning had manifested to try to fill a void she'd had in her heart long before she'd lost Kevin, but there was no use reflecting on it. What was the point?

After the accident, Margot had refused to buy another car. Everything she needed was within walking distance except the grocery store. All her shopping was done through an online ordering system, but she missed picking out her own fruit and vegetables. Sometimes, she would suck it up and order a car, and do her shopping herself. Today, she decided to go to the store. What else was she going to do with her afternoon, after all?

Shopping killed two hours and eating a late lunch took care of another, leaving the remainder of Saturday and all of Sunday. Weekends were painful. Annoyed, Margot eventually grabbed her laptop to do some work. At least that would take another couple of hours.

At the close of the endless day, Margot took care of her tattoos. The white marble tiles and floors in the bathroom echoed the sound coldly as she set a jar of coconut oil on the counter. After removing her t-shirt, Margot stood before the mirror. Her reflection revealed a ghostly figure with filament-thin lacework traversing her skin. The white on white was difficult to see at first, and her skin was still a bit swollen, but when the eye focused on it, it became clear. It was like light had wound itself around her body, as though magic had put the design there. It was the exact effect she had been hoping for. As the swelling went down and the redness subsided, her body and the ink were becoming one, the lace was part of her. Her veil had become a shroud of interwoven scars, interring her with her loved ones.

Chase was doing a flawless job. The man was a true artist. He was also a genuinely good guy. Margot felt guilty for being standoffish with him, but it was for the best.

So, his parents had died in a car wreck. It seemed uncanny, but she was sure it was true. He had said the words with practiced grace and genuine bravery. He'd been orphaned at seventeen. It must have been so hard for him to deal with the logistics of a funeral, the estate, all the things you had to deal with when everyone you love is dead, emotional dysfunction aside.

Perhaps, to some extent, it explained Cassidy. Maybe Chase wanted to help someone, to fix someone, to right some wrong within the world. What Chase was too good to understand was that some people are too broken to be fixed.

Sunday morning, Ginny called and forced Margot to join in an antiquing and cliff-walk adventure with her and Henry, the fiddler. Margot tried everything short of faking an illness to deter Ginny's enthusiastic invitation, but to no avail. When Ginny dug her heels in, there was no stopping her.

Margot hated being in the car. She fought her own sense of panic for miles and miles. She tried not to think and tried instead to focus on her breathing, as they drove south along the coast. The forty minute drive was interminable, but at the end of it lay lovely Ogunquit. The infinite variety of blues and greens that swept out before her in a graceful arc filled Margot with a rare moment of peace. They walked for miles.

Henry, it turned out, was a real gentleman. He doted on Ginny, complimenting her every ten minutes, holding her hand and offering gum. He included Margot in every conversation with admirable grace. Never once did he allude to her accident, to her loss, yet every consideration seemed to ensure he was taking care of her. It was touching, rather than annoying.

"How long have you been playing music?" Margot asked him as they walked along the cliffs at the water's edge, the surf crashing against the rocks below.

"Since I was ten or so," he replied cheerfully, absorbing the sunshine. "I saw some band playing bluegrass and I was hooked."

"That's sweet," Ginny interjected.

Margot involuntarily rolled her eyes and instantly regretted it. Thankfully, Ginny hadn't seen her.

"Do you play any instruments, Margot?" Henry asked, trying to continue the conversation.

"Not anymore. I used to play drums and piano, but that was ages ago."

"She's amazing, actually. She blew people out of the water on the drums, and she can play anything on the piano with sheet music."

"What kind of music did you play?" Henry asked, looking interested.

"Punk rock, mostly, with some math rock and indie thrown in. My influences were bands like Slint, Jawbox, Fugazi, Jawbreaker, June of 44, stuff like that."

"I don't know who any of those bands are except for Fugazi," Henry laughed.

"No one who isn't into that stuff knows about it. You don't hear it on the radio."

"What do you like about that kind of music?" Henry persisted.

"The complexity, the layers, the heavy sound, the energy, all of it," Margot replied, forgetting herself.

"It's your math brain, right, Margot?" Ginny added.

Ginny's enthusiasm embarrassed her once more, and Margot's cheeks warmed. Shyly, she nodded in agreement. "Yeah. It's the math brain. I fundamentally understand the patterns in music, you know?"

"I do know. I can repeat almost anything I hear by ear. Always was shit at reading music though. That's the art brain," he quipped, eliciting a laugh from both women.

"Ginny played French horn in high school," Margot commented, trying to turn the conversation away from herself.

"Yes, I did," Ginny agreed. "I was horrible. I think my teacher actually used the term tone deaf."

"That's so mean," Henry added, putting his arm around her shoulder. "Who would do that to a kid?"

"That's what I thought! Couldn't she have lied to me, at least?"

Henry kissed Ginny on the head with a look of such devotion, it twisted Margot's insides painfully. She didn't want to be jealous. She saw more of her old friend Ginny when she was with Henry than Margot had in years. She was thankful for it.

The spark of new love Margot had seen between Henry and Ginny continued to trouble her the next day. How she hoped Ginny wouldn't rip Henry's heart out. Ginny's record with men was pretty horrific. She had left a trail of devastation in her wake. Henry wouldn't be the first broken heart, but he might be the sweetest. Maybe Margot needed to start a support group for Ginny's castoffs.

Ginny had been different, though, with Henry. She seemed genuinely interested in him. There was less preening, less over-the-top showiness when Ginny was with him than was usual when she was dating a new person. She seemed at ease, very much herself. Margot wondered if the two of them had a real connection. She hoped so.

The dinner Margot ate after work was utterly uninspiring. Margot had loved cooking for Kevin. The praise he'd given even her most flawed attempts at cuisine was off the charts. Their meals together were some of Margot's favorite moments. Now, cooking was drudgery. She avoided it at all cost, which left either getting takeout or preparing something very basic. Often, she resorted to yogurt and fruit, or bagged salad mixes with precooked chicken. It was miserable.

After her meager dinner, she took *War and Peace* down from the shelf and started in where she'd left off months ago, wishing it was still winter. She turned on her remote-control fireplace and the gas whooshed the flames to life. Margot settled in with the Russians. They, at the very least, understood torment.

Not even *War and Peace* made her feel anything that evening and when she did finally go to bed, Margot barely slept. When she awoke Tuesday, the only thing that dragged her from her bed was the prospect of the tattoo shop. Chase would start on her back tonight and she couldn't wait.

Halfway through the day, Jim visited her to get an update on her progress with the new client. "I've found some interesting numbers," was all she'd tell him.

"You're going to have to give me more than that." Jim's animated face was reddened with excitement.

"Why do you care about this particular client so much?" Margot asked impassively.

"This is one of the biggest clients we've had walk through the door. Their holdings are incredibly diverse. If we impress them, they might transfer work for all their various businesses, and we'd be in good shape."

"We're already in good shape," Margot returned.

Jim shook his head at her and said, "You're hopeless."

"That's true," she replied without thinking. She glanced up in time to see Jim smile wistfully.

"You know that's not how I meant it," he said.

"I do." Margot faked a smile. Not long after, Margot took off. She stopped by the bar before heading to see Chase. Her usual booth was taken, so she sat at the bar.

"What'll it be, hon?" the bartender asked. She regarded Margot with dark, watchful eyes, set into a gorgeous face.

"Scotch and soda, please."

When the bartender returned with the drink, she said, "I'm Sheila. Chase told me you're the gal who kicked Cassidy's ass." The woman's vibrant smile took Margot off guard and put her at ease at the same time.

"Yeah, I didn't exactly kick anyone's ass, but she landed a solid punch on my lip. That was interesting."

"What's your name?"

"Margot. It's nice to meet you, Sheila." Margot put out her hand and Sheila shook it.

"I hope you don't mind me asking, but why do you come here? You don't seem like our usual type."

"I guess not," Margot said with a half-smile. "I like the music you play."

"No. Really?" Sheila's expression was one of shock. "Don't tell me you're a little punk under all those fancy blouses and designer handbags."

Margot knew her cheeks were ablaze. She couldn't bear to reply.

"I'm teasing you, Margot. I'm glad you're here. And I'm glad you like the music. Any requests?"

"Sure. You played Jawbreaker a while ago, and it seems apropos after Cassidy's assault."

Sheila laughed. "Unfun or Bivouac?"

"Unfun."

"Coming right up." Sheila headed to her phone which lay on the back counter and within a moment, the rough-voiced angel Blake was singing songs Margot had grown up loving.

At six o'clock, Margot tucked a twenty under her empty glass and slid out of the bar. Chase was waiting for her outside with a smile.

"Why are you telling people about me?" was Margot's abrupt greeting. Chase's smile disappeared.

"What?"

"Sheila. Why were you talking about me with Sheila?"

Chase shuffled uncomfortably. "I wanted to see if she knew you."

"Why?" Margot demanded.

"I don't know. You'd left and I was still thinking about our conversation when I headed over to the bar. You go there and I didn't know if you knew Sheila yet."

"I do now. She played Jawbreaker for me."

"The band?"

"Yes. The band. Listen, Chase." Margot took an aggressive step forward and pointed her finger at him. "You don't know me. You don't know anything about me. I'm figuring a lot out right now and I don't want you involved in my shit. Please. I like your work a lot, I want to keep doing this, but my life is my private business."

Chase looked horrified, but his expression slowly transformed to anger as he studied her. "You push people away, Margot. I get it. You're hurt, you don't want to let people in. I've been there. I understand. It's taken me almost twenty years, but I'm learning not to push people away anymore. I'm sorry if my approach to my work is too personal for you, but that's who I am. I actually care about people."

Margot was stunned into silence. She'd not meant to confront him. She hadn't given it any thought at all before the words spilled out. Chase had been only kind to her and she kept treating him like dirt. He was right, all she did was push people away. When would it end?

"I'm… I'm so sorry," she said and started to turn away.

Prepared to go all the way home, to forget about the rest of the tattoo, to forget about Chase, Margot took one step away before Chase said, "We have an appointment, Margot. Come on in." He didn't wait for her as he opened the door to the shop and went in.

By the time Margot followed him in, he'd already set up the tools and gotten her the plum shawl. Holding it in his hands, he offered it forth. "You ready?"

"Yes."

Margot avoided her own gaze in the mirror as she changed. Her skin, however, she could stare at all day. Thankful she hadn't kept walking she pulled the curtain of the dressing room aside and met Chase's gaze.

"So, you like Jawbreaker?"

"Yeah." She walked towards him and sat in the chair.

"You like a lot of late 80s and early 90s punk?"

"I do."

"So do I. Fugazi was always a favorite. All those bands on SubPop were great."

"Most of them," she said with a faint smile.

He arranged some tools and put on his gloves. "Jawbox?" he asked.

"Loved them. *Static* is still one of my favorite songs."

He nodded in agreement. "Not that we all have to look our

type or anything, but how'd a little punk girl turn into a chic accountant?"

"How do you know I'm an accountant?"

"Your card," Chase said, eyebrows raised.

"Right. I love the music, hate the lifestyle. When I was deciding what to do after college, it was between being an accountant or an attorney. Numbers won. Now I investigate fraud, and it's actually pretty punk."

"I bet they never see you coming."

"They don't." Margot finally smiled. "The last guy I nailed looked like he wanted to murder me on the spot. It was like being betrayed by a Goldendoodle."

Chase laughed out loud. "You're more like a Thayer angel than a Goldendoodle."

"I don't mean to be an asshole to you," Margot said, hanging her head. "As I said, I've had a hard time controlling my feelings lately."

"If you ever want to talk about what happened, I'm here."

"No offense, Chase, but you're my tattoo artist, not a therapist."

Chase shrugged. "You'd be surprised what people tell me."

"No, I probably wouldn't," she stated firmly. "Nothing surprises me anymore."

———

Chase worked on Margot's back for hours, unwilling to stop when the stenciled template ended. He wasn't afraid anymore. The patterns were becoming a part of him. Their mysterious language was clear now and he could speak it more fluently. He remembered a particular scroll from the lace, and he went to consult it, leaving Margot looking confused.

"What are you doing? Are we done?"

"No. I'm going off book. I wanted to look at the lace. I had an idea." As he said this, though, it finally hit him why she was tattooing the lace on her body. It was a wedding veil. Her wedding veil. And she'd lost her husband. How had he not put it together? "You know what, never mind. I'll do some more drawings of the new idea and pick up here next time."

"Are you sure? I can keep going."

"I am. I lose track of time sometimes. Let me clean you up and wrap you."

As Chase put on new gloves and took care of wrapping Margot's swollen back, the compulsion to hug her to him was overwhelming. He wanted to take care of her. She was so small, so lost. He fought the urge to tell her he knew about her husband's death. She was so sensitive. He needed to take it slow with her, win her trust little by little.

Once he was done wrapping her he said, "There, Margot. You're set. I have to say, it looks beautiful."

She glared at him uncertainly for a moment before she said, "Thanks." She slid off the chair and swept into the dressing room.

"Do you ever go to shows?" he called, as he cleaned up.

"Not in a while. You?"

"Yeah. Some good bands have been coming through Portland lately. We could catch one sometime, if you want."

"I don't think so," Margot said, but her voice sounded unsteady, uncomfortable. Chase knew he shouldn't push her.

"Let me know if you change your mind."

Her silence was answer enough. What was he thinking? He had dated so many women who didn't fit him. They didn't think like he did. They might seem to like similar things on the surface, but when you dug down, they were selfish or looking for him to be something he wasn't.

Margot was a closed book. She had only opened up to him in the smallest ways. What was so attractive about her? Yes, she was beautiful. Yes, she was sad in a way he could understand. Yes, there was so much more to her than she had showed him, but none of that mattered anyway. One, he had resolved not to date clients any more, and two, Margot didn't want anything to do with him. Chase remembered the sharp clean lines of Dr. Kevin Morrison's shirt, his chiseled features, his crisp good looks. Chase was scruffy in comparison. Of course he was not Margot's type, in addition to the fact that she was a grieving widow.

Margot left the changing room looking guarded. She set down the shawl and handed him the cash. He chose not to mention that he'd spent more time on her than usual. She'd been overpaying so much anyway, it barely mattered.

As though reading his thoughts, Margot said, "I know you gave me extra time tonight, so I added the difference."

"You didn't have to do that."

"The work looks great. See you Friday?"

"Sure. See you Friday."

Chase's heart sank as Margot left once more. There was a deep silence in her wake he couldn't reconcile.

The next evening, after work, he headed to his apartment upstairs to get ready for band practice. Jake had reluctantly agreed to give Bryce one last chance. They'd texted back and forth with him all week and he'd promised he was clean. Chase was almost out of hope for this band, but he needed to try.

The new song had been in his head all day and he was excited to play it again before the guys got there. Each time he played it, the music grew and changed and morphed like a living thing.

He played it through a few times before restlessness took over. He ate a quick dinner then picked up knitting needles to pass the time. Knitting always made him think of his mom. She'd loved him so much and the longing for her had not abated with time.

After his parents died, Chase had floundered. A few years later during college, he went to a knitting club with a girlfriend as a joke. As he'd cast on those first stitches, though, it was like his mom was communicating with him. There was something of her to be found in the act of knitting. Long after the girl had broken up with him, Chase continued going to knitting club. He learned how to make tiny baby hats, like the ones his mom had made, for the preemies at the NICU. The hats were so small they barely took any time at all, and in his mother's honor, he donated the hats every few months.

Chase cast onto his needle, divided the stitches on to two more, and joined them into a round. He knit until he heard the guys jostling into the downstairs landing. *Here we go,* Chase thought. Never before had he been so apprehensive about seeing his band mates. Would Bryce be too high to play? Would he be a shadow of his old self looking through dead eyes? Or would it suddenly be okay? The loud crash from the stairwell did not bode well.

"You fucker," Jake yelled.

"That was so not my fault, dude," Bryce slurred.

Chase's heart sank as he bolted down the stairs. "What's up?"

"He dropped my amp," Jake said, looking furious and disgusted.

"Why was he holding your amp?" Chase asked, immediately regretting it.

"I was grabbing the mic stands and shit. I thought he could handle it."

Bryce wavered, looking pale and hollow. His eyes were sunken and red, ringed by dark circles. He was completely strung out. Chase's compassion was replaced by anger when Bryce leaned against the wall and closed his eyes.

"Sorry, Chase. I'm done with this shit. Anna wants me to move to Charlotte with her and I think I'm gonna say yes. There's no way this band is ever going anywhere with this asshole."

"Are you sure?" Chase asked, noting the desperation in his own voice. He and Jake had been buddies forever. "I mean, you're here, we might as well play. Bryce can take a hike."

"Fuck it, man. What's the point?" Jake turned, readjusted the strap of his bass case, and grabbed his amp. Looking back over his shoulder he said, "I'll keep in touch. Don't feel bad, Chase. It's not about you. It's been coming."

"Okay, Jake. Good luck."

Chase was strangely emotional as Jake walked away. He'd lost fucking everyone. Who did he even have anymore? Who were his friends? His family? This sucked. Jake had been drifting away for months, but this would be the end.

Chase turned back to Bryce. "Dude, go home."

"You've got my drums up there."

"What? You want to carry them home?"

"No, I guess not."

"I'll bring them by your place next week," Chase said, his voice betraying how gutted he was. "What a waste. You've got so much talent. Get clean, man."

Bryce wavered and stumbled back out the door. Disgusted, Chase locked it behind him and went back up the stairs. The loft was even emptier than usual. The drums sat forlornly in the corner. He didn't even have the heart to break down the kit.

After Chase finally went to bed, the light from passing cars slid over his ceiling like liquid silver. The sight usually pacified him, lulling him to sleep, but tonight he lay awake with only his preoccupations for company.

His thoughts drifted back to his mother. What would she think of him now? He fervently hoped that, wherever his parents were, they were proud of the man he had become, despite the teen he'd been. It was the best he could hope for.

NINE

When Margot got home from the tattoo shop, she headed directly to the basement. *Unfun* had been in her head since she'd left the bar, and when Chase had said he loved Fugazi, Margot's stomach had clinched with excitement. She hadn't shared it with him, but Fugazi was her all-time favorite band.

Buried in a corner of the basement, Margot found boxes of her old CDs and records. The collection wasn't bad. A rare Helium seven inch with a B-side track called *Termite Tree*, her favorite song an age ago, caught her eye. Every one of Fugazi's CDs, all of which contained songs she loved, were together in the first box she opened. There was a ton of great music here.

Since Kevin died, Margot had cocooned herself in silence. She couldn't bear to play classical music on their sound system because it reminded her so much of him. Silence had suited her depression so well.

Lately, though, she'd been seeking out the noise and bustle of the bar. Was it about the indie and punk music they played? Had she missed it that much? Margot resolved to bring all her old CDs and records upstairs to see. Maybe she could reclaim the music she loved.

Kevin hadn't liked any of it. Classical music was his preference, and by preference, Margot now realized it was the only thing he listened to. From the time they'd met, he couldn't tolerate the music she played, usually turning it off within a song or two. He'd never gone to a show with her. She'd never asked.

When she was at his place, in the early days of their relationship, they'd listened to classical while he studied for his boards. Later on, when they lived together, he'd needed to concentrate on reading medical journals in the evenings. Margot's loud music was a distraction. She'd been only too happy to put it all away for him. Little by little, she convinced herself Mozart was her thing. She began practicing complex pieces on the piano, mastering one after another, to Kevin's delight.

Now, as she listened to the scratchy, living vinyl, the sparse rock beat driving the drawling vocals on *Termite Tree*, Margot remembered why she'd loved this music so much. It was still alive in her. It coursed through her body like oxygen.

Helium had broken up long before Margot had found this little record. She'd been a preschooler when it was recorded, but when she saw it as a teenager, she remembered hearing about the seminal indie band. They were a Boston legend. She'd gotten the record home and listened to it immediately, finding that the song on the B side was a lost gem. She was still proud to own this fragile masterpiece in plastic.

The raw record, a simple plastic disc with grooves physically etched into it, exhaled through the mechanism of a thin, metal needle. That tiny needle was incredibly powerful, as it amplified into reality, ephemeral or otherwise, a song made by a killer band nearly thirty years ago. It had lay dormant all this time, awaiting the touch of the needle to bring it back to life.

"Carve our initials in a tree, one for you and one for me, oh, we'll leave it for the termites to eat..." Margot sang along unselfconsciously. The words were so simple, so sweet, she smiled. Maybe Chase would like the song. He had popped into her head, as though he belonged there with the music. His presence was almost comforting.

Music had been Margot's entire world all through high school. Bands would play in Boston and she'd take the train in with a few friends to see the all-ages shows. She'd go home with the tunes in her head and the drum riffs in her hands. The next morning, she'd head to her parents' basement and play what she could remember of the songs she'd heard. Drums are lonely without other instruments, though, so her friends would join her after school to jam. It was a terrible racket, but Margot had learned how to negotiate through music and how to tolerate a certain amount of chaos as they all learned together.

The summer between high school and college, Margot had worked at the Trident Booksellers and Cafe in Boston, on Newbury Street. The place was insane. People came and went all day long, all in search of something. Coffee, inspiration, a rare copy of some random treatise on the Druids, by far the oddest request, whatever they were looking for, the tide of people in and out of the store was incessant. Margot had loved it, had thrived on it.

After work, she'd meet up with Ginny and they'd get discount sushi and go to whatever show was happening that night, if Margot didn't have band practice. When Margot's band was playing out, she'd make Ginny tag along. They were inseparable and their world revolved around Margot's love of music. With a pang, Margot realized that falling in love with Kevin had altered her relationship with Ginny long before his death. After all, Margot had been the first to change. Ginny had simply followed along.

Margot listened to *In on the Kill Taker* by Fugazi next, reveling in the familiarity of the songs. They were like her own breath, her own thoughts manifested in music. At one of the last shows Fugazi played in Boston, at Mass Art, the teenaged Margot had almost been trampled in the pit, but just as easily as she'd been knocked down, she was pulled back up. A big guy had grabbed her from the floor and set her aside like a doll and kept dancing. It was exhilarating.

Margot listened to all her Fugazi songs, then moved onto Jawbox, Dinosaur, Jr., Sonic Youth, Pavement, Sebadoh, The Descendants, all the indie and punk she'd collected in the years before streaming music. She'd forgotten it was a work night, she'd forgotten to eat dinner, she'd even lost track of the pain in her back. The hours ticked by unnoticed. The music sustained her like a heart transplant.

Berklee College of Music in Boston had been a lesson in defeat for Margot. Her concentration had been percussion, with a focus on piano and drums in the rock style. She loved that she could major in such a thing. Her dad said it was impractical, that her natural talent for math should be her focus. What he hadn't understood was Margot's propensity for mathematics was what made her such a good drummer.

Most of the men she was in school with, however, saw Margot as an interloper. She'd had to work twice as hard to be considered half as good. She could keep up with any of them, but they were intimidated and therefore intimidating. It drove her crazy.

After years playing with small-scale bands, Margot couldn't take the inter-band fighting, politics, and posturing. After graduating from Berklee, Margot stopped playing music out. She'd still go see her favorite bands play, but playing music lost its luster. Margot didn't find the same joy in it anymore.

She'd continued working at Trident a few days a week all through college and after. That's where she met Kevin. He came in to take a break from studying for his medical boards. He was older than her, already finished with medical school and ready to start his residency at a hospital in Cambridge. Margot was smitten at first glance. His clean-cut good looks, his kind eyes, the brilliance he exuded from his very being, she couldn't get enough. He'd been taken with her from the start as well, but if it's one thing residents don't have an abundance of, it's free time to date cute girls from coffee shops. They had to work at it. Once they had sex, though, the work wasn't work anymore. It was passion.

They dated for five years while Kevin completed his surgical residency. Margot had meanwhile gone back to school and gotten her Masters in accounting. They couldn't bear to be apart. In retrospect, Margot knew she would have made a good litigator, but law school would have meant so much more work and she didn't want to be away from Kevin any more than necessary. She never regretted spending her time with him. She especially didn't regret it now.

In the middle of the night, Margot finally sensed herself in time and place again, now with an unanswerable question in her mind. Had she put herself on hold in order to fulfil a prewritten, albeit short-lived destiny with Kevin? She'd stopped playing music all together soon after they'd met. Instead of reclaiming what she'd wanted to be, she'd become everything he'd envisioned her to be. Successful and chic, driven yet domestic.

Now that he was gone, she'd come unmoored and was utterly lost. Somehow Margot forgot she'd had some kind of self before Kevin. As Ian MacKaye intoned the tortured lyrics to *Waiting Room*, Margot realized her true self had been in stasis for a decade. *My time is like water down a drain,* he sang, she felt. Something of her former self began to surface, whatever was left of it. However it ended up looking in the shadows of her new life, Margot needed to reclaim the best of what she'd been before Kevin. As she considered how to do this, her best intentions were stifled by the question of who she could be. If not a wife, if not a mother, if not a caregiver, then whom? Who was she now? What did she want? This non-life, this hiatus from attachment to reality, was not sustainable. *I'm gonna fight for what I wanna be…*

Shadows floated across the ceiling of her darkened living room sporadically whenever a car drove by. The headlight beams tangled with tree branches creating an interwoven network of confused lines and bright spaces, like a maze comprised entirely of dead ends. For so long, Margot had been utterly trapped in her web of loss and grief, the bright spots fleeting by like beacons every so often, but never sustained enough to take hold of. Could music help her find a way out?

Morning found her still on the floor of her living room, surrounded by a scattering of music, vinyl and CDs alike. Kevin had never understood her desire to have a real stereo with a turntable rather than some piped in music from hidden speakers connected wirelessly to his various playlists. On a stereo she had insisted, however, buying herself a state of the art system. The music had held her like a blanket all night, and it held her still. She'd moved into the post-punk indie-emo stuff Kevin had been almost able to tolerate, finding in Seam's *The Trouble With Me* a comfort she had not expected. The soft drone of the last song had lulled her nearly to sleep as the sun rose.

When the CD ended, Margot sat up, neatly stacked the CDs on the shelf next to a decorative pile of books topped with bleached coral from a reef she'd never visited and put the vinyl back in the record box. She stretched her stiff back, bending left then right, and went upstairs for an abbreviated shower. The lack of sleep seemed to be having the opposite effect on her, as she didn't feel desperately tired at all. In fact, she felt almost alive. It was a nice change.

Taking care of the tattoo on her back alone proved somewhat difficult. Margot hadn't thought to ask Chase about it, and he hadn't mentioned any different instructions. After doing her best to apply the antibiotic cream, she put on a pair of tight black pants, a dove grey oversized sweater, and flats. As she applied her makeup, Margot examined her eyes as though for the first time. Their unusual color, the exact hue of a sapphire lit from within, looked bare, empty. For the first time in years, she heavily outlined them in black eyeliner, added a thick layer of mascara, and stood back to admire the effect. Without meaning to, Margot laughed. She looked so young, so different. Yet, so familiar, so much like her old self. No one at work would have the audacity to comment. She pulled her hair back into a severe ponytail and headed downstairs.

With her coffee and her bag, she left the house in an unusual mood. The morning colors spoke volumes of how much she'd missed during the year. A house down the street had planted tulips en masse, drifts of pink and white flowers waved daintily to her from impossibly thin stalks. They would be decimated by the next hard rain, but for this moment, their cheerful greeting had its intended effect. Margot's smile lasted for several blocks. It must have been a record.

As she walked, the drum parts on some of the albums she'd listened to stuck in her head. Later in the day, at her desk, she rapped out the beats of some of the changes on Fugazi's song *Epic Problem*, singing along, *And inside I know I'm broken but I'm working as far as you can see...*

Why had she let a bunch of stupid guys in college keep her from playing an instrument she loved, anyway? Why was she always so defined by men? In retrospect, it seemed totally foolish that she'd stopped playing drums. They were her first true love. Playing complicated rhythms, collaborating with like-minded musicians, writing and creating original music that might someday sustain another lost soul, these were the things Margot had been lured in by from the beginning. Had she ever even tried to explain this to Kevin? Or had she simply let go of the one thing that had made her special?

Kevin had encouraged her to play piano. He'd sat night after night with his eyes closed, listening to her play. Margot had loved playing for him. You didn't need a band to play piano. It was not collaborative at all. Piano was about the pianist learning to understand another person's music and to perform it competently. Maybe other people, the virtuosos, found true comfort in that kind of expression, but only with drums had Margot ever experienced a complete oneness with her music.

On a whim, after work, Margot took the bus to The Drum

Shop. As she walked in, the familiar sense of feeling totally out of place crept up on her once more. Firmly, she pushed away the sensation, reminding herself she had nothing left to lose. Not a thing in the universe. Unbridled, she sat down at a kit and started to play the riff from *Epic Problem*.

Margot didn't like the kit. She moved around the store until she found a used kit in the back. It was dinged up but it was from the sixties and sounded good. It had a full, mellow sound none of the new drums had. Was it the old wood? New wood might not have the same level of density in the growth rings as old wood. It would have an effect on the resonance. Maybe. Was that right?

"You sound great," one of the sales people said to her as she adjusted the snare.

"Thanks," she replied with a genuine smile.

The guy was young, probably twenty or twenty-one. "What year is this set?" she asked.

"Sixty-eight. It's eighteen hundred."

"Go get your manager for me, if you would," Margot said in a firm voice.

The kid walked away looking confused. When he returned, he was accompanied by a guy in his thirties who looked like he might know his shit.

"I'd like to make you an offer for these drums. They're pretty banged up, but I like the sound, and I need a kit. I'm hoping you'll take fourteen hundred, keeping in mind I'm also looking for traps and cymbals."

The guy didn't even blink. "Done. Let's call it a manager's discount."

Smiling wide, Margot said, "Well, thank you very much. I feel like I'm supposed to be here today. Also, I don't have a car. Can you deliver everything?"

The manager's eyebrows raised and he laughed. "Sure. Leave your address. I'll bring it all by myself."

"Great, thank you. I'm Margot."

"Steve. Good to meet you."

Margot tried out every cymbal in the store, settling on a used Zildjian ride and a fancy new Paiste crash, along with a decent used high hat and all the stands. She almost forgot to get a seat. Instead of the black one, a pink leopard print swivel stool caught her eye. Once she had sticks and a drum key, she was set. Handing over a pristine Amex, she paid the bill, left her address, and told Steve she looked forward to seeing him.

By eight o'clock, she had a complete drum kit set up in the middle of her living room. She started with paradiddles, frustrated by how out of practice her body was. She practiced along with some CDs, tried out some fills, listened in for the more complicated riffs. All in all, by the end of the night, she was keeping up with most of what she listened to.

When Steve had dropped off the kit earlier, he'd asked her how long she'd been playing drums for. When she told him she'd gone to Berklee over a decade before, he smiled and looked at her anew. "Who are you playing with now?"

"No one yet."

"Here's my card. I know at least three bands looking for a drummer half as good as you. What are you into?"

"Punk, indie, emo, anything not classic rock or country."

"Seriously, if you're interested in a gig, email me."

"Thanks. I'll think about it," she answered, genuinely flattered.

Now, as she lay the sticks down on top of the snare, she did think about it. Would it be the same trouble as last time around? Would playing with adults be different from playing with self-obsessed college students? Should she give it a try? Playing was so much fun. How had she forgotten the joy of it, the way time slipped by when she was part of the music? It made her feel something akin to hope. She would brush up on her skills and consider her options, thankful she still had options. No more time down the drain. It was time to pull herself together.

On Friday Margot wore jeans to work again. This time, it

seemed more natural. She'd paired them with a nice shirt, but she suddenly didn't want anything to do with her work wardrobe anymore. It was all so reminiscent of Kevin, of her old life, all painted in unobtrusive neutrals, a palette of ecru, shell pink, light beige. No actual color anywhere.

After Wednesday's experiment, she'd toned down her eye makeup, but not by much. Margot didn't want to analyze this new trend towards color, but she'd been nearly transparent for long enough.

Tonight was to be her last session with Chase. He would finish the designs on her back, wrap them over the tops of her shoulders and connect them to the front, binding off the lace edge with filigreed decoration. He would etch the final marks of her past, her grief, her loss, upon her very skin.

There was something bittersweet about the ending of this process. The pain had been so physical, such a jarring distraction from the numbness, she had welcomed it, longed for it. She knew she'd miss it. The past two nights, however, she had taken that longing for physical suffering and channeled it into something new, something creative. An outlet.

The drums were a discipline, and she was ready for them to possess her again. As the record player's needle had connected with the grooves of her vinyl, and Chase's needle had connected her body with the past, music would connect her firmly to the present. If a drummer tried to think too far ahead or stopped to analyze what she played, she would not be able to play even a simple beat. To be in the moment with the rhythm, beating out sixteenth notes, laying down a complex pattern with your whole body working in unison, was the freedom of playing music, and in particular, drums.

Chase waited for her outside his shop once more. He looked depressed. His normally excellent posture was downcast and his eyes were sad. Margot wondered if it had anything to do with this being their last session. They would part ways afterwards, right? Was there an alternative? Did she even want to explore alternatives?

"Hi, Chase," she called cheerfully as she approached.

"Evening, Margot. Ready?"

"Yep."

They followed their usual protocol. Margot undressed in the dressing room and put on the shawl. She lay face down on the padded table so he could work on her back. Chase washed her with the green soap, shaved her, washed her again, and applied the alcohol. With each step, Margot unwrapped a secret gift, one layer revealing the next, until Chase's hands were on her once more, resting gently, as he steadied himself for the fine lines he was drawing. Margot focused in on the sensation of the needle piercing her skin, its sting now so familiar, so welcome. The gift revealed itself fully as she realized Chase was not drawing a shroud, as she had once perceived it. Nor was he drawing the lines of the past, a simple record of lives and loves, lived and lost.

Rather, this was the sensation of growing through pain, the sensation of mindfulness in the present moment. Margot had lost sight of this as a semi had barreled through metal and glass and human life. As long as we live, we are each a part of this world. Whether we choose to be present in it is the determining factor of our happiness, of our usefulness. Margot drew the lines into her imagination along with Chase, following the intricacies of his work, as organic as the flight path of a honeybee, as geometric as the sacred ratio of Phi. She wanted to be present. She was choosing, now, a year after the accident, to live.

As Chase drew over her protruding shoulder bone, without protective fat beneath, the sensation was piercingly, shockingly painful. Margot gasped and his needle immediately ceased.

"Margot?" he asked, jolted into concern.

She leaned up on her elbow and looked at him with tears in her eyes. The tears weren't from the pain. They were about moving through it. She sat up, reached out, and placed her palm against Chase's stubbly cheek. "It's okay," she said. "It's just, well, thank you, Chase. For everything."

———

Chase had been feeling low all day. The breakup of the band had gutted him, and Bryce had looked a thousand times worse when Chase had returned his drums. He was barely conscious, with tracks up his forearms and used needles scattered around the filthy apartment. Unsure what to do, Chase had called 911 and they'd arrived and taken Bryce to the hospital. Chase might have felt better about it if he hadn't called later in the week to find Bryce gone. His roommate said he'd skipped town, left everything behind, and no one had heard from him.

Now, Chase was facing down his last session with Margot. Although he'd tried to avoid it, he'd grown attached to her. It definitely wasn't fair to make assumptions about what she needed or wanted, but Chase found her compelling. She had shown no signs of feeling anything but respect for him as an artist, so he realized his feelings were probably way off base. Everything seemed to be circling to an end around him. He was lost, rudderless.

Chase was going to miss seeing Margot. Maybe they would see each other around town, but the intimacy of tattooing her, the closeness of her body, of her consciousness within his realm, would be sorely missed. There was no way for him to express this to her, however, without seeming like a creepy weirdo. So, when Margot showed up, he greeted her and got down to work.

Chase lost himself in the drawing, in the design of the lace, in the drone of the machine he held in his hands, in the warm, yielding flesh beneath it. When Margot gasped, something seized him deep inside, an awful gripping of his heart within his chest, knowing he had hurt her. Ironically, he'd been hurting her all along, but she'd shown no signs of extreme discomfort since the first moment his needle had pierced her skin.

Now, as he slid the machine over her shoulder, her thin, pale skin drawn tight against bone, she gasped with shock at the sudden difference in discomfort. Leaning up to look at him, her unusually large eyes brimming with tears, her expression bore no signs of anguish. Instead, she fixed him with her steady gaze, her expression almost loving, and touched his face. He'd not experienced a touch so tender since before his mother had died. His breath caught in his chest, he closed his eyes to Margot's touch, trying to steady himself as the world tipped beneath him. Her words, softly floating through the charged air, reached his mind, his heart, ecstatic.

"Thank you, Chase. For everything."

All her pain surged through his body and joined with his own. "Margot," he whispered, his eyes still closed, her hand still resting upon his cheek. He put his own gloved hand over hers and held her to him, afraid to open his eyes, afraid to breathe, afraid she too would dissipate and leave him alone. Impulsively, he lifted her hand from his cheek and kissed her inner wrist, the spot directly over her pulsing heartbeat. When he opened his eyes again, the spell was broken. In her expression, he read an infinitesimal moment of surprise before her hand slipped from his and she turned away once more.

Chase had to take a few deep breaths to steady himself before he could continue. If he was ever going to tell Margot how he felt, it needed to be now. He took the chance.

"Margot. This is our last session."

"I know. I appreciate all you've done. You are a true artist, Chase." Still turned away from him, her voice was soft and sweet.

"After Cassidy, I thought it would be best not to ask out my clients, but after tonight, you won't be a client anymore. I'd like to get to know you better. Would you…"

"Don't, please," she interrupted, her back still to him. "I can't."

He sensed her withdrawing. He was losing her. He had to do

something. "Margot, I know about Kevin," he said quietly. "I understand how much you've lost and I'm so sorry."

"You understand?" she demanded with vehemence, abruptly alighting from the table. Facing him, fiercely clutching his mother's purple shawl to her breast, she said, "You could never understand what I've been through. Who I am. What, did you Google me? Did you look me up? Did you find out all the grizzly details of Kevin's decimation? His complete and utter fucking demise? And what? Now you think you know me? You don't know a God damn thing, Chase."

Her hands were trembling, ice white with the strain of clutching the shawl to cover her body. Her eyes brimmed with unshed tears. Chase panicked. "Shit. I shouldn't have mentioned it. Please sit down and let me finish. I'm so sorry."

"We are finished. I'll mail you a check." She turned and walked away. From within the dressing room, Margot withdrew her clothes and purse, then strode through the shop still undressed, still wearing the shawl.

Chase, knowing he couldn't let her leave like that, sprang to action. "Woah, wait. We're *not* finished. You can't leave like that. At least I have to wrap you. I'm not going to be responsible for you getting some horrible skin infection out there."

"You are not responsible for any part of me. You've done enough."

Margot stormed out the door, the shawl draped around her, the skin of her back swollen beneath fresh ink. The bells on the door rang out violently as they clattered against the glass.

Jesus. What had he done? How stupid could he be? She was gone and there was nothing he could do about it now. As the piercing sound of the bells faded into silence, Chase slammed his fist into the shattered vinyl of the chair.

"Fuck," he roared. His heart ceased beating the moment the door slammed behind her.

Margot was furious, horrified, blindsided, and nearly hysterical. She half speed-walked, half ran home, tightly clutching the shawl to her. That bastard. He had violated their contract. He wasn't supposed to *be* someone to her. He was supposed to do his fucking job. Why couldn't he stick to the job?

Who did he think he was, anyway, pretending to understand her experience? Kevin was hers alone. She was not willing to share him casually in conversation with anyone. Losing parents was different from this. Totally different. Margot's world had been shaken upside-down and emptied out, then shredded and set ablaze. There was nothing left but ashes. Literally ashes. *All my love in ashes.*

What did Chase want from her anyway? She had nothing to give. Her back stung in the cool night air as the raw wound screamed from her skin, unfinished. When she burst through her front door, she slammed it shut behind her, locked it and fled upstairs, shedding the shawl and her belongings as she ran. After washing with antibacterial soap, Margot applied a generous layer of antibiotic cream. As her fury subsided, she looked in the mirror. Her naked skin radiated beneath a yoke of beautiful designs, white on white, lost light now gleaming from within her body.

Chase's lovingly crafted designs were part of her now, his interpretation of the veil had brought its lines to life. Why did he have to mention Kevin? Why did he have to ruin this too?

As Margot stared at the flourishes in Chase's lace, her mind flashed back to the moment where she'd put her hand to his cheek. This was her fault. She'd broken their contract first.

Her heart sank as she thought about what Chase might be feeling, how she had hurt him, yet again. He didn't deserve it, but Margot could find no words to mend the rift and no energy to undo what she'd done. Loss, compounded exponentially by this new obliteration, set upon Margot with a weight so heavy she could barely breathe.

TEN

The year anniversary of the car accident came and went. Margot worked so hard she didn't have the energy to focus on it. It was a moderately successful strategy, leaving her exhausted by the end of every work day. She saved enough energy, however, to practice the drums. She played along to Chavez, Hey Mercedes, Death Cab for Cutie, old punk, new emo, everything she could find with real drums played by talented drummers. The complexities and nuances were expressed in her language. Drummers communicated through the mathematics of rhythm, the coded time signatures flirted with her like a dare. Can you figure this one out, little girl? Six-four on the high hat and four-four on the kick. Can you do it? How about the jazz-style improv right in the middle of Grizzly Bear's *Three Rings?* Can you figure that puzzle out? Sometimes her mind could grasp what her body could not. Practice, however, gained Margot incremental ground. She was starting to feel almost competent again, if not creative.

By the time she went to bed each night, the leaden grief in her heart had been transposed into drum notation, ticking away in her mind as she lay in bed, eventually unraveling into static like the crashing waves against some distant shore.

June passed, July turned up the heat to a simmer, and Ginny finally got her way when Margot accepted her invitation to meet for drinks. Since the altercation with Chase nearly two months before, Margot had been walking home a different way. She hadn't been to the bar, preferring a beer while she played drums instead. Since she barely looked at herself in the mirror, Chase was becoming less and less present in her mind, although when she thought about him directly, she was stricken with a pang of regret for how things had ended, and with a less discernable longing. It was hard to admit, but she missed him.

Ginny's hair was longer. Her curls looked looser, more natural. Her skin glowed and she seemed in every way more robust. Margot figured this had something to do with love. Henry had taken like a good skin graft. He was always with Ginny now. In fact, they'd made plans to meet up after Ginny had a drink with Margot.

Margot sat at the bar because the place was unusually crowded. Ginny bounced up to the empty seat beside Margot and kissed her friend.

Ginny leaned back and looked Margot up and down. "You look so good. How is everything?"

"I'm doing better," Margot said, honestly.

"It seems like it. I'm so glad."

"How are things with Henry?"

"Great," Ginny swooned. "He's so sweet to me. I wonder if that's what I've been missing all along. All the guys I've dated put up some kind of front, too cool to let me know they were actually *feeling* something. That part of Henry's male brain must be missing because he can't seem to help himself. He seems to like me a lot."

"Obviously. That was clear the first time I saw him with you, not long after you met. He can't take his eyes off you."

"He can't, can he?" Ginny replied, giggling.

Margot smiled. "I'm happy for you guys."

"He's never going to be rich, you know," Ginny commented

wistfully, gazing up at the ceiling.

"He's rich in other qualities. Better ones," Margot said.

"You're saying that to make me feel better."

"Feel however you want," Margot stated. "But he's good for you."

The two friends drank their usual drinks and talked amicably, as though they were seeing each other for the first time in years. Ginny was much more herself than she had been, and she assumed Ginny felt the same about her. It was nice to have her friend back, even for an hour.

Eventually, Ginny checked her phone. "Gotta go, but this was so fun. Can we do it again soon?" Ginny stood and hugged her.

"Definitely," Margot replied with a genuine smile. "Say hi to Henry for me."

"I will."

Margot looked up at the retro clock behind the bar and found it was still early. Sheila sauntered up. "Hey there, Margot. Want another drink?"

"Sure, Sheila. Thanks."

"So, where've you been?" Sheila poured her scotch and soda and asked, "I haven't seen you in a while."

"I've been keeping busy. I started playing the drums again."

"As in a full kit? What, like punk rock?"

"Yeah, I'm more into the math rock and indie stuff these days, but I love it all. I studied music at Berklee before I became an accountant."

"No shit. That's so crazy. You should play with Chase sometime. He's an incredible guitarist."

Margot's throat dried up at hearing his name, but she nodded and said, "I didn't know he played."

"Yeah, he's been in like a million bands, but the guys are always idiots and screw it up. His last band was good, too, before they imploded. I know Chase has been itching to play."

"I'll keep it in mind."

Sheila wandered off to tend to her busy bar. Chase was the real deal. It had been obvious from the beginning. He was genuine in all his actions and words. He was a creative dynamo. And Margot had been awful to him. She felt terrible.

"Hey," said a voice to her right.

Margot turned to find a man sitting close by. He was youngish and sporty, good looking but forward.

"Hi," Margot said, trying not to sound too friendly. She didn't feel like talking with a stranger.

"You come here a lot?"

The line was the oldest in the lexicon of pickups. Margot forced herself not to roll her eyes. "I used to."

"My first time. It's pretty gritty."

"It's not a sports bar," Margot answered sarcastically, without a trace of a smile.

Not knowing how to respond, the guy played it off with a laugh. Margot looked towards the door, wishing Ginny was still here. She'd know how to put this asshole off without any fanfare.

Turning back to her drink, Margot decided to cut it short. She downed the remainder, took out her wallet to pay Sheila, and tried not to look uncomfortable. The guy kept talking, clearly hoping Margot would find something about him interesting. She answered his questions in monosyllables.

Sheila came over and looked at Margot, scrutinizing her. "You okay? You don't look great."

"I'm going to go," Margot answered, finding the words thick upon her tongue. The edges of her vision started to dim, and she wavered upon her seat. Holding out some cash to Sheila, she paid for her drinks and started to stand up, saying, "Shay hi to Chaaasse for me."

"Here, let me help you," said the guy who'd been talking to her, his voice echoing faintly, filtering through a haze in her mind.

"I'm fine," Margot said, but she didn't believe it anymore. The last thing she remembered before her mind went totally dark was a desperate wish for time to reverse, to bring all her love back, so that she didn't have to navigate this world alone.

———

Chase's habit of standing outside his shop for four or five minutes at a time between customers and again at the end of the day stemmed back to when he'd smoked. Leaning against the wall of his shop, he watched the people go by. He said hi to all the ones he knew and to some he didn't, and generally found a sense of peace in the connection it gave him to his community. Besides, the air conditioner in the shop had broken a few days before, and Chase had been sweating his balls off through client after client.

He'd seen his last person a little while before. This space on Friday evenings had been reserved for Margot, and the emptiness of her absence still plagued him. He hadn't seen her since that last night, since the disastrous landslide precipitated by his own unwillingness to sense her pace, her need for a slower closing of the distance between them. He'd fucked it up royally and he wished he could undo the moment. Wishful thinking.

Scanning the street, he watched the people coming and going from the bar. As if on cue, a man exited with a blonde woman whose arm was draped limply over his shoulder, her wilting body barely able to set one foot in front of the other. They turned towards him and with a sickening shock, Chase realized it was Margot.

His first instinct was to turn away, it was so hard to see her with some jock asshole instead of what? With him? Then he set aside his own hurt feelings long enough to see the obvious truth. Something was not right.

"Hey, man," Chase called, getting in front of the guy who held Margot up like a ragdoll.

"Dude, you're blocking my path. My girl and I are going home."

"Like fuck you are, buddy. Margot?" Chase leaned in and tried to see into Margot's eyes.

Margot looked up, her eyes unfocused, her head lolling dangerously upon her slender neck. "Chaaassse," she said, drawing his name out into a long, slurred blur. "I don' know 'im." She stumbled forward, her heel turning on a loose brick. Chase reached forward to steady her, but the guy pulled her back.

"Let go of her right now, man," Chase said in a low, dangerous voice.

"Fuck off," the guy answered and tried to walk around him.

Sheila burst through the door of the bar looking frantically both ways, zeroing in on the scene in front of the tattoo shop. Bounding over she grabbed the man's arm and said, "You drugged her, you son of a bitch! She'd only had two drinks. She's not drunk. You're one of those roofie date-rapists. Chase, call the police."

Chase took out his phone but before he could dial, the guy shoved Margot towards him. Chase's phone jolted from his grip and smashed to the sidewalk below as he caught the limp Margot. Sprinting away, the man was out of sight in a mere moment.

"Jesus," Chase muttered, trying to hold Margot upright then giving up and lifting her into his arms.

"If you hadn't been out here, he would have…" Sheila's eyes were frantic, wild.

"It's okay, Sheila. Thank God I was here."

"I have to go back in, are you okay to take care of her?"

"I've got this. She's important to me, Sheila. I'll keep her safe."

Sheila moved forward and put one hand on his shoulder. "Thank you for being one of the good guys." Looking down at the unconscious Margot, she said, "I'll come up and check on you guys after work."

"Okay. I'll leave the back door open."

Sheila picked up Chase's broken phone. "You're gonna need a new screen."

"Bring it up later, I don't want a pocket full of broken glass."

With a long look of concern at Margot, Sheila nodded and turned away. Her shoulders drooped as she hurried back into the bar.

Chase maneuvered Margot into the shop, laying her on the reclining chair while he closed up. He locked the front door and took her up the back stairs to his place. He lay Margot on his bed, fully clothed, and covered her with a soft blanket. As he gazed down at her for a moment, his heart clenched in his chest.

Margot's face was pearly white, in complete repose, like Juliette asleep in Romeo's arms. What kind of monster would hurt this lovely woman? Why? She was such a fragile soul she was for tending like a rare orchid. The thought of the asshole who'd drugged her raping her, violating her, casting her out onto the street afterwards, disposable, like a piece of trash, sickened him.

He could call the police, but Sheila had his phone. They wouldn't be able to prove anything anyway, and it had been too dark to get a close look at the guy. He'd move on and do it to some other poor girl. Chase was utterly furious.

Reaching down to touch her throat gently, Chase checked to make sure Margot's pulse was strong. He didn't think she needed medical attention, but she'd be in rough shape tomorrow.

"I'm sorry, Margot," he said, softly. "I never meant to push you away. I'll try to do better."

Restless, Chase paced around the loft, ultimately heading to the fridge for a beer. He plugged in his guitar, turned down the amp, and played softly until Sheila came up hours later.

"How is she?"

"She hasn't moved."

Sheila felt Margot's forehead. She exhaled a deep breath, as though she'd been unable to breathe for the past hours. "I'm going to take her to the bathroom and take off her shoes, at least. You don't have a pair of sweats or a t-shirt she could use, do you?"

"She's going to swim in them, but sure."

As they lifted Margot to a sitting position, she opened her eyes half-way and mumbled something incoherent. Chase helped Sheila get the semi-conscious Margot to the bathroom where she tended to Margot's needs. Chase lay out the sweatpants and t-shirt on his bed, along with a pair of white tube socks. From the bathroom, Sheila called, "Chase, can you help me get her to the bed? She's out cold again."

"Yeah, okay." He swept Margot up into his arms, carried her across the room, and gently set her back in the bed. Sheila undressed Margot, and Chase looked away. Although he'd already seen a good amount of her luminous skin when he'd tattooed her, he wanted to protect her privacy.

When Sheila was done dressing Margot in Chase's clothes, she came over to Chase at his kitchen island and asked, "Is that lace tattoo your work?" She gestured to the resting Margot.

"Yeah."

"Man, you're fucking good. It's absolutely magnificent."

"Thanks, Sheila. You're a sweetheart, you know."

"Yeah, yeah. Don't get sappy on me." Sheila lay Chase's broken phone on the counter, accepted a glass of water, and looked back at Margot as she drank it. "She's a punk rock drummer, you know."

"No shit," Chase said, his heart clenching again. What an enigma Margot was. He had seen a glimmer of her feisty power when she'd confronted Cassidy, but never would have dreamed Margot was a drummer.

"Yeah. She told me tonight, before everything happened. I told her she should play with you." When Chase didn't reply, Sheila changed the subject. "Do you have ibuprofen?"

"Yeah. I'll give her some as soon as she wakes up."

"She'll need it. I gotta go. I'm already late and Dianna gets worried. You going to be alright?"

"I'm fine. She'll be okay by tomorrow."

"Thanks, Chase. You're a sweetheart, too, you know," Sheila added with a wink. She disappeared down the back staircase and out into the night.

Chase resumed his seat by the window with a fresh beer and played guitar until two a.m., at which point he forced himself to lie down on the couch. Sleep remained elusive, however.

Chase's thoughts turned involuntarily to his parents. They had been such good people. When everyone else's mom and dad had been getting divorced, his parents had seemed to love each other more and more with the passing years. He and his sister had always rolled their eyes at their public displays of affection, embarrassed by how comfortable their parents were with each other. There was nothing they wouldn't have done for him.

Chase was a senior with the whole world ahead of him. He'd recently applied for college. He fought with his dad almost daily over the stupidest things. And then, suddenly, they were gone.

Everything Chase had held as solid was an illusion. His grief was a monster raging in his body, threatening to consume him. Somehow, since his sister had already moved out the year before and started college, her grief seemed so much more adult than his. Chase was still a child in comparison, throwing tantrums and punching walls. There was no erasing the all-encompassing loss, returning each night after school to an empty house where dinner had always been cooked and laughter once had abounded. All was silence, emptiness, and he'd been lost.

Art had saved him. The sentiment was a cliché, but it was true. Sketchbooks full of angry drawings, dark designs, a record of his most painful moments, still lay packed in a box of things from his old life.

He received his acceptance letter to Pratt Institute for the Arts two months after the funeral. He'd wanted to shout to his dad, "Look, I did it. Art isn't a waste of time. I'm really good at it!" But he was gone. Chase couldn't prove anything to him, couldn't apologize to him, couldn't make amends. Instead, Chase emailed his sister, followed up on the acceptance letter with the school, and prepared to begin his new life.

Tattooing had been the perfect way to take the money he'd inherited and the art degree he'd almost finished and combine them into a living. He bought the Congress Street building during the real estate crash in Portland and had never looked back.

As he lay on the couch in the dim evening light he listened to the soft breathing of a woman he cared for only feet away upon his bed. What did he want now?

———

Margot awoke to a blankness of memory she'd not experienced since the accident. Suddenly, her eyes were open, fixed upon a far-off, darkened ceiling she did not recognize, in a bed that was not her own. Breathing hard as panic rose within her, she tried to master herself before making any sudden movements. What had happened? The last thing she remembered, she'd been at the bar with Ginny, and when she'd left, Margot had talked to Sheila, and then to some random guy. The guy. The guy. Who was the guy? She couldn't even recall his face. Sporty clothes, clean-cut, white, and maybe good looking, but other than that, his features were a blur.

Gasping, she realized what had happened. Had he drugged her? Was she in his apartment? Had he…

Movement to the left, a shadowy figure approached. Margot screamed, sat up in bed, pulled the covers to her chest, and tried to get away, all before she recognized the voice.

"It's okay, Margot. You're safe. It's Chase. You're okay. This is my apartment."

"What the fuck?" she yelled out, still gripped with panic. "What happened? Why am I here?" Her voice shook, her hands trembled, her head pounded, like it had been crushed in a vise.

"Some asshole slipped something in your drink. He was

walking you down the street like a ragdoll and I stopped him."

"What?"

"He was trying to take you somewhere, but you were incoherent. Then Sheila burst out of the bar and told me he'd drugged you. The guy threw you at me and bolted."

"I don't remember anything," Margot cried, in full-blown alarm. "I, I…"

"It's okay. You're safe. I took you upstairs and lay you on the bed until Sheila could come up. She helped you in the bathroom, she dressed you in my clothes. Can I get you some ibuprofen?"

Margot bent over, put her hands on her head, and squeezed. Chase's calm voice was filtering through into her consciousness, but nothing could calm her down. He left and returned a moment later with a glass of water and a bottle of Advil.

"Here," he said, gently, handing her the pills first and then the water. Her hands shook uncontrollably.

"Thank you, Chase." Her throat felt too tight to swallow the pills, but she managed. Tears prickled behind her eyes as she realized exactly what the guy would have done to her if Chase hadn't intercepted him. "You saved me. Like some fucking fairytale knight. I'm too stupid to take care of myself. That man would have raped me, Chase. I can't imagine surviving that after…after the rest of it." Her voice broke as she said, "Thank you."

"I would do anything for you, Margot. You need to know that. But now, you should rest. You're safe."

Chase took the glass from her unsteady hand, leaned over, and planted a feather-soft kiss upon her head. Margot lay down once more, tears finally spilling down her cheeks. As her throbbing head shifted positions on his pillow, Margot needed to close her eyes and sleep. Within seconds, she was out, giving herself over to the darkness. It enveloped her completely.

Full daylight spilled through the rear windows of Chase's wide-open loft when Margot opened her eyes once more. The ceiling above was unbelievably high and covered in painted, pressed tin. The designs in the tin were of flowered wreaths with egg and dart decorations around the edges. It was charmingly feminine and very old, what Margot had seen written up in design magazines as the ultimate in shabby-chic. Chase was not the shabby-chic type, so it amused the fuzzy Margot.

Chase sat in a chair pulled up close to the bed. Was he actually knitting? He looked peaceful in the halo of light surrounding him, highlighting his handsome profile. Margot's gratitude for his heroics deepened and she wanted to apologize for storming out on him months ago. She'd regretted it ever since.

Margot shifted up against the wooden headboard, and from her higher angle, she could now fully see the work in Chase's hands. He was making a hat. A tiny, pink hat. The sight of it, with its familiar color and its exact shape, set off a depth charge deep in Margot's psyche, shaking the very foundations of her soul.

"Where did you get that?" she asked ferociously, ready to spring from the bed and grab it from his hands.

"You're awake," Chase said, smiling at her. His smile disappeared as he took in her expression.

"What are you doing with my hat?"

"Um, I don't know what you mean, Margot. I make these hats for the hospital. For the preemies. My mom taught me to knit a long time ago, and when I make these I think of her. It's a pastime."

"I don't understand. It was that exact one. How?"

Margot's mind rebelled. She couldn't piece together what she was seeing with the sliver of memory she'd suddenly unearthed. She couldn't understand what was going on.

Chase, looking alarmed and confused, held up the hat which clung tenaciously to the thin, pointed needles. A delicate line of pink yarn hung from it like a fuzzy umbilical cord. Slowly, Chase proffered it forth.

As Margot's hand took the velvet-soft object, as she held the smallness of it, the deep familiarity of it, a tsunami of grief struck Margot's solar plexus, knocking the very breath from her lungs. She gasped for breath, for a grip on reality. The animal cry Margot released rent the air. She remembered. All at once, she remembered everything her mind, in some kind of amnesiac mercy, had held back from her.

The baby. Her baby. Holding her tiny baby, her impossibly small child, in this exact hat. The image was so intimate, so tangible, so physical it tore at Margot from the inside out, from the cavity where her soul had shared a sacred space with that of her unborn child. Margot held the hat to her breast and wailed.

———

"Jesus. Margot, what is it? What?" Chase said, panicked. He sprang from his chair and sat upon the edge of the bed, unsure what to do as the woman before him unraveled, clutching his knitting in her pale, shaking hands.

"My angel," Margot sobbed, uncontrollably. "My tiny angel. Why? Why?" Curling forward into a ball, Margot's body shook with the violence of her sobbing. Chase firmly silenced the voice of doubt in his heart, as he put his arms around her, gathered her to him, and held her as tight as he could.

As he held her, Chase finally understood the true depth of Margot's grief, of her loss, of why she pushed everyone away, of how she'd been so broken. His heart ached for her. Margot had not only lost her husband in the accident, she had lost her child.

Chase held her as a year's worth of unshed tears and pent up misery spilled out against the soft pink yarn, against his steady arms, where the names of his mother and father were drawn in coded designs. He rocked her and kissed her hair as she wept, and when she was spent and her body had gone limp, he held her still.

When Margot eventually stirred, she looked up at him with crystalline, distant eyes. She was utterly bereft.

"Talk to me, Margot," he said gently. "Tell me about your baby."

She closed her eyes. Her jaw tightened. She might tell him to fuck off, that it wasn't his business, that he had no right to ask. He braced himself for this final rebuff, but she surprised him. Margot opened her eyes and sat up. Reluctant to let her go, Chase held her hand firmly as she began to speak.

"I think, somehow, after everything happened, I blocked this out. Maybe my mind was trying to protect me. I don't know."

"You lost your baby during the accident?" Chase asked softly.

"No, it was so much worse than that." Margot paused and shuddered. "You know, I never even told anyone about her. Kevin and I hadn't told anyone we were expecting. Things were so rough at the beginning. She was our secret, growing tenuously within me. We'd finally gotten past the five-month mark and it had started to feel real. She was real. We even decorated her nursery." Margot stopped to wipe fresh tears from her eyes. "We were on a drive, out in the country. It was finally springtime. Kevin was in the passenger seat since I always felt better driving because of the nausea. Out of nowhere, a semi sped into our car. Its breaks had gone out and it plowed straight into us. Kevin died instantly." She paused and swallowed.

Chase reached out and took the glass of water from the bedside table and handed it to her. She took a sip and continued, "I was airlifted to the hospital, broken, half dead. They performed a C-section, but my uterus was damaged from the impact of the dashboard and the steering wheel caving in and crushing me." Margot hesitated, her voice breaking in agony. "They took my baby from me, and when I woke up she was dying in an incubator, on some other floor of the hospital, alone."

Margot's breath was ragged, as she relived this horror.

Sobbing, she forced herself to continue. "I screamed for her. I forced the nurses to bring me to her, and even though I was just out of surgery, full of broken bones, clouded by morphine, they did as I asked because they respected Kevin.

"She was tiny, so unbelievably small, badly hurt and struggling. I held her through the glove in the side of the incubator." Margot gulped back another sob, but continued, unable or unwilling to stop now. Chase squeezed her hand. "I begged them to let me hold her, to feel my skin against her skin. She needed me. My baby needed me. She was all alone in that fucking incubator when she needed to be inside of me. She needed her mom." Margot bent forward, clutching at her abdomen, consumed with the pain of her memories, with the anguish of it all. "I was hysterical as she slipped away from me. Then it was over. They handed me this lifeless, miniscule form in a tiny pink hat."

Margot went silent. Chase could barely breathe, it hurt so much to imagine. He put his arm around Margot and held her close. Eventually, when she could speak again, it was with a hushed, desperate voice. "It was so wrong. It was so wrong for her to die." She sat up a little. "I had her cremated with Kevin. If she couldn't be with me, then at least she could be with her dad." Her voice breaking once more, she said, "She was all I had in the universe. She was all I ever wanted, and I broke her. I couldn't keep her safe."

"You didn't break her, Margot. It wasn't your fault." Chase's words were vehement, his tone stern. "None of this was your fault."

"My only job in the world was to keep her safe. I failed. I lost her. I lost everything." Tears streamed down Margot's cheeks, her expression tortured, and she shook with fresh grief.

Chase held her as tight as he could in his steady arms. "Oh, Margot. I am so sorry," he whispered into her hair. "I am so sorry."

Finally, she said, "I don't want your pity, Chase. I don't want it."

"Listen to me, Margot," he stated in a firm, deep voice. "This is not pity. I care about you. This is what it looks like when people care. Nothing I say or do will bring your family back to you. We both know that. But talking about it, remembering it, bringing it all back out into the open will help you find some peace."

"I don't think peace is possible."

"It is. Your mind couldn't deal with Kevin and the baby's deaths at the same time. You had to put this aside until you were strong enough."

"I am *not* strong enough," Margot answered. "Look at me. I can't even keep myself safe in a fucking bar."

"That predator had nothing to do with your inner strength. He was looking for someone to hurt."

"Wrong place, wrong time, just like the truck," she said forcefully, but her body was losing any energy she had been filled with during her adrenaline spike.

"There's nothing we can do about that. Fate or whatever it is that spared you both times has you here for a reason. Maybe you need to figure out what that reason is."

"It hurts too much," Margot said, desperately.

"I know," Chase said, kissing her head softly once more. "I know it hurts."

After a while, Margot wiped the tears off her cheeks. She looked terribly pale and ill. Looking down at herself in his crumpled, oversized white t-shirt, she said, "May I use your bathroom?"

"By all means. It's over here." Chase was hesitant to let go of her, so he led her by the hand to the bathroom in the far corner of the loft. "Let me know if you need anything."

"Thanks," she said, still unable to meet his eyes.

Chase gently rested his palm against her petal-soft cheek and tilted her head up. "Thank you for sharing your story with me. That took an unbelievable amount of courage."

Desperate grief flared in her eyes before exhaustion took its place. She nodded once and turned away.

———

In the bathroom, Margot relieved herself, washed her hands and face, and looked into the mirror. There she was. Nothing had changed, yet everything had changed. She had been kidding herself for months, thinking she could get better, get over it all, that music would ever heal the gaping wound in her soul.

How had she not dealt with the baby's death? How crazy would a person have to be to put it completely out of their mind like she had? How had she ignored the bittersweet memory of holding her baby, even after it was all over, of holding the last person in the universe she could love? She'd locked the memory up along with the nursery door and had ignored it every day for over a year. How had she disregarded her tortured uterus, the place where possibility had once grown, where a future of love and family had nestled? Everything was torn apart, severed from her, shredding her entirely.

While she'd been grieving Kevin's death, her mind must have blocked out everything else that had happened. Daily, she'd fought back the oblivion, telling herself she could survive without him. But now? The delusion had shattered. She'd lost her precious baby. Nothing would ever be all right again. Not even her body could protect the child from a hideous death, alone in some fucking machine, clear acrylic separating her from the body who had nourished her, who had grown her, who had loved her with every ounce of energy she could muster. It hadn't been enough.

The entire ward went still when her baby's heart had stopped. The last sound was the wail of a lost mother, the bereft woman in the wheelchair, her hands helplessly pounding against the incubator. When they handed Margot her lifeless child, silence descended. It settled into Margot's core, smothering any joy she would ever feel again with grief. Silence had remained. How light she had been, her tiny baby. Margot had never spoken the name she'd chosen aloud. She hadn't even told Kevin that she'd decided already. There was only silence left, in place of life.

Now, reality foisted itself upon her and Margot's stomach turned. As she threw up its bilious contents, sweat broke out on her forehead. She was acutely ill as the poisoned drink left her system. No words could describe the vileness of the man who had done this to her, who would have done so much worse.

Why couldn't they have let her die with her baby? Shouldn't they have known she couldn't live without her? That they couldn't live without each other? Margot, shaking and sick, her knees wobbling, threw up again. There was nothing left. She crumpled to the bathroom floor where she remained until she could breathe again.

After an age of agony, Margot stood up, flushed the toilet a few times, steadied herself against the sink, and washed her mouth out with Chase's toothpaste on her finger. She washed her face again, wishing for her bathtub and soap, or even better, for a loaded gun so she could finally end it all. No more pain.

Then, she thought of Chase's arms around her. He'd held her, strong and steady and silent. He'd saved her from yet another layer of agony by stopping that monster the night before. What was she supposed to do now? A 'thank you' seemed terribly inadequate, but it was all she could muster for the time being.

Gathering her strength, Margot dried her face, brushed out her ratty hair with Chase's tiny man-comb, and steeled herself. She'd come this far, she could go another step. And maybe even another. One foot in front of the other, she walked to the bathroom door, holding Chase's gigantic sweatpants tight around her waist with one hand, and opening the door with the other.

Chase stood at the kitchen island, bathed in cheerful morning sunlight, pouring coffee. He'd made a piece of toast for her and had set it on the bar side of the island.

He looked up as she approached, his eyes sad and concerned. "Toast?"

"No. I should go home."

"Not until you've eaten something." Chase said the words firmly. She was too spent to fight.

"I'll try, but I feel awful," she remarked as she sat down, preempting talk about anything else, anything real. She'd already shared too much. Lifting the warm toast to her mouth, she took a bite and then another, instantly feeling better as it hit her roiling stomach.

"I also made you tea. I figured coffee might be a little too much on your stomach."

"That was very thoughtful. Thanks." She accepted the steaming mug, smiling involuntarily at the image on the side of the cup. It was a vintage Ziggy mug bearing the inscription, *Good morning, sunshine.* The sun was smiling at a relatively cheerful looking Ziggy.

"Why doesn't he ever have pants on?" Margot wondered aloud, sipping the tea.

"What?" Chase asked, the glimmer of a smile on his unshaven face.

"Ziggy. No pants. Ever. It's weird."

"I never thought about it."

"Well, it's weird." Margot forced a smile and met Chase's gaze. He looked tired. There were dark circles under his eyes. He'd been up most of the night caring for her, and this realization produced a fresh wave of guilt in Margot.

Chase took his coffee from the counter, walked around the island, and sat next to her on the other diner stool. "Is the toast helping?"

"Yeah. Sorry to be such a pain in the ass."

"Margot, listen to me. I care about you and nothing will

change that. I'm here, whenever you're ready to let me be your friend."

Staring down at her half-eaten toast, which was kind of in the shape of a screaming man, Margot said, "I'm not sure when I'll be ready to accept that offer. Friendship is a two way street and I'm a bit of a dead end at the moment. But thanks. For everything."

"I told you, you're stronger than you realize. You're going to be okay. You'll never be the same, but you will be okay."

"We'll see," she said quietly.

Chase patted her hand and took a sip of his coffee.

After a quiet moment he asked, "Do you actually play the drums?"

Margot nodded her head weakly. "Did Sheila tell you that?"

"Yeah. She told me last night. She said you play and are looking for a gig."

"I'd been thinking about it, but what's the point? I've been delusional, apparently. I need to get a grip on reality, not just distract myself."

"Music is not just a distraction. It's creation."

Margot was too exhausted to debate the point. Instead, she asked, "Are you working on anything new?"

"I've been hashing something out for a while," Chase said sheepishly.

"Play it for me," Margot requested.

Cradling the mug of hot tea to her chest, she shakily got up, crossed the room, and sat on his couch, on the side closest to his amp. She felt small and she shivered slightly in the airconditioned room. Chase noticed and retrieved a small, hand-knit blanket from the back of a chair. He draped it gently around her shoulders and sat down in an armchair. After plugging in the guitar, he turned on the amp with a startling pop.

Chase tuned up and played a song he knew she knew. It was *Want*, the first song on Jawbreaker's *Unfun*. Chase smiled at her cheekily. Margot shook her head, unable to resist a faint smile in return.

After *Want*, he played a song she didn't recognize. It was a haunting melody in a minor key with chords of such dissonance they clenched at Margot's heart, but the bridge had the sweetest resolution. This was Chase. He was present in every chord. You didn't know what he was going to do or say, but you could count on it being beautiful.

Before the final notes had fully faded, she demanded he play it again. Chase complied.

This time, he sang along. Softly, nearly inaudibly, he sang the melody, intoning words of love and loss. His music was nothing at all like the guys she'd played with in college, whose chords had the predictability of pop music and whose lyrics were meant to be marketable. This was different in every way. It was not trying to be anything, and in its originality lay the artistry. When Chase played the bridge this time, Margot teared up.

"When did you write it?" she asked when he finished for the second time.

"Right after I met you. I came back to a theme I'd been working on. Then, it all came together after I started work on your tattoos."

"Oh." Margot had felt the unspoken connection of his music to her, to her pain and loss through Chase's pain and loss. Now, though, she saw it was something deeper. A connection of personality, of mind, of music. There'd always been something unique about Chase, whose talent and ingenuity transcended the typical. He regarded her for a moment before he started playing again. Margot wanted to say something, but she was tongue-tied. Instead of trying to find the words, she watched him and listened to him. His music coursed through her body, filling spaces she thought would remain empty forever. Maybe she didn't need to say anything after all. Maybe she could simply be here, in the present, without any connection to the past or the future. Only now. In a moment of music.

ELEVEN

Chase had always been thankful for the guitar. It was his preferred method of communication, aside from drawing. Words, however lovely they could be, always seemed to get him in trouble. He could write lyrics to songs, but he'd found that when he wanted to communicate a feeling, music was the only way.

Margot sat, listening while he played, her attention rapt. He could talk for ten years and never say as much as he could with these chords. And here was a woman who understood his language. He could see it in her expression. With each progression, she seemed to sense his story. She understood and participated in the emotion of the music. He didn't want to stop, and she didn't seem to want him to stop. So, he played for an hour. Songs he'd written ages ago, songs he loved by other musicians, songs that bubbled up in the moment. And there Margot sat, listening, feeling.

The sunlight shifted from its oblique angle through the back windows and began winding its arc over the top of the building. Soon, it would blaze through the front windows, creating a golden nimbus of light in his loft. It was his favorite thing about living here. The light was perfect.

Margot, however, was the luminous moon on a cloudless night. Her beauty transcended the realm of what Chase had come to think of as humanly possible. She seemed spun from white light. Her eyes, though haunted, were so expressive they spoke volumes. As she sat watching him, listening intently to his songs, his connection to her grew. He was telling her everything he couldn't say but longed to. He was playing it all for her and somehow, miraculously, she understood.

As he finished a song, Margot stirred as though from a trance. "Thank you for playing for me. You're very talented. But I have imposed on your kindness quite long enough. I should let you get on with your day. Thank you for taking care of me."

"Please, don't go," Chase said, surprised at the force with which he said the words. "You don't need to leave. It's Saturday and I had nothing going on at all. I rent all the spaces downstairs out on Saturdays. Stay."

Margot considered him. She looked around and seemed to lose some of the wind that had stirred her. "Are you sure?"

"I have never been more certain of anything in my life. I want you to stay. Please."

Leaning back on the couch once more, looking rather like a nestling wrapped in a blanket his mother had made for him when he was a child, she nodded her head and said, "I don't want to go home right now anyway."

"I've wanted an opportunity to apologize to you for two months," Chase said. "I am so sorry for driving you away. I should have understood how you were feeling."

"Please don't apologize," Margot replied, softly. "That was all my fault. I overreacted and I've felt terrible about how I treated you. You didn't deserve it and I'm so sorry. I was awful to you. Sometimes I think everything good in me died during that accident. I didn't used to be such a bitch."

"You're not a bitch. You're hurting."

"I am."

Chase was quiet for a moment, but eventually he said, "After my parents died, I had to live in our family house alone. My sister was away at college, so I filed to be an emancipated minor, but every night I came home to a house full of ghosts. Every fight I'd ever had with my dad echoed through the place. Every sweet smile of my mom's was like a knife in my heart. Their love for me lingered there, mixed up with my guilt. It was awful. The second I graduated from high school, I sold the place and moved away, hoping to outrun that sense of loss."

Margot's eyes were distant, fixed upon something outside the window, maybe farther. "It can't be outrun, can it?"

"No."

"I'm sorry you had to go through that," Margot said, looking at him again. "It's so sad. You never got to apologize to your dad."

"I didn't," Chase said, swallowing hard. "I was a terror. So disrespectful, so disdainful. I fought him on everything. He didn't deserve any of it." Chase looked away, unwilling to let Margot see the true depth of his guilt over that part of his life.

"If there is anything left after all this," Margot said, gesturing around, "his spirit will be up there looking down with pride about the good man you have become. We're all awful as teenagers. He probably had the same fraught relationship with his own dad. Don't let the guilt of it eat at you anymore."

Chase nodded, trying to rein in his emotions. "I try not to."

"Did you move to Portland right after that all happened?"

"No. I went to Pratt for illustration and design, but I kind of foundered in New York. After three years I quit, moved up to Portland, and bought this building with money I had left from my parents' estate and the settlement from the accident. There was already an existing tattoo shop downstairs, and this space had been storage. I interned with the guy who owned the shop and when he moved on, I kept the place going. I put in the kitchen and the bathroom up here and made it my home. I decided against walls for a bedroom because of the great sunlight in here all day, so that's why the bed is in the far corner."

"I love it. It's very cool. I always wanted to live in a loft in Boston. By the time I lived on my own, though, I was with Kevin. Lofts were definitely not his style."

"What was his style?" Chase asked cautiously.

"Clean lines, pale colors, minimalist décor. His aesthetic definitely rubbed off on me. He was older than me. I looked to him for a lot of things I probably should have figured out for myself. One thing we never agreed on, though, was music."

"Really? What did he like?"

"Classical, jazz, every once in a while something folk-pop like Mumford & Sons. He thought the music I liked was noise. I couldn't explain the nuances of Fugazi. I couldn't get him to hear the complexity in Hey, Mercedes. He tuned it out. And eventually, I boxed everything up and put it away. I don't know why."

"Love makes us do strange things, doesn't it?"

"It does. How long have you been playing guitar for?"

"Since I was eleven. Art and music were my whole world as a kid."

"I hear that. All I wanted as a teenager was to play in every band I could. Then I got into Berklee, but it wasn't the scene I'd imagined. There was something missing. Looking back, I blamed everyone else. All the guys, all their sexism and exclusion. Maybe, though, whatever I was looking for in them was missing in me. I had no self-confidence. I had no idea how to stand my ground in a band or take on the criticism of the male drummers surrounding me. So, I turned to piano, found it less fulfilling, and eventually moved to accounting."

"I wondered how you ended up in accounting," Chase said, his eyebrows arched.

"Not as glamorous as rock and roll, that's for sure."

"You could make anything glamorous."

"Chase, please," Margot said, looking down at her folded hands. "Don't say things like that."

"Sorry, but I think the world of you."

After a long silence, Margot said, "You're an incredible guitarist. Your songs speak to me."

"I'm so glad you like them," Chase said, genuinely relieved.

"Would you mind getting me a glass of water?"

"My pleasure. Do you need anything else? Something to eat?" he asked, looking concerned.

"Nope. Just the water. Thank you."

Chase poured her a glass of water and handed it to her. Then, he sat beside her on the couch. "You look tired. Please lie down if you need to. You had a rough night."

"The morning was rougher," she said, apparently before she thought it through, for she gave him a sidelong glance of apology. "I am tired, though."

Margot set her water glass on the table and leaned her head against Chase's shoulder. He shifted his arm so that she could rest against his chest and he put his arm around her. He held her tight. His heart was racing, his breathing was a chore to keep even, and Margot's hair was so close he could smell her shampoo. He kissed her head lightly. She settled in even closer.

Within another moment, her breathing slowed and evened out, the tension dissipated from her muscles, and she was asleep against his body. The feel of her there, her warmth, her slight frame, her sweet scent, Chase was consumed with the desire to protect her. He held her softly against himself, shifting slightly into a more comfortable position, and leaned his head back against the couch. Staring at the ceiling, he thought of the women he'd been in love with. Considering his age there weren't that many of them.

Sara had been the most promising love affair he'd had. She worked at the museum in the curatorial department doing installations. Their relationship had lasted almost three years, one of them in marriage, but somewhere along the line Sara had decided she wanted kids and hadn't told him. Chase absolutely didn't want to be a father. Was it any wonder, after the relationship he'd had with his own? As things with Sara deteriorated, it always came back down to that factor. It was a difference so essential, so all-encompassing, that once it was discussed, the disagreement led to the demise of the union.

Sara had been sweet. Kind and nurturing. She, in fact, was a lot like his own mom. Was that why he'd loved her so much from the very beginning? Had he been looking to replace his own mother? It had never occurred to him before, but now it made so much sense. It was also totally fucked up. Chase didn't want to deny Sara the chance to be a mother, even though it broke his heart to let her go. It still hurt to think about. He honestly hoped she was happy and fulfilled in her new life.

As he succumbed to exhaustion, Chase's memories faded into dreams. With Margot tucked beneath his arm, their breathing synched up inadvertently. Fully engulfed in this peaceful state, they slept together on the couch.

———

Margot woke up tucked under Chase's arm, her head against his chest. The heat of his body had warmed her to the core. His scent was completely comforting, so utterly male. She breathed him in and tried to suppress a flutter of attraction. He'd fallen asleep holding her, and now he lay with Margot draped around him, their bodies like one being. Margot ran her hand along Chase's forearm. The patterns drawn there were frenetic, colorful, a lot like him. Was there something written in the designs? Was it a code? She wasn't sure. As she rested her slender fingers against his wrist, his pulse thrilling beneath her fingertips, her own heart skipped a beat as she remembered him kissing her in the exact same spot. She'd been drawn to Chase from the beginning, but weren't they too different?

Over time, Margot had chameleoned into something very like Kevin, but when they'd met she'd been a little punk girl slinging coffee and listening to wild music. Kevin had tamed her, somehow, and in her love for him, she had become his mirror image. Was the difference between her and Chase actually the difference between Chase and Kevin? Maybe, essentially, Margot was more like Chase than she had ever been like Kevin. That idea was disconcerting. How had she become someone new, slowly over time? Who was she now? It didn't matter anyway.

Margot was too broken for any of this. She should get out of here before Chase read the wrong meaning into her weak moment. As Margot began to extricate herself from beneath his heavy arm, Chase sleepily shifted and pulled her to him even tighter.

"Margot," he whispered, still wrapped in his dreams.

Margot gasped. She needed to go. Now.

"Chase, wake up. I have to go."

He started and sat upright, Margot still in his hold. "Sorry, was I snoring? You okay?"

His kind brown eyes met hers. The warmth and comfort of Chase's body was endangering her composure, as Margot's heart tugged from beneath her grief. Whatever this feeling was, she was not ready to explore it, but at the same time, she could no longer deny her connection to him. She needed time.

"I need to go," she said miserably.

"Really? I wish you could stay. I can make you some soup if you're ready."

Margot didn't know what to say or what to do. Why had she let this go on so long? She was going to break his heart. She saw it in his eyes. As she was about to stand up, though, the thought of him being the only person who knew about the baby hit her. They had shared something essential of themselves during these harrowing hours, and nothing could change that. Margot struggled for purchase as her world underwent yet another seismic shift, from solitude to solidarity.

The feel of Margot's body against his was indescribable. Chase didn't want to let her go. In fact, as he'd awoken from a chaotic dream, her name had tasted like honey on his tongue.

Margot now looked into his eyes as he held her tight. She was struggling with herself; he could see it. The desperate desire to kiss away all her sadness, to remind her what it was to feel love again gripped him. But Chase knew that if he kissed her now, he would lose her forever. Pulling back, keeping his deepest desires in check, he simply stroked her cheek and tipped his forehead to meet hers.

"Do you want to leave, Margot?" he asked, gently.

She barely seemed strong enough to nod her head in the affirmative.

"Then I will walk you home."

"You don't have to do that," she replied, her voice cracking.

"Please. I want to. What if we have soup first and then go? Does that sound good?"

Margot nodded again and Chase chanced one last squeeze, saying, "We're still among the living, Margot. We cannot live like ghosts." He stood up, crossed to the kitchen area, and took a couple of cans of soup from the cabinet. "Chicken tortilla or tomato?" he asked, holding them both up.

"Chicken tortilla. Thanks."

"Campbell's finest, coming right up."

After they ate together, Chase put on his shoes while Margot dressed in her clothes from the day before. She looked a bit stronger than she had. Color had returned to her cheeks, her gait wasn't wobbly, and she seemed more like herself. It was a relief.

Before they left, Margot took Chase's arm in her surprisingly strong grip and said, "I cannot understate my gratitude, Chase. You saved me from something truly horrific last night. You were like a guardian angel. I'll never be able to thank you enough. You know what he would have done to me. You are such wonderful person, and I'm lucky to know you." Margot threw her arms around him and squeezed. It was so out of character, Chase was floored. He hugged her back and kissed the top of her head. God, how he wanted to kiss her in earnest.

"I know I said this, but I care very much about you. I'm thankful I was outside the shop last night. I think I would have killed anyone who hurt you."

"I have been all alone for so long. It's nice to have someone in my corner." She released him with an embarrassed expression and withdrew once more into her guarded state.

They walked slowly, side by side, all the way to Margot's house in the West End. It was a beautiful summer afternoon; the bustle of the city gave way to a more peaceful feeling as they entered the residential area tucked up behind Congress Street. When they approached Margot's house, Chase said, "Woah. This is your place?"

Sheepishly, as she fumbled in her bag for her keys, Margot nodded her head. "Would you like to come in?"

"Sure. It's beautiful."

The double-door entry way led into a pure white foyer with white marble floors. A round, antique table stood in the center of the gracious space, an empty crystal vase in its center. Beyond was a gracefully rounded stairway curving up to the second floor. Margot pulled off her heels and put them on a rack in the deftly hidden coat closet. Barefoot, she looked diminutive in the cavernous space. She led him into the living room, which was also done in whites and greys with a tiny pop of muted color here and there. Yet, incongruously situated in the corner of the room sat Margot's drum kit.

Chase laughed and said, "I somehow didn't expect it to be sitting right there. I love it. Sparkly."

"Yeah, I was fourteen when my dad bought me my first kit at a second-hand shop. It was total crap. I played some good drums at Berklee, but I sold them when I left. This time I went with a classic. It's a Ludwig '68 in Sparkle Blue. When I was in school, these would have seemed like a splurge."

"It's all relative, isn't it," Chase said, wistfully. "I'd really like to play with you, whenever you're ready."

Margot nodded her head and continued their tour, heading to the kitchen. "Can I get you anything? Scotch or yogurt?"

Chase wondered if she was joking. He brazenly walked over to her fridge and opened it. She hadn't been kidding. In the fridge he found a bag of kale salad, a couple of apples, and some plain yogurt. The scotch stood on the counter by the fridge. "I don't know what to say."

"I used to love cooking for Kevin. Now, I eat to sustain me, but I don't like to cook for myself."

Chase resolved to cook a real meal for her soon.

Margot poured them each a glass of water and rubbed her eyes wearily.

"Is your head doing all right?" he asked her.

"I might take a couple more ibuprofen. I think a bath and a good night's sleep will help too."

"Okay. Do you need anything at all before I go?"

Margot considered the question, finally answering, "No. I'm fine, thanks to you. I'll see you out."

At the door, Chase panicked. When would he see her again? The thought of waiting for a random encounter terrified him. He wanted a plan. "Are you ever going to let me finish the tattoo?"

Looking up at him, her limpid eyes forlorn and weary, she smiled slightly and said, "Sure."

"Tuesday?"

"Okay. Tuesday. Thank you again, Chase. I owe you so much."

"You owe me nothing." Chase removed his business card from his wallet. "Here's my cell number, in case you don't have it. Please call me. Or text me. Anything. I want to know how you're doing."

Margot nodded, taking the card.

"Promise."

"Okay," she said. "I'll let you know how I am. See you Tuesday."

Hesitating at the threshold, unsure whether he should hug her or leave, Chase looked back at Margot framed in the doorway. Against the monochromatic background, it was as though she was the only color in a black and white photo. He put his hand on his heart, bowed his head slightly, and said, "Talk to you soon."

———

Margot had been holding her exhaustion at bay, but as Chase left, it overwhelmed her. She locked the door and headed up the stairs. She drew a hot bath, added lavender bath soap, and stripped off her clothes. To think of what she might be doing right now, feeling right now, had Chase not intervened, sickened her. She had no recollection of leaving her drink unattended. She had been right there the whole time. The guy who'd drugged her must be an expert at going unnoticed, which meant he'd hurt other women before and he'd do it again. Margot had gotten lucky, but she wished she could remember the guy well enough to give his description to the police.

Margot splashed some warm water up over her arms, relishing the feel of it on her skin. The feeling reminded her sharply of how she'd bathed while pregnant. The memory came like a blow.

Almost every night, she would take a relaxing bath after work. She'd fill the tub with water and her favorite rose-scented soap, and she would luxuriate until Kevin found her, sometimes hours later, shriveled up and blissed out.

For the first three months, no sign of the baby growing within her had been outwardly visible. Her body was so slight it took forever for the baby bump to show. Once it did, though, Margot couldn't leave it alone. She would rub her belly gently and talk quietly to the little being who had taken up residence.

Maybe it was the pregnancy hormones, but Margot was in a happy fog most of the time, detached from reality just enough to dull its edges. She sang the baby songs and told her stories. Margot was used to spending a lot of her time by herself because of Kevin's schedule, but now she was never alone. Little One was with her, keeping her company. It was the most tremendous sensation.

The first scare in her pregnancy had come early on with some minor spotting. The doctors were worried. They did sonograms and tests, put Margot on bed rest for a week, and when they checked again, Margot's body had stabilized. They told her the pregnancy was viable, but tenuous. It was hard not to get her hopes up, but she couldn't help it. She loved this little baby to distraction.

The second scare came with a fall on the ice. It was a late winter storm, the brick sidewalks had turned into frozen ice luges, and Margot had lost her footing walking home from work one evening. She'd lain on the sidewalk gripping her abdomen, spasming in pain, terrified. A passerby had called 911. Kevin was at the hospital and met her in the ER.

"I told you not to walk home on the ice," he'd said harshly, instead of greeting her.

"I thought I'd be all right. I've been walking on ice all my life," she'd replied, angrily.

"I don't want anything to happen to you, honey," he said, his tone softening. "Or to her." He lay his hand over Margot's, which lay over her tummy.

"I'm so sorry." Margot had burst into tears.

They kept her in the hospital for a few days and told her not to fall again or she could indeed lose the baby. Margot had been so careful after that. She'd taken zero risks and things were looking like she might make it full term.

Now, with the water surrounding her like embryonic fluid sustaining her sadness, the deep well of grief over losing her baby threatened to drown her. Blocking it out had only prolonged the inevitable crush of sadness. Margot needed to deal with it. But how? She didn't feel strong enough. She fervently wished her mother was alive. She would have helped Margot through the all-consuming loss. Maybe she would have been able to help Margot find a way forward, but what did it matter? Her mother was gone. Wishing Kevin or the baby or her parents were alive made her feel worse. No, Margot was alone. She'd alienated most of the friends she had left, with the exception of Ginny.

Ginny would listen to her story if Margot could muster the energy to tell her. Maybe Ginny could walk into the nursery alongside Margot for moral support, to help Margot face the un-faceable. Ginny was so happy, though. Margot didn't want to unnerve her.

What about Chase? He'd said to ask for help. He'd literally begged Margot to call him.

That led to the next quandary. How did she feel about Chase? Thankful, assuredly. Connected? Definitely. When he played the song he'd written, Margot knew it was meant for her to hear. She'd known from the first chord. Margot got the feeling Chase wanted more than friendship, but she wasn't sure when, if ever, she would be emotionally available for the simplest platonic relationship, let alone romance.

Sinking under the soapy water, Margot wondered what to do. It would be horribly unfair to string Chase along, making him think there was a possibility when there wasn't. Yet, some part of her was deeply drawn to him. She wanted to know him better. He understood a part of her no one else could fathom.

There didn't seem to be any fair way to handle the situation with him but to squash her own budding desire for a friendship and not see each other. Tuesday, after he finished the tattoo, she would tell him that this was the end. Wasn't it better to end things now rather than later when he'd become even more attached to her? She would sacrifice her own attachment to him in order to preserve his future wellbeing. It was the right thing to do.

Resolution in place, Margot was now doubly bereft. Could she ever be whole, able to explore her feelings like normal people did? She had been stripped of love for so long. Margot added it to the long list of things in her life that were unequivocally, irrevocably unfair.

After her bath, Margot hesitated at the closed door to the nursery. She put her hand to the wood, trying to honor the torrent of emotions swirling within her. When she finally went to her bedroom, Margot climbed into her bed naked and fell asleep. She slept through the afternoon, through the night, and well into the next day. Sunday was dreadful. Margot tried to go for a walk to the water, but she found no comfort there. There was no comfort anywhere, her grief for her baby was so consuming. Nothing could get her past it.

Monday morning, Margot awoke disoriented, slightly panicky, and then the tsunami of sadness hit her again. Although her clock said 8:12, Margot couldn't process it. She had no idea what day it even was, and it took a moment before reality hit her. She was supposed to be at work in less than an hour.

"Shit," she muttered and launched herself from the bed. After a quick shower, she dressed, grabbed her phone and keys and her unfortunately empty coffee mug, and sprinted out the door.

Portland had a good number of coffee shops to choose from, but Margot's need was dire. She walked into the first one she saw and filled up. They had a selection of natural breakfast replacement bars on the counter as well, and since her stomach was eating itself in desperation, she bought one of those as well.

At her desk, she consumed the bar, drank all the coffee, and headed to the breakroom for more. It seemed like everyone else was in a trance. The hushed environment, the muted office colors, the impossibly bright blue sky out the windows in contrast, it was all too much. Margot was ready to burst at the seams.

I had a baby, once, and she died, she wanted to scream.

How could life simply continue on as though nothing had happened? How could she pretend everything was all right? Nothing was all right. Margot had held her still, beautiful child in her hands, her tiny eyes closed, her tiny lips parted, her perfect hands dreadfully small. She had never felt the gentle touch of her mother's skin. She had never seen her mother's loving face. She had never heard her beautiful name. She had died and Margot had been left with nothing.

Rushing back to her desk before anyone could comment on her disintegrating state, Margot breathed through a wild panic attack. Her heartrate was erratic, her breathing shallow. Her vision tunneled. She tried to calm herself down. She tried to tell herself she was okay. But she wasn't okay. Through the strangling tears, Margot whispered, "Amandine. I named you Amandine."

Jim lightly knocked on her door, but it was a sound in a different dimension. He opened the door slightly and poked is big red head through the crack. As he saw her state, he burst into her office, closed the door, and rushed to Margot.

She had never touched Jim before with the exception of a handshake, but he was like a bald, sweaty bear. He hugged her tight as though he had been expecting her to crumble for the past year and was shocked she hadn't.

"It hits everyone differently," he whispered into her hair as she cried.

"I am so lost, Jim."

"I know, Margot. I know. I'm here for you. I've been waiting for you to break."

When the panic subsided and the grief ebbed away slightly, Margot looked at her boss. "I'm sorry you had to see that."

"You're a human. We're here for each other, you know. That's what people are supposed to do."

"I know, but I never wanted to be weak," Margot said, miserably. "I tried to hold myself together here. I have a job to do."

"You've done it flawlessly, too." His words terrified her. Why was he speaking in the past tense?

"You're not firing me, are you?" Margot exclaimed.

"For crying at work?" Jim's eyes went wide. "I'd have to fire ninety percent of the staff, including myself. We've all been kicked around, some more than others. You more than most. But we get through it. You're not fired." Then, in a cheeky tone, he added, "This time."

Despite herself, Margot laughed.

After Jim left her office, Margot slowly began to function once more. She checked her email, read through some documents, and realized she hated it all. Where she had found comfort during the past year, Margot now only found tedium.

While walking towards Chase's shop the following evening, Margot was seized with nervousness. What would he say to her? It was so awkward after everything he'd seen her through, after telling him everything, after sleeping in his bed, in his arms. Margot blushed at the memory.

She spotted him from a few doors down waiting for her, leaning against the side of the building. What an objectively good looking man he was. She'd known that all along, but now it seemed so obvious. His broad, muscled chest, his perfect proportions, his rakish curls, his expressive eyes. His overwhelming magnetism. Margot's gait slowed. Her palms grew sweaty, and her heart was racing, like she was an unhinged teenager. The sobering reality that she was anything but hit her hard and her step faltered.

Chase's smile, however, remained steady. His warm expression drew her closer, erasing her unease. How was she ever going to end her friendship with him after tonight? She didn't know if she had the courage.

———

As Margot approached, the early evening sunlight gilded her hair from behind. Her beauty took his breath away. The pain in her countenance was unmistakable, but she still looked like an angel. Angel of Lost Children, he thought, harkening back to his art school days. Somehow, the fanciful, resplendent images of Byzantine seraphim didn't hold a candle to Margot's glory.

Neither of them spoke as she stopped before him. Chase had lost the capacity for words, taken instead with the physical beauty of the moment. They regarded each other with shy, wide eyes, and Chase was shocked at the strength of his attraction to her.

Finally, he smiled, nodded to her, and ushered her into the store.

Once they were inside, Margot reached into an oversized butter-yellow purse and drew out the plum-colored shawl. She handed it to Chase. "Sorry I had it for so long. I should have returned it ages ago. I was too, I don't know, too mad, too embarrassed. I hope you can forgive me."

The contrition in her sparkling eyes was genuine, he was certain. Chase accepted the shawl and said, "It was my mom's. She made it, actually. It's one of only a few things I kept. She was always cold. She wore this around all the time."

"She must have been a good mom."

Chase swallowed hard. "Why do you say that?"

"Because she raised a good son."

"Thank you, Margot." Chase smiled sadly. "That means a lot to me. Are you ready?"

"Yes," Margot replied. Chase handed the shawl back to her and smiled. "This is a better color on you than the green one I have in there."

———

Margot accepted the shawl once more and retreated into the dressing room. The ridges of her ribcage arose sharply from beneath her taut, nearly translucent skin. Her eyes traveled down to her concave stomach. It was gaunt, unappealing. She'd been hollowed out, so what was even left?

Margot unbuttoned her pants and slid them down from her hips slightly. There it was. A jagged C-section scar just above her pubic hair, where the doctor had cut her baby from her. She was sewn back up unceremoniously, like a tattered ragdoll, leaving her an empty carapace. Margot ran her fingers along the scar. It felt as deep as it looked. It was still a little pink but fading into white. So many scars.

She buttoned up her pants once more, wrapped herself in the shawl, and returned to Chase. He was ready for her. Their process was a comforting ritual. Washing her with the green soap, shaving and washing again, drying her off, disinfecting her skin with alcohol. Purification. Applying the lotion, the stencil, the pressure of application. Transformation. Peeling the paper off like a reptile sloughs off its old skin to make way for the new. Metamorphosis.

As the machine's needle pierced her skin, however, Margot was thrust into a new realm of pain. The bright hospital lights blinded her, consciousness ebbed and flowed, she became aware long enough to see the doctors rushing around her like electrons around a nucleus. Positioning her, prepping her, stabilizing her heartrate, taking notes. Every part of her body hurt. Weren't they supposed to sedate her? Had they tried? Whatever they'd done hadn't worked. Then a knife screamed into her body, sliced open her skin, her organs, her broken, torn-up, nearly crushed uterus. They took out her little baby. Margot was filled with the compound agony of separation.

Chase's voice filtered into her consciousness. She was on his chair, staring at the overhead lights, the knife still so fresh, so present, that she clenched her abdomen expecting to find what? A hole? A bloody cavern?

"Margot, Jesus. Margot? Can you hear me?" Chase's voice was laced with concern. He came in and out of focus for another moment as Margot's mind reconciled itself to the present. He cradled her head in his arm.

"The surgery," Margot gasped for air. "I remember the surgery. I must have blocked that out too. They cut me open and took my baby out and I felt everything. I had been unconscious, but I came to right as they cut me open. I watched them take her. I don't know why they didn't have me sedated, or maybe they did. There was so much blood. I must have gone into shock. The doctors were talking loudly, barking orders, trying to save me. Trying to save the baby." The words came out of her like a bloodletting, a rush of poison from a festering wound. Tears streamed down her cheeks and into her hair, rivulets hot as blood. "How did I block everything about her out?"

"Your mind was protecting you. It was a horrific experience."

"I'm so sorry you had to see me like this. I don't even know who I am anymore."

"Do not apologize for anything. It's going to be okay." He shifted her forward gently, then he sat on the chair next to her. Chase put both of his arms around her and held her tight. "Go ahead and cry, Margot. You have to let the pain out somehow." His tone of voice, dripping with honeyed sympathy, infuriated her.

"Stop it, Chase. No pity, remember?"

"No, Margot. You've been through hell. Now it's time to admit it and deal with it."

"Don't tell me how to handle it!" Margot shouted. She unraveled herself from his embrace. If she didn't immediately replace this cancerous sorrow with anger, it would kill her. She would die right here from the sadness of it all. It would finally consume her.

"Don't push me away, Margot."

Looking him in the eye, Margot saw something she didn't deserve, but it was a revelation. Chase didn't only care for her superficially. He cared for her unconditionally. Her fury at him, at the life she'd unwillingly clung to, deflated as she searched his compassionate eyes.

She was so lost. So alone. Shouldn't she let him care? Margot, exhausted from the flood of memory, unwillingly surrendered. Chase, at the very least, didn't deserve her anger. He was too good.

Margot hung her head. "I can't live like this." Her voice sounded small.

"You can. You will. I'll be here for you."

"I'll never be what you want me to be." Margot stared up at the ceiling. "You're attached to some idealized version of me, but I'm empty, Chase. I'm broken." She looked him dead in the eyes. "I have nothing left to give."

Chase stood and came forward, leaving a space between them. "I don't want anything from you, Margot. I care about you. I want to be here for you, however you need me to be."

"It's not fair to you. You deserve to invest your energy in someone who makes you happy, someone to love, someone to marry and start a family with."

"I don't want a family," he stated earnestly.

"What do you mean?"

"I mean I never want to have kids. Ever. Did you ever stop to wonder why I'm not married?"

Margot was shaken, shocked. Softly, she answered, "Yes, I wondered."

"I've been honest with every woman I've ever dated, but somehow they think they'll change my mind. I *was* actually married. My wife's name was Sara and we loved each other. But in the end, Sara decided she wanted more than I could give."

"Jesus. I'm so sorry. Why on earth don't you want kids?" Margot regretted asking as soon as the words had left her mouth. It was none of her business, after all.

Chase hesitated and then answered, "I told you, my relationship with my dad was complicated. Then, my parents died. They left me. That loss eviscerated me. The guilt tortured me. I never want to make anyone suffer like that, even inadvertently. Life is too ephemeral, too uncertain. I can barely take care of myself, let alone a child."

"Oh." Margot ran her hand along her abdomen again. "That, I understand."

"Listen to me, Margot," Chase said, gripping her shoulders. "You're not broken. You're healing, little by little. In the end, you'll be a different version of yourself. You will find a way to honor your loss and forge ahead, however you can."

"I'm not strong enough."

"Yes, you are. You aren't made of lace. You may feel fragile, but you're stronger than you think. You've already lived through the worst of it. You have nothing left to lose."

He was right. She had nothing left to lose. "What am I supposed to do with that?"

"It's a blank slate." Chase took his hands from her shoulders and gestured to the walls of his shop. "What has every artist and musician for centuries done with pain?" Chase's earnest eyes bored into her with the question.

"Create."

"When you're ready, you will too. Let me walk you home."

"What? No. What about the tattoo?" she asked, alarmed.

"I can finish it any time," Chase said, trying to placate her.

"I want you to do it now," she said forcefully.

"I'd need to disinfect you again. It will ruin the stencil."

"Then tattoo it freehand. I trust you."

Chase looked at her hard. He peered into her eyes, trying to read her. "It won't be exactly symmetrical. I want it to be perfect for you."

"Perfect? Nothing in this life is perfect," she stated vehemently. "Do it."

Chase hesitated for a moment before he did as he was told and began their ritual once more. This time, when the needle entered her skin, just over her shoulder, Margot breathed deeply and focused in on the pain. It had been her only reason for coming to Chase in the first place. It had come full circle now, for now the physical pain had finally freed the last of the emotional heartache she'd buried so deeply. Although Margot didn't understand it, she was thankful. Maybe someday she'd try to explain it to Chase.

———

Each night for the past few months, to quell his spinning mind, Chase had filled sketchbooks with patterns of lace. In the beginning, he had drawn solely from the veil, for it was a wealth of designs. He had drawn it as part of his job for Margot. As he internalized its fragile beauty, the scant single-thread netting connecting the larger elements, holding it all together and asking for nothing, the netting had become as important to him as the flourishes. Its understated power was elegant, ephemeral, and tenuous, yet resilient enough to bind the lace as a whole.

Now, on Margot's shoulders, Chase drew boldly, confidently. The lace had become so much a part of his drawing vernacular, he had no trouble articulating the designs in ink freehand. He filled an arabesque heart-derived shape with the single needle lines of the netting. The result was superb. He supported the heart with other elements, scrolls, flowers, spirals, picot edging, but the net had become the focus within the heart, with its gauzy, subtle texture. It was the might of the entire piece.

Once he'd drawn enough on one side, Chase switched to the other, balancing out the work and maintaining its essential symmetry. Margot sat unbelievably still throughout, as though in a trance. Chase worked for hours, connecting the designs on the front of her body to those on her back.

As he approached the final moments of his work, his heart constricted. He didn't want to be finished. He didn't want to say goodbye to Margot. The tattoo had given him an excuse to be with her. They were only bound by its tenuous threads. Would Margot let him go now that they were done? Holding on tighter wouldn't help. Chase turned off the machine, cleaned off her blood from his final lines, and sat back to admire the work. It was some of his best.

Handing Margot the mirror, he asked, "What do you think?"

She examined her shoulders, one at a time, angling the mirror to reveal some of her back as well. "It's perfection. I can't believe how beautiful it is, Chase. Thank you. You are such an artist."

"I'm so glad you like it," he answered, genuinely relieved. "Let me wrap you now. Then, if you'll join me, we can get a drink next door."

Margot shifted, hesitating before she answered.

Chase, afraid she would outright deny him, said, "I do this with all of my long-term clients when we're done. It's like a rite of passage."

"All right." This seemed to placate her. "That sounds fine."

While Margot got dressed, Chase took the box with the veil in it from the closet where he'd had it carefully stored. He put the box on his desk and on top of it, he placed a single pink rose, from which he had removed the thorns. When Margot pulled aside the curtain of the dressing room, the first thing she saw was Chase behind his desk. Then her gaze travelled down and alighted upon the rose. As she approached the box, Chase's pulse raced. He was more nervous than when he'd proposed to Sara. More nervous than when he'd spoken at his sister's wedding. His palms were sweating, his muscles were clenched tight. Still looking down, Margot picked up the rose, breathed in its sweet scent, and held it to her cheek. After a moment she looked into his eyes and with deep feeling said, "Thank you."

"Shall we?" Chase smiled at her, relieved.

Margot cradled the box and the rose in one arm and linked her other with Chase's outstretched arm. Together, they walked next door.

The bar had emptied early because it was a Tuesday evening,

so there were a couple of booths to choose from. Sheila waved to Chase and Margot as they came in, and Margot waved back reservedly. They walked past the bar to the booth in the back corner, where Margot set the box down on the seat and sat next to it. Chase sat across from her. He fidgeted, looked up at the chalkboard menu, and glanced around the room.

"You okay?" Margot asked, a smile tugging at the corner of her mouth.

"Yeah, I'm fine. I can order for us. What would you like?"

"I'm still not up to snuff from the weekend. How about a soda water with lime?"

"Done. Anything to eat? Would you like to share something?"

"If you get something, I'll have a bite of it."

Chase bounded up to the bar, ordered their drinks and a plate of fries, and sat back down again, setting the soda water before Margot like an offering.

"Can you tell me something?" Margot looked at him as he settled his surge of restless energy. "And please forgive me if it's too personal."

"Nothing between us is too personal at this point. Ask me anything." He leaned forward; his arms folded on the table.

Margot looked down at her hands and then up at him again. "You're not defined by your loss. How did you get through it?"

"Time, I guess. I mean, my parents died almost twenty years ago. I don't see myself as having gotten through the loss, necessarily. It's more like I learned to live with it. It's unchangeable. What else could I have done? I had to make the best of it. The first years were so hard. I was angry and miserable, but I've always had music and art. They've provided an instant community wherever I went, which helped a lot. I made friends, played with people, and after I sold the house, I never looked back. I didn't want to be defined by it, like you said. At some point, I chose to live in a way that would make my parents proud."

That statement had an effect on Margot. She stiffened, shifted, looked down. "I'm sure you've made them proud."

"I hope so."

"Tell me about Sara."

Chase hadn't been expecting to hear Sara's name on Margot's lips. "Why?"

"If you don't want to…"

"No, it's fine. I… We haven't talked in a few years. She remarried; she has two kids now. From what I hear, she's happy, and I'm happy for her."

"What was she like, though?" Margot persisted.

Chase thought about Sara for a moment, trying not to let his feelings show. Ending things with Sara had broken him. "She was kind. She *is* kind. She's smart and funny but also sarcastic, and when she wanted to, she could cut to the quick. I could never keep up. I'm smart, but not word smart, if you know what I mean."

"I do. It's the theory of multiple intelligences. Some people have kinesthetic intelligence, some verbal, some visual, and so on. You obviously have music and visual intelligences, but I'd score you high on interpersonal intelligence as well. You truly care about other people."

"That's intelligence?"

"It is, according to Howard Gardner."

"And he was…"

"A professor of education at Harvard who wrote a bunch of books on the topic. Early on, I'd thought about being a music teacher so I took some education classes. I don't know why I remember it all." Distractedly, Margot took a sip of her soda water, removed the lime from the rim, and put it to her mouth.

Watching Margot bring that sour fruit to her lips knocked a hole in Chase's chest. Margot was absolutely dazzling and seemed totally unaware of it. He swallowed hard. "What kind of intelligence are you?"

"Analytical. Numbers make sense to me. And music. I

understood music from the time I was a little kid, you know? The two kinds of intelligence are linked deeply for me. I can't imagine separating them."

Sheila brought the plate of fries to their table, along with Chase's beer, and sat down next to Chase. Smiling, she said, "You look better, Margot. I'm so sorry about what happened the other night. I haven't seen that creep back in here, but if I do, I'm calling the cops."

"Thanks for looking after me. You guys saved me. Literally."

"Chase had it all under control, didn't you, buddy," Sheila said, punching him lightly on the arm. "You knew something wasn't right."

"Yeah, I did. I'm so glad we stopped him," Chase said.

"Me too," added Margot.

"You kids enjoy yourselves. Fries and drinks are on me tonight."

"Thanks, Sheila," Chase called after her as she headed back to the bar.

After the fries, Chase noticed how exhausted Margot seemed. He said, "I'll walk you home."

"You don't need to, I'm fine. Besides, you live next door." She gestured vaguely upwards, towards his place. "You're already home."

"I want to walk with you if you don't mind. It's a nice night and there's nothing I'd rather do."

"I can't argue with that, I guess," Margot said, smiling.

Together, they walked through the balmy summer evening. The air smelled like the ocean. Nothing else compared. When they arrived at Margot's house, Chase fidgeted uncomfortably behind her while she opened the front door. Cool air spilled from the dark house. This vibrant creature would soon be sucked back into the mausoleum beyond. It was horrible. No wonder she was still so sad all the time, coming home to this place. It was so big, so cold, so colorless. It wasn't her at all.

Margot turned towards him. "I guess this is goodbye." Her

voice betrayed her. She sounded desolate. "Thanks for everything, Chase."

Chase took a tentative step forward. "This evening was the end of our business arrangement. I consider this moment the beginning of our friendship."

"I can't promise you anything, like I said. I have nothing to give." Margot's expression was miserable.

"Do you have tea?"

Margot couldn't help it. She laughed out loud.

"I guess I can manage tea. Come on in."

TWELVE

Together they walked to the kitchen, turning on lights as they went. Margot set the box with the veil on a counter and took the rose to the sink where she filled up a slender crystal vase with water and put it in. Its blush pink was the only color in the entire room.

"Mint or Sleepy Time?" Margot asked.

"I'll take the Sleepy Time. Thanks."

Margot filled a copper kettle with tap water and set it on the stove. The fire from the gas burner beneath crawled up the edges of the kettle, licking it, caressing it.

"Something you said earlier got me." Margot moved about the kitchen like a tiny ghost. "You said you hoped your parents were proud of you."

"I do hope that. Every day. It's what kept me from making terrible decisions after they died. Well, most of the time."

"I think I want that too."

"To make your parents proud?" Chase asked.

"Them and Kevin," she replied.

"So, what would they want for you?"

Margot considered the question. "They wouldn't want to see me like this. Like I've been. Kevin wouldn't even recognize me.

But for the past year, letting myself be happy has felt like a betrayal."

"Kevin loved you. He wouldn't want you to suffer any more than you already have. Love means wanting the best for someone. Wanting happiness for them. You got to live, and he didn't, Margot. It's not fair, but that's where things are. Now, you have to decide what you want to do with your life. Who do you want to be?"

Margot considered the question for a long moment. "Kevin was attracted to the spirited, funny person I used to be. I can't imagine why *you're* still here, considering what dismal company I am now. I wish I could spark myself back to life."

"What are the things you used to love? Before everything happened?"

"We loved to drive along the coast and look at the cute towns and the water," she answered. Then she paused and said, "But before I was with Kevin, it was always music. Music was my everything."

"And now?"

"I don't know anymore." Margot hesitated. "I need to tell you something. I didn't come to you for a pretty design, you know. That's not what the tattoo meant to me, especially at the beginning."

"I know. Your energy was different from anyone else I've ever worked with."

"I came to you for the pain, Chase. How fucked up is that? I came because nothing else made me feel alive. Physical pain was the only thing that made me feel like a human anymore. After you started tattooing me, the pain of it brought me back to my body, like I'd hoped it would. I'd been totally disconnected. All I could feel was heartache, devastation, emotional anguish. The tattoo became a physical outlet for all the emotional pain. It was helping, I know it was."

"I'm so glad. What happened?"

"I was getting a little closer to figuring it all out. I had made more progress since meeting you than in the entire year before. After we talked about Jawbreaker, I came home and dug out all my old music. I think I told you, Kevin hated punk, so I had put it all away after a while. We always listened to classical together because that's what he loved. After a while, I forgot how important music was to me. But when I listened to some of my favorite songs, like *Waiting Room* and *Termite Tree,* it was like a call to my old self. Music started to replace the pain I'd been seeking. I think I'm still in there somewhere. Listening to all the music I love, I was finding *me,* whatever me is left, somewhere underneath all the misery."

Chase nodded his head, looking at her with expressive, kind eyes, patiently waiting for her to continue. The kettle whistled, startling Margot. She turned back to the stovetop, picked up the kettle, and poured water into the two mugs she'd placed on the island. The stream of hot water steamed in the chilly air. With the teabag steeping, she handed him a mug and took one to herself, still standing on the far side of the island.

"Then, that fucker drugged me. Being knocked into such a vulnerable state again cracked open my psyche and let the rest of my experiences come forward. All the feelings I'd buried. All the grief and misery of losing my baby." Margot's voice broke at the last word. Then, softly, she continued, "I've never shared this with anyone, but her name was…" Margot's voice cracked again, and she paused to swallow. "Her name was Amandine. It means Loved One. She was so small, Chase. So beautiful. So perfect. Your little pink hat fitted her perfectly. Thank you for that."

Chase nodded, his heart screaming inside his chest as Margot's sapphire eyes brimmed with tears.

"I don't know if I can get over losing her, that grief feels so deep. I don't know how I could have blocked out the surgery, along with the baby, but I did. This I do know, however. It wasn't the physical suffering I was blocking from my memory, although that would have been reasonable. I can't even describe the depth of that agony. No. It was her. I was blocking out *her.*

It's so horrible. My mind had me convinced I hadn't lost her, like she'd never existed. That's so fucked up. My sweet baby doesn't deserve that. She deserves a mother who loves her no matter what. Blocking so much out for so long, I feel like an amnesiac getting to know her life again. Except in my life, there's nothing left."

"That's not true," Chase said forcefully. "You are still here. You can be anything, anyone you want to be."

"I don't know what that is anymore. I thought I was meant to be a mother."

"Margot, you will always be Amandine's mother. You love her more than anything. I can see that. Your mind was protecting you all this time. You would have broken otherwise. It was too much. You needed time to heal from everything else and now you can begin the healing process for losing her."

"I'm not sure I can do it."

"You will," Chase assured her. "I have faith in you. And, in time, you'll figure out who you're meant to be."

Margot, still lachrymose, took a sip of the tea. The steam curled around her. "God, I hope you're right."

———

Chase only left once Margot promised to call him the following day. By that time, it was late, she was bleary and tired, and she had all to do to lock the door and get in her bed. Dreading the prospect of work, she considered calling in, but that seemed too self-indulgent. After all, it was her choice to get a tattoo on a Tuesday evening, befriend her tattoo artist, and relive some of the most horrible moments of her life. Margot was too exhausted to think about any of it. She closed her eyes and the next thing she knew it was morning.

Memories came to her little by little. First Chase, their talk, his kindness. Then, as the tenderness of those moments faded, they were supplanted by her suppressed memories of the surgery, then the baby, the baby's death. Would every day start this way from now on? Margot stared at the ceiling, shattered by the intensity of her memories. Her heart had been torn in half that awful day, ripped from her body along with her baby. She sat up feebly, wondering how someone could live with half a heart. She swung her legs over the side of the bed and padded silently down the hall to the locked door at the top of the back stairs. She leaned her cheek against its smooth, white surface, ready to cry, but no tears came. Instead, she was raw, hollow, bereft of all feeling, even the sadness she'd been gripped by for so long. Being with Chase always tricked her into thinking she could be whole again. How could she now that her heart was so damaged?

Yet, Chase believed in her. He saw something in her, some possibility, some spark. Was he wrong? Margot desperately wanted to believe him. She desperately wanted to heal, to love again, for what was the point of having lived if she could not love?

THIRTEEN

Leaving Margot alone was impossibly hard. Chase walked home, wishing he could have stayed with her, wishing he could have held her again like he had the morning she'd been at his loft. She shouldn't be alone with her memories, alone with her loss, but even as he thought it, Chase understood that everyone is alone with loss. Nothing could change that aspect of humanity.

When Sara divorced him, Chase went into hermit mode. He was so depressed. For a moment he'd had everything a man could want. A pretty wife, a successful business, a band to play with, but it was all such a lie. It was incredible how his mind had hidden from him all the signs that Sara was unhappy, that she longed for more. They'd fought more and more as their love died a slow, agonizing death. Only afterwards did Sara explain how she'd felt betrayed, how she'd assumed Chase would mature with her, not remain some overgrown child. Her desire for children overrode all feelings of love for him, and when she couldn't change him, she instead set about destroying him.

It was years before Chase could forgive Sara for putting him through that slice of hell, but had he forgiven himself? Had he actually healed? Maybe the string of destructive, crazy girlfriends since, including Cassidy, had been a manifestation of his guilty conscience for unknowingly misleading Sara or raising false hopes that he was ever likely to be a father. More likely it was a result of his fear of abandonment, a fear too often reinforced with loss. Was he trying to replace his family? Was he looking for something that had been taken from him too early on to recognize that it could never be replaced?

What did all this mean with regard to Margot? She was lost. She needed a life raft, something to bring her back, a reason to live. Would she use him for this and then leave him like everyone else? Could he handle it if things with Margot did move forward? Or worse, if they did and then she left him? His budding attachment to her was different from anything he'd felt before, it was so intense. It seemed a lot like love. It was terrifying, but Chase was a moth, inextricably drawn to Margot's flame. He was willing to risk anything to be with her.

Morning brought little comfort. Chase lifted weights, went for a run, and came back sweaty, but ultimately feeling no different than he had when he left. Restless, he showered, made some strong coffee, and headed down to the shop early, where he sketched until his first client came in. The joy of tattooing made time pass like a dream.

At lunchtime, Chase went upstairs, made himself a sandwich, and sat at the table in the sunshine. As he ate, he focused on all the things he had to be grateful for. He had his own business, his own apartment, he was healthy and strong, he could express himself musically and with ink. As he focused upon this thankfulness, Chase finally found the calm he'd been missing since leaving Margot's side.

That evening, as he sat down to eat dinner, his phone rang. It was Margot. It was only after he'd stopped wondering if she'd actually call him that she did.

"Hi there," Chase said, accidentally allowing his excitement to infiltrate his voice.

"Hi there," Margot repeated. Her tone was markedly reserved.

"I'm glad you called," Chase said, risking honesty. "I wasn't sure you would."

"You made me promise," she said, cheekily.

"I know," he said. He got up and started pacing in front of the windows. The phone felt awkward in his hand, against his cheek. "How was your day?"

"The same as usual. Yours?"

"It was okay. I worked on a sleeve, a couple of small pieces, and had time in between to sketch. Not too bad." There was a pause as Chase waited for Margot to speak. When she didn't, he asked, "Are you still there?"

"Yes. But I'm not sure what to say. People don't talk on the phone anymore, you know."

"I know. We're being very retro." When Margot didn't react, Chase said, "I have an idea. Tell me a story about your childhood."

"Um," she said, uncertainly. "Like what?"

"It doesn't have to be much, or very interesting. Whatever comes to mind." Chase perched on the high swivel stool at his drafting table, waiting for Margot to think of something. It squeaked indelicately as he spun towards his sketchbook.

"Okay," she finally said. "We went to Belgium when I was around ten. My grandmother hadn't seen her family there in twenty years. My mother hadn't seen any of them since she was a child. I didn't speak French or Dutch, I wasn't sure what to expect. My dad went along with the whole thing, saying we could all use a change of scenery. When we got there, everyone spoke perfect English, they were all nice, and we went to all these churches and museums. It was a beautiful place."

"What city were you in?" As she spoke, he opened his sketchbook and began doodling. "Describe it."

"We stayed in Bruges. It's a tiny medieval town that hasn't changed too much in about five hundred years. They have a lace museum where old ladies continue the old ways. They make bobbin lace and needle lace."

He smiled and said, "I don't know the difference."

"Needle lace uses a needle with a single thread wound around in knots, whereas bobbin lace uses many threads attached to bobbins that you wind around pins to make a design." Margot's interest in lacemaking wasn't academic. It sounded personal, as though she were reciting words her grandmother had taught her. "Both kinds of lace are very complicated to make," she added.

"I can imagine," he said. Chase wondered which type of lace her veil was, but he didn't want to ask. Instead, he changed the topic from lace back to the scenery. "What else did you see in Bruges?"

"The buildings are old, and there's this wall around the city punctuated by windmills. It's so European, so different from America, even America's oldest stuff."

Chase paused his sketch and said, "That makes me think of the Minus the Bear song where they talk about a park bench older than our country. Is that what you mean?"

"Exactly. I love that song. Everything there is beautifully designed, thought about, cared for. They value history."

As they'd talked, Chase's drawings had grown together, connected by the patterns he'd memorized from Margot's lace. "I'd like to see Belgium," he said.

"I'd like to go back. Maybe someday." After a thoughtful pause, Margot added, "Okay. Your turn to tell a story."

"Okay," Chase said, but now that it was his turn, he couldn't think of anything to say. His line wandered into a nervous border, picking at the edges of the paper. "This is so weird. In high school, all my friends talked on the phone with girls every night, but I never really did. I was too busy drawing and playing in bands to talk on the phone. So, I guess this kind of thing is a first for me."

"It was your idea, need I remind you." The sarcasm was thick in her voice. He could imagine her narrowed eyes and sly smile.

"I know. Okay. Your vacation story reminded me of going to the Blue Mountains on a family trip once. We drove my dad's sedan. My sister Caroline and I had the back seat, but we were crammed in with a bunch of bags because they didn't all fit in the trunk, and everyone was miserable after eight hours of driving each day. We were a close family when we were really young, but Caroline and I bickered the entire time. By the end, my mom yelled, 'This is the last time we're ever driving on a family vacation together!'"

Margot giggled. "Was it?"

"No, we just kept it under five hours after that."

"Do you remember the Blue Mountains?"

"Nope," Chase said wistfully. "Only the car trip. I got gum in Caroline's hair. My dad, who was usually lighthearted and even keeled, was so pissed."

"How did Caroline take it?"

"We eventually laughed about it, but it took some time." The memory made him smile.

"Chase?" Margot asked, sounding far away.

"Yes, Margot?"

"Thanks."

His heart tugged inside him and he laid down his pencil. "For what?"

"For reminding me I'm a human," she answered.

"Anytime."

"Chase?"

"Yes, Margot?"

"I'm a tired human."

Chase smiled, picturing her fading into sleep's oblivion. "Go to bed."

"Okay. Talk again tomorrow?"

"Tomorrow it is," he said gently.

"Good night."

"Sweet dreams."

After she hung up, Chase's heart ached. He closed the cover of the sketchbook so he wouldn't have to examine the evidence of how his mind processed his aching desire, rendered in lines. In the semidarkness of his loft, he played some sad songs on his guitar. No person had helped Chase through his grief as much as having music and art as outlets for his feelings. Would Margot ever see her way through this newest round of painful memories and emerge on the other side of her drum kit? God, he hoped so. It would help her healing continue.

FOURTEEN

Summer was passing. Margot and Chase talked on the phone every night. Margot's intense sadness was fading slowly, if at all. Work had relaxed again after Margot had routed out the culprit of fraud at the company Jim had been courting. Their thankful CEO then signed onto the firm for all their accounting needs. It was a coup. Jim gave Margot a large bonus as thanks. She was proud of the work, but after the glorious bust, everything had calmed down into a torpid, stagnant well of boredom, with one featureless day folding into the next.

Upon returning to her desk after a long walk at lunchtime one afternoon, Margot checked her voicemail to find something out of the ordinary.

"Margot, I need you to call me. As soon as you can."

Ginny's voicemail was urgent, even by Ginny-standards. Margot had three missed calls from her in addition to the voicemail and a string of texts. She shut her office door, dialed Ginny's number, and stood at the window watching the end of another August speed by unappreciated. The phone only rang once before Ginny picked up.

"Margot, I'm so sorry to bother you. I need you." Ginny

burst into tears on the other line.

"What happened? Are you okay?" Margot's concern was intense, as her stomach tightened with dread.

"I need to see you. Can you meet me?"

"Sure," Margot agreed. "Where?"

"Can we meet at your house?"

"Sure, after work?"

"No. I need you now."

Margot was so alarmed she agreed. Leaving work wasn't a big deal, especially since she rarely did so. Margot stopped by Jim's office and let him know she was heading home.

"I'm going to head home if that's all right. A friend is in crisis mode and I need to see her right now."

Jim looked up at her with concern. "No problem, Margot. Is everything all right?"

"I hope so."

Margot walked home as fast as her high heels would allow. As she passed Chase's shop, a disconcerting swoop of emotion hit her. Was it longing? Attraction? The uproarious desire to burst into his shop unannounced? What the hell was that about? Margot put her tangled feelings aside with difficulty. Ginny needed her. She forged on.

Ginny was pacing on her stoop when Margot arrived.

"Jesus. I forgot you don't have a car. I would have picked you up," Ginny said. Her hair was wild, her face bore no trace of make-up. In her trembling hands she gripped a plastic shopping bag from the pharmacy.

"What's going on, Ginny?" Margot asked unsteadily, opening the door. Ginny stormed in behind her and lost her shit.

"Jesus. What happened?" Margot slammed the door shut and threw her arms around her distraught friend.

"Come with me to the bathroom," Ginny said through her hysterical hiccupping sobs. She pulled Margot through the house by the wrist and into the guest bathroom on the first floor, where she opened the shopping bag and dumped out ten pregnancy tests of all brands on the counter.

A wave of dizziness took Margot as all the air was sucked from the room. She placed a pale hand on the rim of the counter for support and stared in shock at the array of colorful boxes. After a moment, she looked up and met her friend's pleading gaze in the mirror.

"Well, let's get on with it," Margot said, as evenly as she could. She picked up a box and opened it, read the directions aloud, and instructed her friend to pee on the stick. Ginny followed her directions, replaced the cap to the test, washed her hands, and stood against the wall trembling. For an eternity, the friends held hands and stared at the little window on the test. When the plus sign appeared, Margot remembered her own tentative elation at seeing that tiny symbol of new life. Ginny, however, turned back towards the toilet and threw up.

"How many tests have you already done, sweetie?" Margot asked, holding back her friend's hair.

"Four. I've already done four. They're all the same."

Shaking, Ginny collapsed, hugging the bowl of the toilet, her tears adding to the contents below.

"You've been sick?"

"Yes," Ginny wailed miserably.

"How long?"

"A little over a month. I missed my period, but I'm not that great at keeping track."

Margot hesitated. Then she asked, "How far along are you, do you think?"

"I have no clue."

"Wow. This is a surprise. I think we need to call your doctor."

Margot helped Ginny to her feet, flushed the toilet, and ran the tap. Ginny washed out her mouth, splashed her pale, splotchy face with water, and turned wild-eyed back to her friend. "What am I going to do?"

"Is it Henry's?"

"Of course it's Henry's." Ginny's eyes were furious.

"How long have you guys been together now?"

"It's been a tad over five months. He's going to run for the hills."

"Like hell he will." Margot patted her friend on the back. "He's in love with you. And he's a good man."

"I haven't called him."

"In how long?"

"All week."

"I'll tell him to come over," Margot said, decisively.

"No. I'm not going to tell him," Ginny said feverishly. "I think I need to end this. I can't be a mother right now."

Margot's legs went weak. A fathoms-deep sadness welled up inside her. Margot had fought so hard to keep her pregnancy viable. She'd fought until the very end. What could she say to Ginny, who had every right to feel the opposite?

"Margot?" Ginny's alarmed voice filtered in and Margot looked at her.

"Come with me," Margot replied, in a flat tone, taking her friend's hand.

Margot went to the kitchen and retrieved a key from a small box at the back of a drawer. Together, the friends climbed the back staircase. At the top, they stood outside the locked door.

Wordlessly, Margot fitted the skeleton key to the lock, trying to steady her trembling hands. Slowly, she opened the door to the nursery. Palest-pink walls suffused the room in a warm, loving glow. Upon the rosy walls, silvery birds flew over billowy white clouds. A white crib with white bedding stood beneath a handmade mobile of silver swallows frozen in mid-flight. Pale light streamed through the blushing sheers at the window, before which, a velvety grey glider sat empty. A little bookcase stood against the wall beside it, its slight collection of unread volumes neatly propped up by porcelain unicorn bookends. Margot had thought it was the sweetest nursery she'd ever seen. She'd attended to each and every detail with the loving care of a joyfully expectant mother.

Ginny looked around speechless. "I don't understand. You and Kevin didn't have…" She spun her head to look at her friend's stricken expression before understanding took root. "Oh, Margot. I had no idea. You lost your baby in the accident?"

All Margot could do was nod her head before her tears began to fall silent into the void. Ginny took her friend to her, their embrace so tight neither could breathe. Together they sank to the floor and sobbed. "I am so sorry. Jesus, I am so stupid. How did I not know?"

"How could you? We never told anyone we were expecting. I had such a hard pregnancy at the beginning, I thought I'd lose her. Then, around four or five months, everything seemed to get better. We thought we would actually have a baby. We decorated her nursery. Then…" Margot couldn't go on.

"Then you lost her in the accident."

"Yes. They delivered her via C-section when I got to the hospital. She lived for a day in the incubator. When I woke up, I screamed until they let me see her. She was so tiny, Ginny. So small. So alone. I couldn't even touch her. She needed me and they wouldn't let me hold her until…" Margot was sobbing uncontrollably, as though all of these words had burst a dam within her broken heart. She'd held it all back too long.

"Oh, Margot, why didn't you tell me?"

"I put it all out of my mind, I guess. I couldn't face losing her and Kevin at the same time. I had blocked it all out. I only recently remembered everything. The surgery, losing the baby, feeling like I'd died along with her. After she died, they finally let me hold her, this perfect little angel. She was so unbelievably small she fit in my hand. I loved her so much, Ginny. I loved her so much."

"It's okay. It's okay. Let it out, Margot. You're going to be okay. I'm sorry I haven't been here for you more. I didn't think you wanted me. I'm here now, though, and I'm not leaving you. I love you."

"I love you too. I'm sorry I pushed you away."

"You have nothing to apologize for."

They held each other on the nursery floor until Margot leaned over and lay her head on Ginny's lap. Ginny stroked her hair. "This is the first time I've been in here since she died."

Softly, reverently, Ginny asked, "What was her name?"

"Amandine."

"That's so beautiful, Margot. Absolutely beautiful. I'm so sorry to put you through this, to bring this all up." Ginny's voice cracked.

"You didn't do anything. I'm supposed to be here for *you* today, and instead I'm crying like an idiot. I'll support you whatever you choose, but promise me you'll think twice before you end things, okay?"

Ginny paused. "I'm so scared."

Margot sat up. She grew pensive for a moment and said, "You're right to be scared. Motherhood, even for the infinitesimal time I experienced it, is an impossibly heavy responsibility. Nothing is ever the same after."

"No. Either way, nothing will ever be the same."

As they left the nursery, Margot's hand lingered on the doorknob. She looked back into the rosy-hued room for a moment and accepted that pain could live alongside her love. Margot did not close the door behind her.

Margot made them tea and they sat close together on the couch, staring at the drum kit. After a while, Ginny said, "I didn't know you were playing again."

"I'm not. Not really. I mean I was, but I haven't in a while."

"I don't understand," Ginny said.

"It's hard to explain. I thought it would help to play again, but then I remembered about Amandine. Nothing seemed to matter after that."

Ginny shifted to stare at Margot.

"What?"

"You were so fierce on the drums. Did I ever tell you how much I loved watching you play?" Ginny looked wistful.

"I don't know. It was a long time ago," Margot added.

"If I didn't, I should have. You were magic. I was always so proud of you. And a little jealous, but mostly proud." Ginny paused for a moment. "I should also tell you I was mad at Kevin for ages, after you got together."

Margot set down her cup and turned to her friend. "I didn't know that either."

"Well, you disappeared. He took you away from me. I only got to see you a little after that, for that whole first year. Then, we sort of came back together, but you were already different."

"I was. I know I changed. I'm sorry I pushed you away." Margot took Ginny's hand. She hadn't thought Ginny had cared at the time. Now she saw she'd been wrong.

"Don't be sorry. Here's the thing. I never understood the kind of pull Kevin had on you until I met Henry. I love him, you know."

"I know. He loves you too."

"I need to tell him about the pregnancy. I'll know what to do after that, but I want him to know." Ginny sounded sad but confident.

"Ask him to come here for dinner. I'll cook."

Margot ordered groceries and spent the afternoon making a salad and dinner while Ginny rested on her couch. Henry came over after work, obviously confused and a little nervous. Margot led Henry into the kitchen, handed him a tall scotch and soda, and said, "Wait here."

Henry looked at the drink, then back at Margot, quizzically.

"Trust me," she said. "You're going to need it."

Margot revived the sleeping Ginny and led her from the den.

"Ginny, are you okay?" Henry said, setting the drink down and surging forward.

"I'm fine. Henry, I have something to tell you." She took a

deep breath. "I'm pregnant with our baby."

The gigantic smile that instantly transformed Henry's worried expression into one of absolute elation saturated Margot with joy and relief.

"What? That's wonderful news!" He picked up Ginny and swung her around, kissing her on the cheek. "Oh," he said, setting her down abruptly. "Did I hurt you? Did I hurt the baby?"

He got down on his knees and listened at her stomach. Ginny laughed. "I'm probably only a few weeks along, Henry. I think she's the size of a pea if that."

"She?"

"I don't know why I said that," Ginny said, her cheeks blazing in embarrassment. "I have a feeling." She looked up at Margot, apologetically.

"I think so too," Margot said, going to her friend's side and kissing her. "I'm so happy for you, Ginny, Henry."

"This is awesome," Henry said, standing up once more. "I am so excited. You are going to be the most beautiful pregnant lady ever. People are going to stop you in the street to touch your belly. I'm going to wait on you hand and foot. Oh, wait!" Henry said, getting back down on the floor, this time on one knee. Taking Ginny's hand in his, he asked, "My darling Ginny, I've never met anyone like you. I love you so much, and I promise to be a good dad. Will you marry me?"

Ginny wavered and went pale. She reached out for Margot to steady her. Henry shot back up to his feet and took her elbow, and together Henry and Margot guided the dazed Ginny to a chair. Margot poured her a glass of water and put it into her hand. "Drink this, Ginny."

Ginny obeyed in shocked silence. When she'd recovered her composure, she looked at Henry for a moment, her eyes full of bewilderment and love. "You'd marry me?"

"I'd be honored to marry you. I love you, Gin."

"I'd wanted to be with you for a few years before we did

that, to make sure you actually want this crazy lady."

"I want you from now until forever." Henry's eyes were earnest.

"You want me to marry you."

"I do."

"Are you sure?" Ginny persisted.

Margot, smiling like a lunatic, interjected, "Just say yes!"

"Yes."

Henry threw his arms around Ginny and kissed her lovingly, passionately. When their lips finally parted, Ginny let out a little laugh. "I'm so glad you're happy. I thought you'd hate me for being stupid and getting knocked up."

"You must know me better than that. It's a beautiful gift. How could I be sad or angry about that?"

Together, the friends ate dinner at the island. Margot opened the door out to the patio, letting in some of the evening's warm air. With all the lights on and candles lit, good food on beautiful dishes, tangible joy blew in with the breeze. Margot was genuinely happy for Ginny and Henry, even if this trajectory was not part of their original plan. But since when did fate stick to the plan?

Ginny looked so content, so peaceful. Henry's goodness, his kindness, was genuinely adorable. Margot loved them both. They'd be great parents.

At the end of the evening, Margot saw them to the door. Ginny turned back and asked, "Are you okay?"

"I am, Ginny. Go. Be happy. I'm happy for you."

"I'll call you tomorrow."

"Okay."

Ginny turned back once more and came towards Margot with open arms. She hugged her tight. "I love you."

"Love you too. Now, Prince Charming awaits. Go!"

After she'd done the dishes and cleaned up, Margot picked up her phone to check her email for work. Chase had texted around four, *I hope you're having a good day.*

Margot hadn't talked to Chase yet, so she grabbed a glass of prosecco, headed out to the patio, and dialed his number.

"I thought you were going to stand me up," Chase said, in lieu of a greeting.

"I had a strange day. Sorry it's so late."

"What happened?" Chase asked with concern.

"Ginny's pregnant."

"Woah. How are you?"

"I think I'm okay. It was a surprise. I ended up showing her the nursery. I told her everything."

Chase was silent for a moment. "What did she say?"

"She had no idea. How could she have?" Margot answered, trying to keep her voice from sounding desolate.

"Then what?"

"Henry came over and instantly asked her to marry him."

"Wow. That's actually kind of romantic. You really did have a strange day."

Margot laughed a little. "I couldn't make this stuff up."

Chase hesitated. "Do you want to come over for a drink or hang out or anything?"

"Not tonight, Chase. I cut work early for Ginny so I'd better not have a late night."

"Okay," he replied, sounding crestfallen.

"Chase?" Margot asked.

"Yes, Margot?"

"Will you keep being patient with me?"

"I care about you, Margot. I will be patient. I promise." His voice was earnest and eased Margot's aching heart.

"Okay."

"Goodnight, Margot."

"Goodnight, Chase."

Margot turned off all the lights and locked the doors. Upstairs, she almost ignored the door to the nursery, as she had every evening for fifteen months. This time, though, she approached, halting before the slice of light streaming out from behind the partly open door. When she entered, Margot found the warm glow of the day had been transmuted into silver, creating an utterly luminous space. The moon shone through the curtains, lighting up the empty glider. Margot ran her fingers along the feather-soft woven blanket draped over the side of the crib. A stirring of air brought the silver swallows floating on the mobile to life for a brief moment as she walked past. Margot sat upon the velvety glider and gazed at the empty room. Her heart was tight in her chest.

"Amandine," Margot said softly. "I want you to know how sorry I am we couldn't have our life together. I wanted you so badly. I miss you, my sweet darling. I miss you so much. I love you more than anything in this universe, and I always will. Chase is right. I will never stop being your mom."

Tears clouded Margot's eyes. What joy it would have been to hold her child in this chair, to rock her to sleep, to cradle her in her arms until she was too big to hold. Margot wanted her baby back so badly.

Now, Ginny would have a child instead. Margot was happy for her, but now, in the silver moonlight, she knew this powerful sadness and loss would remain, despite her best wish to be happy for her friend. Maybe she should give the nursery contents to Ginny. They would at least see some use. Could she part with them? So much of her love and her sense of expectation had gone into those objects.

But they were only objects, after all. Margot finally stood up and crossed the room. The mobile's silver swallow caught her eye, glinting ethereal in the diffuse moonlight. Another idea struck her. She would need Chase's help once more.

After work the following day, Margot stopped by to see him. He was cleaning up after his most recent job and when he looked up, their gaze met across the room. His affectionate smile was all Margot needed. She smiled back.

"Hi there," he said, removing his gloves and putting them in the trash. "To what do I owe the pleasure?"

"Hi, Chase. I was walking by and wanted to say hello in person."

"You walk by every day and don't stop in. What's different today?"

Embarrassed, Margot said, "Today, I want to hire you for another tattoo. Would that be okay?"

"Yes, it would be okay," he said gently. "What do you have in mind?"

From her bag, Margot removed the silver swallow she had taken from the mobile. "This."

"What is it?" Chase asked, taking it from her hand, treating it, as he did all things, with the utmost care.

"It's from Amandine's mobile. I've decided to give everything from the nursery to Ginny and Henry. Everything but this. I want you to put it on my body in white ink like the lace. Above my heart."

Chase looked up and met Margot's eyes. Unable to keep her tears at bay for a moment longer, she smiled through them as they slipped from her eyes.

"Come here," Chase said, pulling her into an embrace.

Margot let herself be held. It was so comforting to be in his arms once more. Trying as hard as she could, Margot pushed away the guilt that always bubbled up when she experienced a glimmer of peace. I deserve to be cared for, she told herself. *I deserve to feel better.*

Chase held her a little longer, finally releasing her with a last squeeze of her arms.

"I sat in the nursery last night. I talked to Amandine for the first time. I made sure she knows how much I love her. Still."

"She knows," Chase said softly. "How could there be any question? She loves you too."

"I know. I could feel it last night. I finally let myself open up to her love."

"Everything happens in its own time."

"How am I going to watch Ginny be pregnant? How am I

going to watch her have a baby without wishing for my own?" Margot choked out the words, fighting the sobs rising in her chest.

"Oh, Margot. I don't know," he replied sadly, pulling her to him once more. "I guess you'll be brave, like you've been all along. Except now, you have me."

───────

How hard, how painful it must have been for Margot to go into the nursery with Ginny. She had confronted yet another part of her past and she'd done it with grace. He agreed to do the tattoo right away, so while Margot was in the dressing room, he got his tools ready.

As Margot emerged from the dressing room, Chase was captivated by the way the plum shawl slipped from her slender shoulders. The white lace spread ethereally over her chest and back. The whole site had healed, and now that no redness remained, the effect was ravishing. Her pearly skin shone soft beneath the white lines, as though the lines were made of light glowing through her body. He realized too late that he had been staring.

"Sorry to stare at you, Margot, but the tattoos look phenomenal. They're so becoming."

"It's all right, Chase. It's your artwork, after all. You should be able to admire it." Margot's demure, almost embarrassed gaze bit into him before she looked away.

He admired more than the artwork. He was completely enthralled with her. With her golden hair tied up in a loose bun, a few strands loose against her cheeks, her neck was revealed in its delicate, elegant, inviting beauty. Margot's fragility was an illusion, however. She was stronger than steel.

"Point to where you are thinking," he said, as she sat down before him, a goddess on her throne.

"Here," she answered, pulling down the shawl to reveal the

lily-pale swell of her breast. "I don't want it touching the lace, but I want it close, right above my heart."

Chase wanted to melt away her sadness, to take her in his arms and hold her forever, to tell her everything would be all right. Nothing in the world would have made him happier.

Instead, he accepted the truth. Nothing was ever going to be the same, the wounds would never fully heal, the sadness would never disappear. So he nodded, his heart shattering for her and for himself and for the world so full of loss and pain and death, and he began their ritual once more. As he started washing her body with the green soap, he hesitated above her breast. "Is it okay if I touch you?"

"You've been touching me for months, Chase. It's okay. I trust you."

Chase nodded. Pushing back all feelings of attraction for her, letting himself feel only the purest love and a genuine wish for Margot's wellbeing, he began again.

Chase did not work from a stencil this time. Instead, he drew upon her freehand, using the silver bird as a template and guide. He embellished with detailed, single-needle feathers, bringing softness and motion to his lines, creating a creature that seemed at once both spirit and flesh, connected to Margot and yet floating from her body at the same time.

Margot seemed entranced, focused on the sensation of the needle, letting it bring her the peace she so deserved. One pain eases the other, it was a fact. He'd never been sure why. As he paused, looking once more at his work, gently wiping Margot's blood from the raised white lines, he had another idea.

"May I write her name in cursive below the bird, with swirling lines connecting the bird to her name?"

Margot opened her eyes and considered his idea. "Yes. I trust you."

"I want to spell it right. A M A N D I N E?" he asked reverently.

"Yes," Margot replied, her voice tight. "Yes, that's right." A fresh tear slipped from her eye. "Thank you, Chase. Of all the people in all the world I could have found to do this work on me, I found you. The one who understands."

Chase couldn't find his voice. It had betrayed him all together. Instead, he looked her in the eye, all his loss written in his expression, on his body, in his heart. He nodded.

Margot leaned back once more and closed her eyes, inviting him to begin. Chase took a deep breath, steadied his hands, and began to write the name of Margot's precious child. Her tiny, lost angel. He brought her name forth in a flurry of swirls emanating from the V-shaped tail of the bird. His lines floated along Margot's skin as though on air. He anchored the lettering into a tiny, outlined heart.

It was perfect. He picked up two mirrors and handed one to Margot. The other he held at an angle to show her the reflection of the reflection, so she could see the name correctly instead of backwards. She smiled and said, "It's perfect. It's absolutely perfect. Thank you, Chase."

Chase nodded once more, cleaned and wrapped Margot, and cleaned up his supplies as she changed.

When she returned, she regarded him quizzically. "Are you all right?"

"Yeah. I'm fine."

"We share something in our pain, Chase. I feel what you feel, and you feel what I feel."

His throat was still tight, too tight to talk, so he nodded and kept cleaning. Margot went to his desk and took out her checkbook, ready to pay him for his time. "Margot, no. I can't accept money. Not for this."

Looking back, studying him, she seemed to understand the gesture. She didn't fight him. "Are you sure?"

"I am. This memorial is my gift to you and your precious daughter." His voice broke as he said that word and he turned away embarrassed.

Margot walked back over to him and put her hand on his back. "Chase."

He couldn't answer.

She turned him around and tenderly wiped away the tears that had finally worked their way free. This time, Margot held him as he wept.

Shocked at the depth of his own raw grief, even all these years later, he wept for the child he'd been once, for the orphaned teen, for the man who held his loss and guilt and sadness inside a prison of flesh. He wept for Margot's lost family, her lost self, for the cruelty of it all. The deluge of long-restrained tears overwhelmed him, cleansed him, and galvanized the connection between them.

"I'm so sorry," he finally said. Margot released him but stayed close. "I've never cried like that. Even after it happened. I guess I was so angry I couldn't feel the depth of the sadness."

"Everybody handles loss differently, I think."

"I guess. Somehow seeing you go through this grief has made mine seem closer, more acute than it was before."

"You were young. Your brain wasn't fully developed. How could it be the same?"

"I guess that's true. Young people are kind of stupid," Chase said, trying on a humorous tone.

"Yes." Margot laughed. "Young people are stupid."

"Fuck it. Do you want to get a drink next door?"

"No, Chase." His heart fell a little bit at her words. "I'm going home. I'm exhausted."

"Sorry. You've had a crazy couple of days. I'll walk you."

"You don't need to," Margot said, gathering her purse.

"I know I don't need to," he stated firmly. "I want to."

Margot hesitated before agreeing. "Okay. Thank you."

Chase turned off the lights, locked the door, and held his arm out for Margot. She looped hers through the crook of his elbow and together they walked into the evening air.

FIFTEEN

Even days later, Margot was astounded by how open Chase had been with his feelings, his pain. How could pain come in so many forms? Margot's pain defined her, every minute of every day, but Chase had not let his pain win. It shocked Margot that he could experience so much sorrow and loss, and still become an overall happy person. It was a wonderful thought.

She called Ginny to check on her. Ginny sounded so much calmer, so much more centered.

"Henry hasn't let me leave his sight. We made an appointment with an OB/GYN for next week and he's going to come with me to that. He even gave me a ring, last night. His grandmother's wedding ring. I can't believe how sweet he is."

"I am genuinely happy for you," Margot said. She was.

"I want to know what to share with you, Margot. How much is too much?" Ginny's tone was tentative. "I don't want to hurt you by being happy."

"How could your happiness hurt me? I admit I experienced a wave of jealousy about the baby, but that's natural, I think. I want you to be happy, Gin. You're the sweetest woman I know."

"Woman, not person?"

"Exactly. You're funny too."

"I love you. It hurts so much to think about you losing the very things that are making me so happy. It's rotten how things work like this. I'd spent years being jealous of you and Kevin. You had something so perfect."

"Nothing is perfect, Ginny."

"That's true," she admitted. "It's just not fair, though."

"No. Life is not fair. But if I don't look forward, I will shrivel up and die. It seems pointless to have survived this long only to give up now. Ginny, I can't wait to meet your little baby. I want to watch her grow up and turn into a person. It's the most exciting thing in the world and I want to be a part of your lives. So yes, tell me everything."

"I'm so glad," Ginny cried, her voice betraying the breadth of her emotion. "I wouldn't want to go through this without you."

When they hung up, Margot turned back to her computer, wishing the day was over. She'd struggled through zombie work mode for endless months, letting the math contain her disorderly feelings. Now, though, it was more tedious than ever. Utterly boring. What had she been thinking? Shouldn't she have done something else as a career with this math brain?

Distracted, Margot's thoughts wandered back to an invitation she had awaiting her at home. It had come in the mail weeks ago, in a silver and white envelope, elegant and terrifying. Was it a wedding for some friend she barely remembered? Would she have to explain Kevin's death in her RSVP? Hesitantly, she'd opened the envelope to reveal something even more unusual. It was an invitation to a reception to honor her husband. The Portland Medical Center had an annual gala event to thank important donors and each year, they honored a prominent doctor. This year, they had posthumously nominated Kevin.

Margot's emotions upon opening the missive had been mixed. The text was very clear, she was invited to accept the honor on his behalf, the event was black tie, she would have to talk to people she barely knew and certainly wouldn't remember. It was petrifying. It was also touching.

Kevin had been an incredible doctor. He'd saved people using new microsurgery techniques he'd helped pioneer. He was an extraordinary person and he deserved to be honored. How she could hold it together alone at such an event, however, was questionable.

Two weeks. She had two weeks to find a dress, write a speech, practice talking about Kevin without bursting into tears. It was a tall order.

Margot closed the spreadsheets on her computer and opened a Word document. She began to write about Kevin, hoping some of what she thought in this moment would make it into her speech. It was comforting to think about him objectively. She'd spent so much time reliving their intimate moments, their love, the grief of losing him. She had not, however, given a great deal of thought to the man himself. Who he was, what made him special, what had made his contributions to his hospital invaluable. Her loss had been so personal. Now, however, she considered how many other people had been affected by Kevin's death, how many patients he would not save, how many doctors he would not influence. It was horrible. A single life had so many facets. Margot wrote as much about her beloved husband as she could.

Then she called Ginny back.

"I need your help."

"What's up, sweetie?" Ginny's voice sounded curious.

"I need a dress. Like a fancy dress for a gala event they're having in Kevin's honor."

"You sound panicked. Are you okay?" Ginny asked.

"Yes, I'm fine. But I will have to give a speech. I'm terrified. I want it over with and it isn't for two weeks." Margot fidgeted with the stapler on her desk.

"Is it black tie?"

"Yes," Margot replied, miserably.

"I have an idea. Let's go down to Boston and find you something special to wear."

"I was thinking I'd wear something of yours," Margot said, sounding alarmed.

"We can take the bus," Ginny cajoled her. "We don't have to drive."

Margot was astounded by her friend's perceptive understanding of her hesitation. "Fine, you're probably right. Let's go down there and find something. When can you go?"

"Saturday?"

"Okay. I have no idea where to shop for something like this, though."

"Yes, you do. Newbury Street." Ginny couldn't hide the amusement in her voice. How much time had they spent together on Newbury street in the old days, with Trident and Newbury Comics at one end and the park at the other? A return to this place would have a circular quality to it that she'd rather not contemplate. But Ginny was right. If she couldn't find a dress on Newbury, the dress didn't exist.

"Jesus. Fine. I'll see you at the bus station Saturday morning. I'll text you about tickets."

"Okay, Margot. See you soon."

On Saturday, Margot and Ginny took an early bus to Boston. They watched the bus's free movie together, making fun of it like teenagers. From South Station, they took the T to Park Street and walked the rest of the way through the park in the sunlight. The Swan Boats were already paddling their endless circles through the pond, ferrying strangers in an infinite loop.

"Do you want a ride?" Ginny asked Margot, jokingly.

"Actually, I do." Margot surprised herself with this statement. "It's been a while since I've had any fun."

"Your bar is low, then. That doesn't qualify as fun, I don't think."

"Let's do it anyway."

They bought tickets and hopped on the next available swan boat. A hundred years' worth of layered paint lay thick and bumpy along the rails and was tacky to the touch. The swans looked tired, but elegant. The teenagers who paddled the boats did so with surprising good humor, considering it was over eighty degrees already. The real ducks and swans who frequented the pond blatantly ignored the boats, suffering their presence with haughty grace. Margot laughed as one duck nipped another duck in the tail, eliciting an incredulous quack.

"You're having fun," Ginny stated, wide eyed.

"I am," Margot answered, smiling out over the water.

"I am too."

The carefree moment reminded Margot of when they'd been young together. "Good," she answered. "Having a kid around is going to make you do things like this all the time."

"I guess that's true." Ginny smiled even wider. "But Henry is kind of kid-like in that way, too. He sees the beauty in things I have always taken for granted."

"You're lucky."

Ginny lay her head on Margot's shoulder and said softly, "I know."

Once they disembarked, the friends walked arm in arm towards the chic shops on Newbury. In the first one they entered, a wave of dread crept down Margot's spine. The dresses were gaudy, showy things, none of which she could abide.

"This is all wrong," she whispered under her breath, tugging at Ginny's arm.

"Try this one on," Ginny said, concealing a smirk as she pulled a black, sequined, floor-length gown with a four-figure price tag off the rack.

"I am not a fucking Barbie, Gin."

"No, but you're the closest thing I've ever seen to one."

Margot shook her head but felt a little flush of thanks for her looks.

"Fine." They brought the dress to the conceited salesgirl, who eyed them up and down.

Languidly, the girl led them to a dressing room and left them alone.

Margot undressed without thinking about it, but when Ginny gasped, Margot's attention snapped to.

"Holy shit," Ginny said, a little too loud. "What is this?"

"What?" Margot asked, genuinely wondering. Then she caught sight of her body, luminous in the mirrors. The tattoos swirled over her shoulders and down her chest in a flurry of delicate designs. "Oh, the tattoos. They're new."

Ginny looked her up and down, tears filling her eyes. "These are the designs from your veil. I remember."

"Oh, Gin," Margot said, her voice catching in her throat.

"You are so beautiful, Margot. I can't believe what you've been through but here you are, strong and lovely." She brought Margot in for a hug. When she released Margot, she looked down again and asked, "Who did them? They're exquisite."

Margot's cheeks went hot. How could she explain Chase? "The guy next door to the bar. His name is Chase."

"He's incredible. What artistry. Well, whatever you wear, we're going to have to show off that incredible work."

"No," Margot said firmly. "I don't want to. It's too personal."

"Margot, there are tattoos all over the top of your body. Every dress we try on will be changed by the look of your lace-covered skin." She paused, staring at Margot's chest, her eyes growing wide. "Is that bird from the mobile?"

"It is."

"You even wrote her name."

"That was Chase's idea," Margot confessed with a tightening in her chest at seeing Amandine's name.

"He is good."

"I think he's in love with me," Margot blurted. Better to say it now then explain later.

"What?" Ginny's eyes were wide, and her mouth was agape.

Margot turned back towards the mirror "I think so, anyway."

"And what do you think of him? And more importantly, why didn't you tell me?" Ginny was only partly joking.

Margot leaned her forehead against the cool mirror glass. "I don't know what to do. We're friends and I like him, but then I feel horrible for feeling anything at all, so I shut it down. I'm such a disaster. I wouldn't wish me on anyone."

Ginny reached forward and rested her hands on Margot's shoulders. "You're an incredible woman. You shouldn't feel that way. He must see you like I see you."

"I guess."

"What do you think of him, though?" Ginny persisted. "Is he nice?"

"He is. He's great. I-I think I could have feelings for him, but I don't know."

"Give it time."

"I'm trying," Margot said, miserably. "But all I can think about is Kevin."

Ginny sat down on the little bench against the wall and watched Margot in the mirror. "Kevin was a dreamboat, Margot. He was perfect. No one will ever replace him. I loved him for the joy he brought you and for the incredible person he was. But he would want you to be happy, love."

"I know," Margot said, but her heart was an empty nest.

Before Margot could sink into a pit of sadness, however, Ginny's buoyant voice said, "Well, my dear, back to the important question at hand. What is that wild, spangled dress going to look like on you?"

Margot shook her head and slipped the crazy dress over her hair. It slinked down over her body, a flawless fit. It was a surprisingly beautiful contrast against her skin. She looked like a sparkly raven.

"Well, you were right," Ginny said, appraising her. "It's crazy."

Both women laughed.

Three more stores worth of dresses held nothing promising and the day's heat was intensifying. "I don't even know what I want," Margot said dejectedly over coffee while they took a little break at Trident for old time's sake.

Ginny sipped her mint tea. "You'll know it when you see it." With a bite of croissant in her mouth, she added, "It will feel like a second skin."

The next stop they made was at Margot's request. "The sign says they specialize in vintage designer clothes. We might have better luck going old school, don't you think?"

Ginny looked tired but smiled indulgently at Margot. "It's worth a try."

The first dress that caught Margot's eye was an inky sapphire silk velvet dress from the 1930s and it looked like something a movie star would have worn. "What about this?"

"Try it on. It looks very small, so it should be perfect on you." She absently patted her belly. Although she hadn't changed sizes dramatically yet, she appeared preoccupied by the coming shift.

As soon as the dress touched her skin, Margot knew it was right. It was formal, elegant, not showy, and the lace tattoo was mostly hidden behind the high cowl neck of draped silk. The fluttery sleeves and dramatic length were glorious.

"What do you think?" Ginny asked, staring wide-eyed at Margot's reflection in the mirror.

"It's incredible," Margot replied, breathless. "I love it. Do you love it?"

"I do. It's as unique as you."

Embarrassed, Margot smiled. "It's also expensive."

"So what? Don't you make a million dollars a year or something?"

"Not exactly, but I'll be comfortable for the rest of my life with the settlement from the accident."

Ginny looked stricken. "Jesus, I never thought about that."

"I don't really talk about it."

After a thoughtful pause, Ginny said, "Well, if you can afford it, that dress is flawless."

"Okay. It's a deal. Let's buy this and get you home."

On the bus ride home, the friends decided to forego the movie and talked instead.

"I've been thinking, Gin. If you'd like it, I'd like to give you and Henry all of the stuff from Amandine's nursery. If you don't have a girl, the crib and blankets and stuff will still work. The glider's comfy too." Ginny raised her eyebrows and her hands in protest, but before she could say anything, Margot interrupted her. "Don't ask if I'm sure because I am. I've given it a lot of thought. I want to see your precious baby enjoy those things. But only if you want them. Please don't feel obligated."

Ginny reached out and took Margot's hand. She squeezed it. "You have always had impeccable taste. I loved everything in that room. I'd be honored to accept whatever you'll send our way. Thank you, Margot."

"I hate to see it all collecting dust when it could be enjoyed."

"That's kind of how I feel about you."

"What do you mean?" Margot turned her head to look at her friend.

"You have this life. It's still yours. It's a gift. Don't waste it, Margot. It's okay to let yourself be happy. If this guy Chase makes you happy, you should go for it."

Margot silently contemplated her friend's words. Choking up once more, she said, "I can't let Kevin go, Ginny. Every time I let Chase a little closer, my love for Kevin pops its head up between us. It feels like such a betrayal. It kills me."

"You know that's not what Kevin would want. He'd want you to be happy. He loved you more than anything," Ginny urged.

"I know." Margot paused. "I loved him too. I still do."

"I'm not saying you have to let that love go. You never will. You shouldn't. But it's okay to love them both."

"Is it?" Margot's voice quavered.

"Yes," Ginny answered firmly. "And love yourself too, while you're at it. You're a wonderful person."

Ginny rested her head against Margot's shoulder, their hands still clasped tight. "Thank you, Gin. You're going to be such a good mom."

"God, I hope so. I'm going to need all the help I can get."

Ginny fell asleep a little while later. Her breathing slowed and evened out, her body relaxed. Margot watched the world fly past outside the windows of the bus, a blur of cars and trees and sky. It was all so surreal. Nothing seemed substantial. Her eyes closed and she imagined Kevin's lips on hers, his love filling her. It felt so close, so real. She wished so badly to have him back it hurt. But Ginny was right. She needed to be loved again.

SIXTEEN

The gala was at the country club in Falmouth. From behind the high windows, Margot watched the expanse of glittering ocean play at the rocky shore. Mesmerized, she didn't notice the man by her side until he set his drink down on the windowsill.

"Margot," he said, by way of greeting, as she turned to him in surprise.

"Aaron. You startled me. I was looking at the water thinking of.... Well, it doesn't matter. How are you?"

Smiling, he leaned in and air kissed her cheek, touching her arm lightly as he did so. The velvet sleeve of her dress pressed against the skin of her arm.

"I'm wondering how you are," Aaron answered, looking at her intently with his icy blue eyes. His handsome face wore a somber expression, so unlike the flirty, frolicking bachelor she'd known before Kevin died. "I should have called you, but I didn't know what to say that hadn't already been said."

"I understand," Margot replied. She remembered a moment when Aaron had imbibed a bit too much at one of her parties, taking her aside in the kitchen and whispering how he wished he could find a woman like her. The moment had passed by barely noticed by Margot, but Kevin had walked in to find his best friend whispering to his wife. He had not been pleased. Margot wondered if Kevin had ever forgiven Aaron for that indiscretion. "I've been getting better."

"Things at the hospital have been different without him. I don't enjoy it the way I used to. I can only imagine what that must feel like with everything else. I've thought of you often, Margot."

"Thank you, Aaron. Like I said, I've been getting better."

Margot wondered whether Aaron would ever settle down. He and Kevin had been residents together in Cambridge, so Margot had watched Aaron play the field for years. He must have dated twenty different women during that time, all of a specific type. Where was his date now, she wondered, scanning the room for a tall, leggy, glamorous woman.

As though he'd read her mind, Aaron said, "I came alone. I've been spending time contemplating what I actually want in a relationship. I'm sure you think of me as a bit of a player."

"Maybe a bit," Margot admitted, meeting his gaze with an embarrassed acquiescence.

"Right. Well, that's all behind me. I'm almost forty, for Christ's sake. I need to figure out what I want the next phase of my life to look like."

"So, what are you looking for, exactly?" Margot's guard was up, although she wasn't sure why.

"I'm looking for someone I can grow old with. Someone who is as beautiful on the inside as she is on the outside." Aaron's gaze bored into her. "I always envied Kevin's relationship with you."

Margot felt the tension grow between them, as though Aaron were asking her a question with his statement. Was he hitting on her? It was so crass if he was. Even the possibility made her nauseous and wildly uncomfortable. When the Chair of Internal Medicine inserted herself into their conversation, Margot's gratitude was immeasurable.

"Margot. I am so glad you came tonight. I can't imagine it was easy, but you have always been up for the difficult tasks. Your strength astounds me."

"Thank you, Dr. Fitzgerald. I hope you've been well."

"You don't need to be so formal with me, Margot. Please call me Talia."

"Thank you, Talia. Kevin held you in the highest regard."

"That sentiment was mutual, believe me. We wanted to honor his life this evening. He was a special person and a truly gifted surgeon. Aaron, all is well, I presume?" The formidable Talia turned her iron gaze upon Aaron, finally including him in the conversation.

"Indeed," he demurred. "Thank you for asking."

"Margot, join me." Talia said, the command in her voice directed more towards Aaron than Margot. "I'd like to introduce you to some people. Also, I'd be honored if you would accompany me at the head table. I have a seat saved for you there."

"Thank you, Doctor."

"Talia," she corrected.

"Talia," Margot parroted, feeling like a grade-schooler. "I appreciate that. Aaron, best of luck in your quest." Margot smiled at him coolly, registering his obvious disappointment, then allowed herself to be led by the silver-haired Talia away into the crowd.

Awash with relief at not being cornered by Aaron all evening, Margot shook the hands of countless people, some of whom had known her husband, and some who had not. Those who had told tactful stories of his prowess with microsurgery, of how many families he had reunited when all had seemed lost. His talents were touted in the most extraordinary terms, all of which Margot believed wholeheartedly. She was so proud of him.

This sharing of her husband with people who knew him professionally was deeply cathartic. She'd held Kevin, and the loss of him, so close for so long. Now, she could actively share that loss with others. She had always known she wasn't alone in her grief, but since it was all she had left, she'd held on to it with a desperate grip, possessive of it to the point of incapacity when it came to talking about Kevin.

Here, however, people wanted to share with her their stories of his genius, of his kindness, of his extraordinary bedside manner. Margot listened rapt, thankful for all of these other sets of perception when it came to remembering Kevin. Their perspectives were less personal, but they rounded hers out, somehow.

When they finally sat down for dinner, Talia asked Margot, "Where on earth did you find that dress? It's extraordinary."

"Thank you. It's from the thirties. I found it in Boston. I had nothing at all to wear to something like this, so my friend Ginny and I took the bus down and did some shopping. It fit well and the velvet is so soft, I thought it would be kind of comforting."

"You look like a movie star. I noticed Aaron Beaman eyeing you from across the room before he went to talk to you. He's got quite the reputation."

"He was one of Kevin's closest friends, so I remember his antics quite well. I appreciate the warning, though."

"He's a good doctor, despite the womanizing. Did I hear him say he wants to settle down?" Talia asked with a glimmer in her eye.

"You heard correctly. I would sooner expect the sun to divide in an epic mitosis than Aaron Beaman settle into a long-term, monogamous relationship," Margot said, shaking her head.

Talia laughed unabashedly and nodded agreeably. "Have *you* met anyone? I know that's forward, but you're so young. It would be a shame for you to spend the rest of your life alone."

"It's hard to think about finding someone new to love in that way. I don't know. I've got a friend and I know he would like it to be more, but every time I think of it, the thought of Kevin stops me in my tracks. Maybe in time."

"I am glad to hear you say you've not ruled it out. Let yourself be happy, Margot. You deserve it. Kevin would want it. You know that."

Her throat suddenly too tight to swallow her food, Margot nodded, fighting back tears. She took a sip of her champagne and excused herself. "I'm going to use the ladies' room. I'll be right back," she said softly, pushing her chair away from the table.

In the rest room, Margot lowered her head and took some deep breaths, trying to calm her mind, to tame her racing heart. It was still such a surprise when the grief swelled up and consumed her like that. Of course she should move on. Theoretically, why shouldn't she? But even the thought of being with someone else was enough to set her into an emotional tailspin.

Once she was calm, Margot touched up her make-up and walked out into the club once more. A tall, bearded man, probably in his late fifties, with greying hair and a creased forehead, left the men's room at the same time as Margot left the women's room. Their eyes met and Margot nodded.

"Ms. Morrison?" he asked tentatively.

"It's DeWitt," Margot corrected gently. "But my husband was Kevin Morrison."

"My apologies, Ms. DeWitt. I'm Sam Monaghan. I'm a cardiologist and I often worked with your husband. He was a wonderful man, and I am so sorry for your loss." The man's tone was genuine.

"Thank you. I appreciate that. I remember him speaking highly of you, Dr. Monaghan."

"Please, call me Sam. May I?" he asked, offering his elbow.

"Thank you," Margot said, accepting. Together they walked back into the ballroom. Sam escorted Margot back to her seat, gallantly drawing out her chair for her.

"Ms. DeWitt," he nodded, taking his leave.

"Now he would be a catch," Talia said, watching him leave.

"He's a widower, and one of the nicest men you will ever come across."

"When did he lose his wife?" Margot asked, having sensed his sadness as they walked.

"Three or four years ago now, I can't remember. Cancer." Talia shook her head sadly. "It was pretty awful."

"That's so sad. Did they have kids?"

"Yes, but they're grown. Not that it ever gets easier to lose the people we love," she added.

"Have you ever been married?" Margot asked.

"Yes. Twice. They didn't take. It wasn't them, mind you. It was work. I am married to my work and they were married to theirs. I firmly believe a marriage takes at least one person to be married to the marriage in order to work."

"I can see that." The woman at her side didn't seem sentimental about it. Or sad.

"Whenever you're ready," Talia said softly. "I will present the award in Kevin's honor to you, and you can have the microphone for as long or as short as you'd like, if you'd like to say a few words."

"Thank you. I'm ready any time."

As Talia stood up and crossed the room towards the podium, Margot's heart started to flutter rapidly once more. She took a sip of her water and glanced around. Most people were focused on Talia, now, but Aaron and Sam, from two separate tables, looked in Margot's direction. She met Sam's glance and smiled faintly. He nodded in encouragement. Talia spoke for a few moments about Kevin, telling what Margot assumed would have been a touching story, but the buzzing in her ears precluded any real listening. She waited until her own name filtered through the white noise of applause, then she stood unsteadily. After another sip of water, Margot removed her speech from her clutch, and walked over to Talia at the podium.

Every person in the room was standing and clapping. Talia handed Margot an etched crystal award with Kevin's name engraved on the front. It reminded Margot of a miniature glass gravestone, but she accepted it graciously.

Talia kissed her on the cheek and whispered, "Are you okay?"

Margot nodded and switched spots with her, accepting her place at the microphone.

"Thank you," she began, clearing her voice as the applause died down. "Thank you all for being here tonight to honor my husband, Dr. Kevin Morrison. Many of you knew him personally and therefore know what a wonderful person he was. He couldn't hide that from the world. When we first met, I could see he was special within the first few moments. His love for the world, his desire to help people, his inherent kindness flowed from his very being. I was the lucky recipient of his love and adoration. I will not shy from saying that losing him was worse than dying. Kevin was all that is good in this world and for a long while, I didn't think I could go on. I didn't think I wanted to."

Margot paused for a moment and looked up at the crowd. She didn't want to stick to her speech, for suddenly it seemed unimportant to list all the great things Kevin had done. Everyone already knew. She wanted to say something else but wasn't sure how to begin.

"I'm a musician," she finally said. "I may not look like it, but once upon a time, I was a punk rock drummer. And if you've ever tried to play drums, you know how all the parts work together to create a rhythm, but that nothing makes sense without the downbeat of the kick drum. I tell you this because Kevin was the kick drum in our relationship, the driving, steady heartbeat. His reliability, his unwavering sense of purpose, his way of always being able to see the good in the world, brought meaning into my life. Losing him was like losing my own pulse. But it has also taught me something. Every single person makes a difference in this world, for good or for ill. Kevin made a difference in my life, but also in the lives of so many others, every day. I know we all feel the emptiness of a world without him. He was kind and generous and talented and fearless. He inspired so many people to live their best lives. Now, I ask in his memory, what can each of us do to make the world a better place as Kevin did? What will we do to honor him? For me, for now, the answer I am coming to is that I must try to live every day of my life like the gift it is, rather than waste it in despair. I must live in the present, doing as much good as I can, as my dear husband did. Thank you."

Still holding the crystal award in her trembling hands, Margot was escorted from the podium by Talia, who had been standing protectively beside her all the while. Another distinguished doctor took their place and continued the proceedings as soon as the standing ovation abated. Instead of taking her back to her seat, Talia led Margot to the bar. She ordered another glass of champagne for Margot and a Manhattan for herself. Without speaking, she took the award from Margot, handed it to the bartender and said, "Keep this safe."

Nodding, the young woman took the fragile object and set it aside behind the bar. Talia led Margot through a side door out onto the expansive bluestone terrace overlooking the bay to the south. The sunset's low angle bathed the landscape in dramatic light, making it seem more like an N. C. Wyeth painting than the real world itself. Livid orange clouds raged against a purple and indigo backdrop that faded to the purest cerulean at the eastern horizon. Every color was represented except green, Margot noticed incidentally, as she admired the view.

"Kevin would be very proud. Your speech was touching." Talia raised her glass. "To Kevin."

Margot nodded and raised her glass. "To Kevin."

"There are few doctors like him. He saw the world with a unique perspective. It made him truly great. As a spouse, I know you understand some of what he did, but from one surgeon to another, I can tell you, he was one of a kind. We miss him every day."

"I appreciate knowing that. Seeing him as a whole person, not only as my husband, has reminded me that the loss was not my own. It was collective. I'm finding some comfort in that." Margot stared off into the sky.

"I'm glad."

"Thank you for staying beside me during the speech. It was kind of you."

"It was the least I could do." Talia turned back towards the room full of guests. Before she walked away, she rested her hand on Margot's arm. "Be well, Margot. Live your life and do not be afraid to move on. Take your own advice. We don't honor anyone by living in the past."

As the evening concluded, Margot stood alone in the foyer, trying to get cell reception so that she could summon a car. She must have looked ridiculous, waving her phone in one direction, then another, because when Sam approached her, he did so with an ill-concealed smile.

"Would you like to use my phone?" he asked.

"No, I'm trying to use one of my ride apps. The reception here is surprisingly bad."

"May I offer you a ride?" he asked, gesturing to the doors.

"That's unnecessary. I don't want to put you out."

He frowned at her playfully. "Ms. DeWitt, it would be my pleasure."

"Goodness, please call me Margot."

"Margot, it would be my pleasure."

Considering him for a moment, Margot acquiesced. She put her unresponsive phone back into her clutch. "Thank you, Sam. I appreciate the offer. I'm in Portland, a few blocks away from the hospital."

"Familiar territory, then."

"Right."

"Wait here," he said. "I'll pull the car around."

"That's very chivalrous, but unnecessary. I am happy to walk twenty feet to your car."

She smiled and gingerly rested her hand upon his outstretched arm as Sam escorted her through the parking lot. When they reached his car, he opened the door for her, and she got in. Pulling the hem of her dress up over the threshold, she held the comforting fabric to her and smiled as he closed the door.

"Did you see the sunset this evening?" he asked as they drove.

"I did. Talia and I were outside watching it."

"She's a formidable person and an incredible doctor. What do you think of her?"

"I like her very much. Kevin always spoke highly of her and of you, Sam. Thank you for looking after me this evening." Margot looked down at the crystal award in her lap. Cradled in the sapphire velvet of her dress, it glinted in the soft light from streetlamps overhead as they drove. From darkness into light, Margot thought. And only in the light do we shine.

"Thank you for saying so. With the younger doctors it's always difficult to tell. Kevin, as I said, was a great doctor and wonderful person. Your speech tonight was lovely. I don't think I would have had the courage to talk about my late wife like you talked about Kevin."

Margot breathed in deeply to control her nervousness being in the car. "I'm sorry for your loss, Sam. Talia told me what happened."

"Thank you. It's been years and I still don't think I have it in me to talk about her publicly."

"I wouldn't have if I'd had a choice. It was the right thing to do, though." Margot looked out the window anxiously wringing her hands as they drove, thankful the distance home was relatively short.

"Sorry." Sam picked up on her discomfort. "I hadn't thought about the reason you don't drive anymore. This makes you uncomfortable, doesn't it?"

"Yes." Why should she pretend it didn't?

"We'll be there soon," Sam said gently. "You're safe, I promise."

"Tell me about your children," Margot said, looking for a distraction.

All too happy to oblige, Sam told Margot about his three children, all boys, all in college or graduate school. She listened obliquely, trying to focus, but not thoroughly able to. As they pulled into her neighborhood, Margot relaxed considerably. When they stopped, Sam got out of the car and walked Margot to her door.

"You'll be happy again, Margot. I promise. But first, you have to give yourself permission to be happy. To decide you deserve it."

Margot turned towards him. "Are you happy, Sam?"

"Sometimes." He paused thoughtfully. "Isn't that the best anyone can ask for? No one's happy all the time."

Despite herself, Margot laughed. "I guess that's true."

"If you ever need anything, even to talk, please call me." He took a card from his jacket pocket and handed it to her.

"Thank you, Sam." She accepted the card and nodded. "You're very kind. I appreciate the ride home. Goodnight."

"Goodnight," he replied, looking pensive.

Margot unlocked her front door as he walked back to his car. Once she was safely inside, he drove away with a final wave. The house was chilly in comparison to the balmy August air outside, and Margot shivered. Her phone buzzed in her purse, distracting her momentarily from the depressing scene of aloneness before her. It was Chase. Margot relished the little flutter in her heart as she saw his name.

"Hi," she answered as she walked into her living room and placed the award on a shelf.

"Hi," Chase said expectantly. "How was it?"

"Better than I thought it would be. Everyone was nice."

"I'm so glad," he said.

"Yeah, I guess." Panicky desperation was threatening to overcome her again.

Chase must have sensed it in her voice. "Margot, what's wrong?"

Hesitating, trying to figure out what exactly was the matter, Margot finally answered, "I want to move forward, but the past is holding on too tight."

"Do you want company?"

Margot hesitated once more. How could she live with herself for stringing Chase along like this? Yet was she stringing him along? Didn't she want to get to know him better? "Okay."

"Do you need anything?"

"I don't know." Margot sat down on the couch in the dark living room.

After a short pause, Chase said, "I'll be over soon."

Margot held onto the dark phone and stared out into the dark street. From its place on the bookshelf across the room, the award glinted in a lonely stream of light. Kevin and Amandine seemed close by, somehow.

"Take care of her, Kevin," Margot whispered. "I love you both, but I need to live now."

A short while later, Chase knocked at the door. Margot went and opened it. When Margot saw Chase's dazed look, his eyes wide, she looked down at herself and realized she was still wearing the sapphire velvet dress. Rather than feeling mortified at answering the door in formal attire, Margot was emboldened. She put out her hand and led Chase into the foyer.

"You are stunning," Chase finally said, by way of greeting.

"Thanks. This is the dress Ginny helped me pick out in Boston. I forgot I was still wearing it. She said it would feel like a second skin if it was right, and it does. Plus, it's vintage."

"It's perfect." Chase fidgeted for a moment before he met Margot's gaze again.

"I'm glad you came over. I like talking on the phone, but I missed seeing you." Margot couldn't believe the words had actually come out of her mouth, but as they did, she knew they were true. Her heartrate quickened as she moved closer to Chase. He did not back away, but he tensed visibly. She placed her hand over his heart, moved so her whole body stood touching his, and lay her head upon his chest. "Thank you."

———

Chase stood frozen for a moment as Margot leaned against him. The top of her head came up to his chin, she would fit into his arms perfectly. Chase mustered the courage to hold her, to put his arms around her, to feel her body against him without letting himself simultaneously embrace the obvious truth.

Her body was soft beneath the sumptuous velvet, the curve of her back drove him to distraction, the vanilla scent of her hair beneath his lips as he kissed the top of her head tore at his heart. His desire for her was barely tamed, simmering beneath the surface like a call to insurrection. He wanted more than anything to kiss her beautiful neck, to taste the secret of her lace-patterned skin, barely visible from the angle at which he stood. He imagined caressing her through the velvet, feeling the rise of her breast beneath his hand, the curve of her lower back, the plush fabric sliding against her flawless body beneath.

As he struggled with himself to maintain control, Margot seemed to be doing the opposite. She tilted her head and fixed him with her gorgeous blue eyes, all the bluer because of the sapphire dress. Her expression was a dichotomy of longing and sadness. Sliding her hand from his heart along his collarbone, up his neck and letting it rest upon his cheek, Margot said, "I don't know how to let myself feel anything but loss. I asked you to be patient with me, but I'd understand if you want to find someone more…accessible."

"I'm not going anywhere. I will wait as long as you need me to."

Chase held her even tighter. Although he had mastered his desire for the time being, he still yearned for her.

Eventually, Margot said, "Let's do something normal people do. Would you like to watch a movie or go for a walk?"

"A movie sounds good." He wanted to keep her close. "Do you have popcorn?"

Margot laughed. "I have no idea. Let me change and I'll look through the cupboard."

While Margot was upstairs, Chase had a vision of her slipping from the dress, velvet flowing like water over her body, leaving her pale skin exposed in the moonlight. It was heartrendingly beautiful, sublime. With an effort, Chase locked this image of her, resplendent in her vulnerability, away. Now was not the time. She wasn't ready. Yet.

Margot returned in jeans and a loose sweater. In the back of her cupboard, she unearthed a half a bag of popcorn kernels.

"These don't go bad, right?" she asked, smiling sheepishly.

"I don't think so. Let's find out."

Margot took a heavy kettle from another cupboard, poured oil into it, and set it on the stovetop. As it heated, Margot put three kernels of corn into the oil. Chase looked at her, perplexed. "Test kernels," she explained. "When these pop you add the rest. That way, none of them burn."

While they waited, Margot melted butter in the microwave. Then she tied a clean dishcloth around the lid of the pot. When the test kernels popped, she added a half a cup of popcorn to the oil and put the covered lid on the pot. As she shook the kettle over the flames, she said, "I put the cloth on the top to keep the steam from getting the popcorn soggy."

"Why do you know so much about popcorn?" Chase asked, smiling from across the island.

"My dad was a big popcorn guy, but he hated air poppers and microwave popcorn. He liked the feel of doing it over the flames."

"Tell me about your dad."

"He was awesome. He was funny and smart, and he loved to cook. He was serious about his work as a structural engineer and said if he got the numbers wrong, people would die. He never got the numbers wrong. I got my math brain from him."

"Did he pass away?" Chase asked tentatively. He realized they'd never talked about her parents.

"Yes. While I was in college. He was such a kind man and I loved him. Losing him was unbelievably hard."

"I'm so sorry. Is that why you went to grad school for accounting?"

Margot shimmied the kettle back and forth across the flames as the kernels within heated and began to burst. The popping was furious, frenzied. "Maybe, in part. Losing him set me back emotionally, that's for sure. Music suddenly didn't seem as important. I couldn't play right after he died. I didn't want to. I missed him so much it hurt. It was my first experience with loss. You understand. Then I met Kevin and loving him eased the sadness somewhat. A couple of years after Kevin and I got married, my mom died too."

"I'm sorry, Margot. That's so sad."

"It was horrible. We were close, especially after Dad died. We loved each other very much."

The popping slowed down and when Margot removed the pot lid, Chase saw a full kettle of white popcorn.

"There," Margot said. She turned off the heat, set the pot on the counter, and removed the melted butter from the microwave. To this she added truffle oil. "Back Bay Grill always used to serve popcorn with truffle oil. I wonder if they still do." She drizzled the mixture over the popcorn, added salt, poured some into a bowl and said, "Voila!"

"I've never had truffle oil," Chase admitted.

"Shit! I should have asked first. I can make more popcorn if you don't like it."

"Let me try it," he said, reaching for the bowl. He tasted it, but moreover, he smelled it. It was earthy and sensual, delicious. "Man, that's good. Thank you for showing me something new."

"I'm so glad you like it. You can pick the movie since I picked our popcorn flavor."

Margot poured them seltzer water and got some napkins, handed the bowl of popcorn to Chase, and led the way to the den.

"What movies do you have?"

"Classics like *Bringing Up Baby* and *The Philadelphia Story*, *Casablanca*… Then I've also got a few modern classics like *The Life Aquatic* and *Bladerunner*. What do you like?"

"I've always liked the Wes Anderson movies. Let's watch *The Life Aquatic*."

"Done. It's my favorite."

Together, side by side on the couch, they watched the movie and ate popcorn. The experience was sweet and tender and awkward. The intense longing Chase felt for Margot was tempered by her need for his patience. These emotions and desires swirled through his psyche, while at the same time he was trying to focus on the movie. Halfway through the film, he reached for Margot's hand. She did not pull away. The simple act of holding hands was perfect. Energy pulsed between them, connecting their bodies so simply, so innocently. Chase was like a much happier version of his teenage self and it made him smile. He never would have thought such a thing was possible.

After the movie, they sat in the glow of the blank TV in silence. Chase had forgotten how sad the ending of the movie was, or he might not have suggested it. Watching life go on, though, despite loss, was uplifting in a way. That was the beauty of Wes Anderson's stories, after all.

"Are you all right?" he asked Margot.

She hesitated for a moment, surreptitiously brushing a tear from her cheek. "I love that movie. It hasn't lost any of its charm over the years. I love the way Wes Anderson builds a parallel world to ours. And Bill Murray? I can't get enough."

"I agree. He's amazing."

"I also love the sugar crabs."

"They're pretty great," Chase agreed. "Seriously, though, are you okay?"

"Yep. Just sad. What else is new." Margot leaned her head back against the couch and stared at the ceiling.

"Tell me about the gala."

"The view was lovely, the food was good, and everyone was very nice to me," Margot replied vaguely.

"You know that's not what I meant."

Margot turned her gaze upon Chase and in her eyes he saw all the feeling she'd held back all night. "I talked about Kevin publicly. It was impossibly hard."

"What did you say?"

"That he was our kick drum. God, it sounds so stupid, now. I should have stuck to my original plan, but something about him being the downbeat in our rhythm together struck me while I was standing there, looking out at a crowd of people I don't know but who all knew him. I've been so lost without him. I ended the whole thing by talking about how everyone has an impact on the world around them. Kevin's impact was gigantic. I mean, he saved lives for a living. Everyone loved him. He was a wonderful person."

"Tell me something about him that I don't know. Build a picture for me."

"Well… He loved his work. He changed the lives of so many people, both doctors and patients. Someone tonight told me how Kevin would intentionally take the hardest patients, people who'd been told they wouldn't survive, and he fixed them. He was gifted."

"It sounds like it. What would Kevin say about you, do you think?"

"What do you mean?" Margot asked, her eyebrows raised.

"I mean if he were here talking about you instead. What would he say?"

Margot swallowed hard. "He'd say I was the happiest person he'd ever met."

"Oh, Margot. I've seen a little glimpse of that happiness. You'll be yourself again in time."

"I need to make meaning in my life, Chase. I need to create positive energy. I've sucked the joy out of every room I've entered in the past year and a half. It's time I did something creative rather than destructive."

"Then play music with me." The thought was like an electric jolt through his body. "Once a week. Twice a week. Whatever you like. It can't hurt to try. Let's see what happens."

"I don't know, Chase. I haven't picked up my sticks since before the night you saved me from that asshole at the bar, since I confronted the full memory of losing Amandine." Margot's tone was heartrending.

Chase leaned forward, his body language earnest. "You will find your creativity again. It's in there, Margot. It never left. It will all come back to you. Let's give it a try, at least. Fridays?"

"I don't have a car. I can't get my drums to your place."

Chase smiled at her. "I can pick you up and help carry everything."

"What if I can't play?" she asked miserably.

"Then I'll serenade you."

Margot giggled. "Fine."

"Good. It's a deal."

Margot was so strong. She had spoken publicly about her deceased husband. He couldn't imagine the courage it must have taken. He would never have been able to talk about his parents publicly after they'd died. It would have torn him apart. All these years later, he still had a hard time talking about them. But Margot was forged differently from him. There was determination simmering beneath her sadness. A transformation was happening inside her and it would take time. Eventually, though, it would burst forth into something incredible.

SEVENTEEN

By Tuesday evening, Margot had logged countless hours agonizing about playing with Chase. What if she sucked? What if he hated her style? What if she hated his? Even worse, what if it was perfect? Then what? Would they play in a band? It sounded so stupid, like no thirty-two-year-old widow should be doing such a thing. Was music even what she wanted?

The entire endeavor seemed impossible, a terrible experiment. She was going to risk everything, her budding friendship with Chase, her own interest in playing music again, on the fragile possibility of their musical compatibility. It was insanity.

The more she thought about Chase's proposition, the more it freaked her out. She should back out now, before it was too late. As she was about to text Chase and cancel, Doctor Sam's words of kindness came back to her, stopping her in her tracks. *Give yourself permission to be happy.* Sam had been through this. He understood. Happiness seemed like an elusive animal, something mythical, unattainable. She couldn't remember what it felt like anymore. Sam had told her to call him anytime if she needed to talk. Maybe he could give her some perspective.

Instead of texting Chase, Margot called Sam.

"Sam Monaghan speaking," he answered, sounding professional.

"Sam? This is Margot DeWitt. I am sorry to bother you."

"Margot," he said, his voice instantly softening. "Hearing from you is the farthest thing from a bother."

"Thank you. You were so kind to me the other night and I wanted to tell you I appreciated it."

"You're most welcome. How are you doing?"

"Oh, you know." She was trying to keep her tone light, but it wasn't working. "Up and down, but mostly down."

"That I understand. Your grief is still so fresh."

"You told me I need to give myself permission to be happy. I keep thinking about that. I want to be happy. I want to live my life. Kevin would be terribly sad to see me languish, I know that. But how do you get past the guilt? How do you move forward with the guilt of happiness, of life, of loving again pulling you back?"

Sam paused for a moment. "Does the guilt make you feel better after you've given in to it?"

"No," Margot admitted.

"Do you know why we feel guilt?"

"Because we're doing something wrong?" Margot conjectured.

"Sometimes, but not always. Often, we feel guilt because in our construct of morality, we are conditioned to think in terms of right and wrong. Guilt is a psychological phenomenon, reinforced by various religions, that has permeated human culture since its inception. Its purpose? To control people more effectively. It works well for the big stuff like murder and theft. People should feel badly about those things, only psychopaths don't. For someone like you, Margot, who hasn't done anything wrong, guilt is a chain around your heart, strangling your potential. Let go of the guilt and you can find something akin to happiness."

Margot was fascinated. She'd never considered the origin of guilt before. She was a critical thinker, how was it she'd failed to question this basic feeling?

"So, what you're saying is that we're taught guilt in society to give us a sense of right and wrong?"

"Exactly. It's not a pure form of expression, nor does it equate one-to-one with morality. Often, it's completely self-imposed."

"So, all the guilt I feel for being alive while Kevin is dead is my own doing?" she asked flabbergasted.

"Maybe not at first, since it's part of the way we're taught to react to life's tribulations, but once you're able to identify guilt for what it is – an artificial, unnecessary, completely destructive construct – you will find it has no value in your life."

"How did you let go of it?" Margot asked, the desperation in her voice unconcealed.

"I work at it every day. When it pops up, I bash it back down. You'll be surprised at how many places in your life irrational guilt can hold you back."

"What if I fall in love again?" Margot asked, involuntarily thinking of Chase. "Isn't that a betrayal of Kevin? Of our love? Isn't that wrong?"

"Love is the constructive force in the universe, Margot. Without it, nothing is worthwhile. You have to let yourself love again in order to be whole. You said it yourself, during your speech. How can you honor the people you've loved if you don't live? And to take it one step further, what good is living if we can't love? How is that a moral choice for living our best life?"

Margot practiced the drums every night that week. Sam's words had taken hold, freeing the frozen creative mechanisms within her once more, and growing into something resembling confidence. Combined with the meditative quality of her practice, something like peace filled her, for while she played, there was room for nothing but music. As the end of the week approached, nervous excitement dominated Margot's heart. On

Friday, Chase came over to Margot's house at six looking as anxious and eager as she felt.

Chase looked out of place in her living room, gathering her drums. He was so big, so colorful, so strong. He lifted the bass drum easily, brought it out and came back, all in near silence. In her faded jeans and a black Misfits t-shirt she'd had since high school, Margot looked like a different person, incongruous to the space as well. She carried out her cymbals. "Fake it 'til you make it" was her new motto.

Together, they delivered the kit to his loft, carrying everything up the steep back stairs. Chase had a concealed parking space behind his building which, for some reason, delighted Margot. Little secrets were slowly being revealed. Once everything was upstairs, Margot set up her drums and sat restlessly tightening the heads, listening for the right sound.

Noticing her nervousness, Chase grabbed a couple of beers and handed her one. They clinked bottles and she smiled uncertainly. She took a long swig of the beer, set the bottle on the floor next to the high hat, and sat back down. Her leg bounced up and down anxiously as she waited for Chase to tune.

"You're nervous," he said, glancing up at her.

"Yes. Please don't judge me. I haven't played with anyone in over a decade."

"I would not judge you, Margot," Chase said. "Everything is okay."

Not sure if she believed him, she nodded her head.

"Ready?" he asked, and played a power chord in G.

Margot giggled. "Yes," she answered, this time with a genuine smile.

"Click it off."

Without hesitating, Margot clicked off a fast four-four and rolled into the steady punk beat from *Want* by Jawbreaker. Chase knew exactly what she was doing and played along flawlessly, singing out the words by heart. She wished they had a mic and a PA so she could hear him better.

After *Want* they played Chase's song and Margot followed along with a steady tempo, trying out an indie fast tick on the high hat, flaming into a couple of improv fills, then onto the ride for the bridge. Chase was smiling like a lunatic as he sang along. When the song ended, he stared at her for a second too long.

"What?" she asked incredulously.

"That was fucking awesome. I wouldn't have thought of any of that, but it was perfect. You are incredible."

"Don't flatter me, Chase. What's next?"

"I'm not flattering you, Margot. You're unbelievably talented. You're a natural."

Margot rolled her eyes at him, but inside she glowed with pride. It was good to hear what he thought of her playing. Chase was impressed. He was also unstoppable on the guitar. When he'd played for her last, he'd played quietly to comfort her. Now, she could feel the raw power of his talent unbridled. He was glorious. Margot closed her eyes and followed him, trying to predict where he might go next.

By the end of two hours, they were anticipating each other's next moves, communicating without words. Margot was exhilarated. Playing with the guys at Berklee had never been so fluid, so natural. So fun. When they finally stopped, Margot looked up at Chase uncertainly, hoping he felt the same as she did.

His smile said it all.

Music bound them in an ecstatic experience in which they were communicating new feelings and ideas, all without words. New songs sprang from their hands and hearts, complex and emotional and brimming with the indie spirit so essential to Margot's love of music. Their shared musical vernacular had set the stage for this natural collaboration, as each song grew organically. When she stopped to consider it, Margot marveled at how the best songs seemed to exist already, somewhere outside of sight and mind, somewhere Margot hadn't known before. But when they played, her soul rang out from its depths.

One night, as they wrapped up a set of new songs, Chase smiled at her in a way that spoke volumes.

"What?" Margot asked, looking at him quizzically.

"I can't get over how fun this is, first of all. I love playing with you. But there's something else going on in our songs, Margot."

"What do you mean?"

"I don't know, exactly. It's strangely euphoric." He shook his head and took a swig of beer. "It's like time wanders away from me while we play and I'm tapping into something, some creativity I didn't realize was there, like an underground spring and you're the divining rod."

"What's a divining rod?" Margot asked with a seductive smile.

"When someone is looking for a water source, they take a stick with a forked branching at the end, like a Y shape, and they wave it slowly over the ground, back and forth. The diviner can feel the tug of water's presence beneath the ground."

"That's a real thing?" Margot was skeptical. How had she never heard of such a phenomenon?

"It is. When I was a kid, my parents had to have a well dug at our camp. I watched the guy they hired find the best spot. He was this crusty old dude in a ripped plaid jacket and Carhartts. He walked around the land with my dad and pointed to some stuff. I was tagging along. The guy turned to me and said, 'Kid, find me a tree branch shaped like a Y,' so I did. He cut it down, held the V end in his hands, and walked it around for a while. When he felt the tug, he said, 'This is the spot.' He said it with total conviction. When my dad questioned him, he explained the branch longs for the water, but he said not everyone can feel the tug. Then he handed me the stick and told me to try. I was terrified of him, but I took it and walked around. Once my mind went empty, I felt a bit of what he'd been talking about. The energy of the water was there all along, hidden below. The stick bent downwards in my hands and I dropped it and stared at the guy who was laughing. 'Kid's got the touch,' was all he said, and that was the end of that."

"That's insane. I've never heard anything so crazy. Have you ever done it again?"

"No," Chase laughed. "But I'd like to try."

"So, what are you saying, Chase?"

"I'm saying you're like the musical divining rod I've been missing all my life. The music is there, inside me, a vein of creativity that runs through my very being. But you can find it and tap into it."

Chills ran up Margot's spine. "I think I know what you mean. I feel the same way about playing with you."

"You had a shitty time at Berklee, didn't you?" he asked.

"Yeah. I had no confidence in my playing, I couldn't find people that wanted the same things musically as I did. Everyone wanted to be huge, popular, the next big thing. And the music suffered for it. Plus, there were a lot of jerks there who either thought they were better than me or hated me because I was better than them. Then my dad died, and I met Kevin, and I lost interest all together."

"Did you ever regret leaving music behind?"

"That would mean regretting every decision I've ever made. Letting go of music led me to Kevin, which led me to Maine, which led me here." She almost said, *To you.*

"No regrets, then?"

"None. I'm starting to understand that I don't get to decide everything life gives me. Control isn't the point. I still don't know what the point is, but when I start listening to my feelings, I start making better choices for my own happiness. Playing with you, being with you, makes me happy, Chase. Everything else aside, how could I regret coming to this?"

Chase crossed over to Margot, took her hand, and led her

from behind the kit to the couch. They sat side by side in silence. Margot had felt the current Chase had been talking about since the moment he'd first touched her, his creativity flowing below the surface, the energy that made him who he was. Margot leaned in and he put his arm around her. She savored the rise and fall of his chest, the soft rhythm of his beating heart, the strength of his body holding her close. They didn't speak. They didn't need to.

Eventually, Chase walked her home. On the threshold of her house, Chase stepped incrementally closer to her. He took her cheek in his palm and said, "Margot." Leaning in, Chase touched his forehead to hers. As though caught in a magnetic field, they came together in a tender kiss.

Margot slid her hand around the back of his head and buried her fingers in his hair. He ran his hands down her back and her knees buckled as she succumbed to his touch. He caught her to him with his other arm. For one blissful moment, Margot kissed him back. She naturally opened to him and pulled him closer.

For one moment they kissed intensely, as the world around them fell away. Then, Margot pulled back abruptly, gasping. Before he could speak, before he could take one more breath, she had slammed the door, locking him out, separating the warm night air, so full of life and possibility, from her inner lair, its cold prolonging the stasis that had frozen her heart.

Heaving, Margot leaned her back against the closed front door. She couldn't catch her breath. What had she done? Margot slid down to the floor with her back against the door and tried not to hyperventilate.

Kissing Chase was a betrayal of Kevin. She had cheated on him. Hadn't she? Did the distinction even matter? She wanted so badly to undo the moment. Kevin had loved her so much. She was so weak; how could she do this to him? He didn't deserve it.

"Why did you have to die, Kevin? I miss you so much," she whispered into her knees.

How could she be so stupid? How could she let things with Chase go so far? Why couldn't he be like everyone else, keeping her and her ugly grief at arm's length? No. He had to nurture her, be kind to her, fall for her.

But she had kissed him back. She had wound her fingers into his hair and pulled him to her, closer.

"Kevin, forgive me," she cried softly, into empty air, into their empty house. She was all alone. The house beyond was so cold, so dark, so big. She didn't want to be alone. She wanted her husband back.

A soft tap on the door behind her scared the daylights out of her. "Go away," she called miserably through the heavy wood.

"Margot, I'm not going to apologize for kissing you. But I can wait."

"You may have to wait forever," she answered.

"I'm willing to take that risk." Chase hesitated, then continued. "I promise I won't kiss you again until you make a move."

Margot deliberated. She peered off into the pitch-black darkness, deep and cavernous. She was so alone. Kevin was never coming back. No amount of crying, begging, or anger at the universe could bring him back. Standing up, she brushed the tears away from her cheeks and opened the door.

Chase stood in a halo of porchlight, looking sad but beautiful.

"I'm sorry I freaked out." Margot stood uncertainly in the doorway. "Kissing you felt like cheating on Kevin. I don't know why."

"You don't need to apologize for anything."

"Yes, I do," Margot said forcefully. "I'm leading you on. I'm letting you think I can be with you."

"Wouldn't Kevin want you to move on with your life?" Chase asked desperately.

"Yes," Margot admitted. "But it hurts too much."

"Everything hurts too much, Margot, but we do it anyway. We push through the discomfort. Look at my fingertips."

"Why?" she asked, raising her eyebrows.

"Look at the callouses. What do you think those fingertips looked like when I first started playing guitar?"

"Raw."

"Exactly. Raw. They blistered and bled. But my skin thickened. If I had given in to the pain, I wouldn't be able to play music. Nothing beautiful ever comes without pain. There is no art without sacrifice. We suffer for it, as we suffer for love. It's all the same."

Margot considered his words deeply. "I know you're right. I'm not going to run away from our music together. I promise."

"Thank you," he said, looking relieved. "I'll see you Friday."

"Yes. Friday."

———

When Margot had slammed her door in the wake of their kiss, Chase was aghast. He'd stood still for a moment, frozen in the blank space between shock and reaction. As the realization hit him that she was gone, that he was responsible for that closed door, his heart twisted in pain. The closed door represented every ending he'd ever faced down. All the loss. A lifetime of dormant grief inundated him. He couldn't lose Margot too. He couldn't bear it.

When she opened the door once more, though, he mastered himself. He was strong enough, even for this. He'd left her, once more, with his promise to wait.

On the way home, Chase couldn't tame his rampaging feelings. He was a caged bird, raging against its bars. Margot had him by the heart. He'd thought the fact she'd nestled up to him after they'd played was a step forward, but the kiss was taking it too far. He understood where he'd crossed the line, but it was getting harder and harder to stay on the right side of it.

Margot was so warm and real next to him, the pure beauty of their music still lingering in the air with them, but his longing for her was becoming impossible to ignore.

Chase called his sister as he walked home.

"Hey, Caroline, it's Chase. Call me when you're free." He left the message on his sister's voicemail feeling like a needy teen. He wasn't sure what perspective Caroline would lend to the situation, but it was worth a try.

"What's wrong," was Caroline's greeting twenty minutes later when she called him back. He was back at the loft, knitting.

"Nothing," Chase lied, setting down the unfinished pink hat.

"Bullshit. You never call without a reason."

"That's not strictly true," Chase said, feeling dejected.

"It's okay, bro. I don't call you either. What's up?"

Chase inhaled deeply and forged ahead. "I met a woman. She's beautiful but emotionally unavailable, with good reasons, but I think she might come around. I like her."

"You sound miserable," Caroline said. "I hope she's worth it."

"Since Sara," Chase began, wincing at her name. "I have only dated crazy girls I knew I didn't have to worry about a future with. I see that pattern now, but I want it to stop. I want something real."

"You deserve something real," Caroline said softly. "What's so special about this girl?"

"She's a musician. She plays the drums. She's absolutely gifted, Caroline. I've never played with anyone like her. We even like the same stuff."

"In that case, she's a keeper!" Caroline laughed. "The stuff you listen to is noise!"

"She loves it all."

"In all seriousness, hon, tell her how you feel." Caroline loved him and it came through in her voice.

"I kissed her tonight," Chase answered miserably.

"And?"

"And nothing. She's not ready. I don't know if she ever will be."

"Is she worth waiting for?" his sister asked him gently.

"Yes." Chase didn't even have to think about it. "She is."

"Then why did you call me again? You already know the answer."

———

Margot tried hard not to let the kiss ruin anything between her and Chase while they played during the next weeks. But Margot sensed something had shifted. One Friday night, Chase was listless and broody at practice. He'd written a doleful new song which he reluctantly played for her. Margot understood it intimately, as though her soul knew exactly what he meant. Through their new PA and mic, he sang of longing. The words were so personal, so much about his feeling for her that she was startled into silence. When she caught the beat back up, Chase looked at her in torment before he finished the song.

They played for a few hours, and when they were through, their eyes met. Chase's expression was unreadable. Margot was concerned. Had she screwed up too badly on that new song? It was rare for her to get so distracted when she played. But the rest of the time, she knew they were breaking serious ground with their music.

Finally, Margot couldn't take it. "What?" she asked unsteadily, setting down her drumsticks. "Did I suck tonight?"

Chase didn't say anything at first, but then he spoke. "No. You were amazing, as usual."

"What is it then?" she asked.

"I'm trying to separate the feelings I'm having right now. Trying and failing."

"What do you mean? I thought we sounded great."

"We did. You're better than I ever imagined." He unplugged

his guitar from the amp and rested it on the stand. "When I first suggested playing together, I assumed you'd be a good drummer, you'd keep up, that sort of thing. Forgive me, but I never dreamed you'd be an actual virtuoso. I've played with a lot of people, but never before have I played with someone like you. I've wished for a drummer as good as you my whole life. If you hadn't stopped playing music you'd be famous by now."

"Don't change the subject," she said firmly. "What do you mean by 'separate the feelings'?"

"Margot, don't press it if you don't want to hear the truth."

"What truth?"

Chase met her gaze and with a tortured expression, said, "The truth of how I feel for you. And playing together has proved to me how perfectly we work together. Our compatibility stretches way beyond friendship or music. I'm... Fuck. This is so hard. I'm crazy about you, Margot. And I'm not sure how to separate that out enough to play with you anymore."

Margot's heart stopped. She knew Chase cared for her. For a long time, she'd known his feelings were deep and genuine and had crossed over into physical attraction, as evidenced by their kiss, but hearing it was quite another thing all together. The awful truth was, she understood exactly how he felt.

Chase wound the guitar cord around his fist and put it in a basket by the guitar. Margot sat impotent behind the drums, her palms face-down on her snare.

"So, it's all or nothing?" she asked, her voice devoid of the emotion raging inside her.

"That's not what I'm saying. But I might need some time apart to recalibrate."

As Margot watched Chase straighten up his things, avoiding her gaze, her panicking heart screamed in her chest, *Don't leave me. Don't you leave me too...* But she couldn't give voice to that plea. Instead, she remained paralyzed, wishing she could go to him, wishing she could throw her arms around him and kiss him. It's all she wanted in that moment.

Then, as though standing on a precipice, an unknown sea stretching itself before her, inviting her to take the risk, she demanded of herself, why not? Why shouldn't she jump? Like Sam said, guilt was a noose. What she needed was wings. Chase was perfect for her. He'd been perfect all along.

In a burst of courage, Margot stood abruptly, her drumsticks clattering to the floor as she crossed the room to him. His eyes were tormented as he watched her come closer and he looked away once more.

"You told me you'd wait. You said you'd wait until I'm ready. I didn't know it would be like this either, and you're probably right, maybe we do need time to think about it, but…" She hesitated, her voice quavering. "Please. Please, don't give up on me."

Chase turned back toward her and said, "I won't give up. But it's just so hard."

Looking into her eyes, he delved her to the core. Margot whispered, "Oh, Chase."

He reached out to touch her cheek but froze before his hand could graze her skin. Margot reached up before he could pull away, put her hand on the back of his, and guided his palm to her face. Closing her eyes, she leaned into his warm touch, savoring the energy surging through his body.

Instantly, she knew she needed him. She wanted him. She couldn't deny it any longer. Margot turned and kissed his palm, his wrist, all along the inside of his thickly muscled, tattooed forearm. Chase gasped and closed his eyes. She kissed him softly at first, then more passionately. When she paused, Chase opened his eyes and met her hungry gaze. She slid her hands behind his head and guided him towards her.

As their lips met, Chase's energy ignited beneath her. Catching her up in his arms, he held her to him, kissing her intensely, ardently, possessing her with his mouth, his hands. Margot kissed him back, every bit as urgently. Gasping for air, she tipped back her head enraptured and moaned, eyes closed, as

Chase kissed her throat with an open mouth, his tongue grazing her sensitive skin. Lower and lower he went until he reached the neckline of her shirt. Done hesitating, Margot tore her shirt over her head. Chase stood frozen, watching her luminous body in wonder.

"You are the loveliest woman I have ever seen, Margot." He looked spellbound. Margot, unabashed, moved into his embrace once more.

Chase ran his fingers over the lace on her shoulders and along her spine, sending tingles down her back. He kissed each curve and flourish, absorbing himself in her patterned skin. The white lace lines almost glowed, like some ghostly creature arisen, one willed into being for this very moment.

Margot, although exposed, felt as she had while they'd played music together. They understood each other elementally. Chase kissed her gently on the lips once more, then again more deeply, stripping away the last of her reservations. As Chase lifted her easily into the air, she felt like she was soaring. Margot wrapped her legs around his body, desperate to feel him against every part of her. He slid his hands down to her back side and held her in mid-air against himself, as they kissed fervently. With her body wrapped around him, he wove a path to the couch and lay down with her on top, giving her all the control.

Margot tugged at the hem of his shirt, lifting it over his head as he leaned forward slightly. The feel of his bare skin against hers was sublime. His broad chest was tattooed with more designs, all kinds of strange pictures and symbols swirling in a matrix of black lines and color. Her pale skin against him looked incongruous, but so alluring. She pressed up against the length of him, straddling him, locking him beneath her as their mouths explored each other.

Chase pressed his hands against her rear, pushing her against his ready body beneath.

Passion boiled inside her as she imagined undressing him and so much more.

"Margot. I want you so badly."

"I want you too, Chase."

Meeting her needy gaze, he whispered, "Then take what you want."

Chase's voice reverberated in her deepest places. Desperately, Margot tried to drive all thoughts of her former life from her mind and stay in the present.

Reaching down, she boldly unbuckled his belt and undid his pants. He followed suit with her clothes, finding her jeans loose enough to slide down over her narrow hips.

Shifting them both sideways, Chase asked, "May I make love to you, Margot?"

"Yes," she answered, her heart racing, her voice wavering, trying to channel the certainty her body felt.

The sensation of his touch after being dormant so long was almost too much. Margot's eyes teared up involuntarily.

He froze. "Are you okay? Am I hurting you?"

"No, I'm fine. It feels… so good."

"Do you want me to stop?"

"Definitely not."

Chase's smile was all she needed in answer.

The rhythm of the ocean swayed inside her as they made love. The pulsating tick of rapid drumbeats filled her like the heartbeat of the world, punctuated by Chase's body against hers. Her heartrate quickened as they groaned with pleasure, with the sensation of becoming one. Margot let go of time and place and guilt and sadness as she gave herself over to the intensity of the moment. For in this elemental union, Margot felt almost whole again.

Margot had not expected to have sex with Chase. Ever. Yet afterwards, it seemed so natural, like they'd been doing it all along. All tension between them dissipated, and now they held each other, naked, sated, in the middle of his apartment with all the lights on, like everything else in all the world had been put on hold while they'd made love.

In her heart, Margot knew Kevin would have wanted her to move on. There's no way he'd want her to be a thirty-two-year-old widow shunning all attachments for the remainder of her life. He'd want her to live. If she'd been the one to die, she would have wanted him to live. What she realized was that her heart was capacious enough to hold the love for both men, and that one did not preclude the other. The realization was deeply comforting, yet despite Sam's words, guilt still gnawed at the edges.

Chase's breathing had finally slowed down and he held her so tightly she could barely move. She knew it was because he didn't want to risk losing her, to risk having her run from him yet again, not after sharing this intimate moment. To set him at ease, she snuggled into him, tracing her finger along the wild designs traversing his body.

She kissed his chest. "Tell me about this one," she whispered.

Awkwardly craning his neck, Chase looked down and said, "Oh, that's the fourth tattoo I got. There's this guy who does work with geometry, numbers, symbolic meaning. He took my parents' birthdays and death anniversary and created this one. The center is the energy of the universe, and everything else kind of orbits around it. I've never been much for the whole ink-some-superhero-on-my-ass-while-I'm-drunk kind of tattoo. Everything means something. It was all important at the time."

Margot kissed the drawing again.

"How about this one?" she asked, leaning over him, and kissing another one of his tattoos.

"The tree, with the roots stretching downwards, and the branches stretching to the sky, all mirroring each other means life comes full circle. It's another early piece and it was about dealing with my parents' death. I tried so hard to understand it, intellectually, spiritually. In the end, though, it sucked, and I wished I could have them back."

"How long was it before you stopped wishing that?" she asked softly.

"Honestly, I still wish it. That never goes away, the gnawing longing for them to come home, whole and happy, like nothing ever happened, like no time has passed. The question is, how we learn to live with it."

"Did you feel guilty?"

He shifted to look at her more intently. "What, about being alive?"

"Yeah, I guess that's what I mean."

"Sometimes," he answered, resting his hand on hers, which still lay on his chest. "But I think you're feeling a different kind of guilt, right?"

"Yes."

"Margot, please know this. You are allowed to be happy." He took her hand in his and kissed it.

"Being with you, when I can get past the guilt, makes me happy, Chase."

"At least now we can work on it together."

"Thank you."

They held each other for a little while longer until Margot shivered against Chase's body. Then he picked her up like a precious doll and brought her to his bed. He snuggled under the covers with her where they held each other tight and kissed, then fell asleep. It was the first time in over a year that Margot had gone to sleep unencumbered with grief.

The enticing scent of breakfast cooking filtered into Margot's sleepy mind before she opened her eyes the next day. Understanding when and where she was in time and space took a moment. No one had cooked her breakfast since Kevin, so her mind automatically placed her into their world together. Opening her eyes to Chase's loft, with the sunlight filling the wide-open space and the feel of an unfamiliar bed, was a shock.

Panic rose up in Margot's heart. What had she done? Why had she let herself stay here? Why had she let herself get entangled with Chase? He wasn't the man she loved. She loved Kevin.

As her mind synched back up to the present, she was beset by despondency once more, tinged this time, with deep regret. Would Kevin understand? Would he forgive her? Did it even matter?

Margot's gaze eventually rested on Chase at his kitchen island. Her heartrate ebbed slightly as she took him in. He was smiling and humming as he cooked. Had she ever seen him look so happy? It deepened her sense of regret exponentially. She didn't want to hurt him. He deserved more. She should have walked out last night and never looked back. Now, it was too late.

Chase looked up and caught her staring at him. He turned off the stovetop and walked over. He was wearing boxers and a black t-shirt with the name of a band she didn't know. He was unbelievably attractive. No wonder she'd ended up here, in his bed. His smile didn't fade as he noticed her dismal expression.

"It's all right, Margot. You were happy last night, and you will be happy again, especially after you taste my eggs."

How could he still be so sweet after reading her mind? It was clear to him how she felt, all raw and twisted up inside, but as he sat beside her on the edge of the bed, and gently stroked her hair, and leaned down to kiss her, all her guilt and apprehension and regret melted away for a single, perfect moment. And in that moment, Margot found a spark of hope.

Chase was tender and loving, while at the same time unyielding. He knew what she needed, and she needed to be well and truly kissed. Eventually, he pulled away and said, "Let's eat and then see what else happens."

"Chase, I don't think I should stay. I need to go home. I…"

He interrupted her, saying, "Eat. Then we'll talk."

Acquiescing, Margot started to get out of bed, but her nudity prevented her. Chase noticed her hesitation and handed her a t-shirt. He turned away while she put it on, along with her underwear, and then they walked hand in hand to the island.

Chase's eggs were indeed fantastic.

"These are too good," Margot said sheepishly, after her second helping.

"You've been missing a person to take care of you, to hold you close. I know I can't replace your husband, and I'm not intent on trying, but I want to give you as much care as you will accept."

Margot shook her head sadly, staring down at the polished cement countertop. "You're right. No one's cooked for me since Kevin. Thank you."

———

When his parents had died, neighbors and friends had come out of the woodwork to take care of him and Caroline. They cooked them more food than the two of them could eat in a lifetime. The siblings had known they were not alone. Chase had never stopped to consider that kind of generosity before, and how he'd taken it for granted.

It broke him that Margot didn't have a support network. Growing up in a place, with your neighbors and extended family all around you, there is always someone to talk to, someone to help you out. Someone to make you a meal.

"No one cooked for you after the accident?" Chase asked tentatively.

"No. I was in the hospital for so long healing, and I barely remember those two months at all. When I got out, Ginny came over a few times and I was horrible to her. I totally scared her away. I pushed every kindness away." Her voice was thick with regret.

"That's changing, though."

"Is it? I almost ran out of here this morning. My instinct is to repel the kindness you're showing me."

"Because it hurts too much to accept?" Chase asked.

"Because I don't want to care about anyone anymore." Margot glared at him. "It's easier to push you away than to let you in, to let you get hurt, to eventually lose you like I've lost everything else."

"I'm not going anywhere."

"Well, I am. I can't do this." Margot got up from the island, put her dishes in the sink, and walked towards the bathroom.

Chase couldn't let her go. He couldn't. He'd never get her back and after last night? After feeling their connection grow exponentially stronger? He couldn't bear it. He'd let Sara go without fighting for her. He wasn't going to make that mistake again.

He got up and stood in front of Margot. "No."

"No?" With an expression of complete shock, Margot stared at him. "What the hell do you mean, no?" Her eyes blazed with intensity.

"I mean no. You're not leaving like this. We've gained ground here, Margot. We're connected. We have both found something we were missing and it's a work in progress. We're an unfinished song, right now. We need to put the time in to see if it's good or not. I think it will be."

"Please, Chase. Please let me go," Margot begged, her fury dissipating, her composure finally crumbling.

"No, Margot. I won't. I care about you and you care about me. You can't push me away. I won't let you."

"You're right." Margot looked up at his broad chest, his strong arms folded over it. He knew he looked like a bouncer and she laughed through her anguish. "You're much too big to push away."

"Stay, Margot." Chase chanced a smile. "Please."

"I'm going to hurt you, Chase," she said desperately.

"I'm willing to take that risk. I have been since the beginning."

Unsure what she'd do next, Chase relaxed his stance, his arms fell to his sides. He was therefore thoroughly surprised when Margot rushed into his ready embrace.

EIGHTEEN

The syncopated rhythm of living two separate and opposite lives turned out to be untenable. Twice a week, Margot went to Chase's house where they ate dinner, played music, and made love all night. Twice a week, Margot came alive again. When the mornings came, however, she sank back into a torpor as sadness settled back into the corners.

All through breakfast on Wednesday mornings, Margot sat quiet, introspective. As soon as she was finished, she would leave Chase and walk to work. On Saturdays, she declined his offers of hanging out, going someplace, doing something. Chase couldn't understand her reluctance to be with him at other times, but Margot didn't try to explain it. She couldn't explain it to herself, so how could she explain it to him? Giving him two days a week, finding joy again, playing music again, feeling alive again, drained her so deeply she couldn't muster more.

The music grew despite Margot's desperation. It flourished wildly, like her own soul trying to escape the confines of her body. While she played, and in her intimate union with Chase afterwards, Margot was free, almost happy. It was the only hope she had, and she clung to it.

Well into September, the air changed, but Margot's battle with herself gained little ground. She was stuck in limbo between the past and the present, between her old self and whatever emergent self she might be incubating. Chase was patient, kind, loving, and attentive, but she knew he wanted more. She could feel it. It was part of why she couldn't give herself over to him completely. She wasn't sure she wanted to. What would be left for Kevin and Amandine if she left them fully behind in the past? Part of her needed to keep them close, keep them tethered, but it was so draining to live two lives, tugged back and forth between them.

Playing twice a week meant leaving her drums at Chase's place. Without them, Margot had nothing else to think about at night when she got home. Sometimes, she sat in the glider in Amandine's room and let the ghosts come to her. Her mother, her father, her husband, her baby. One at a time they alighted and were gone, leaving nothing but pain in their wake.

Ginny came over a few times for takeout, but even she sensed Margot's continued unhappiness.

"I thought things were getting better," she said one evening over Thai.

"I'm not sure what you mean by better," Margot said. "I've felt guilty since I started seeing Chase, and that hasn't changed. In fact, I think it's gotten worse."

"Sex is not that big a deal, Margot." Ginny shook her head. "You've found someone who makes you feel good, someone you really like, and you have sex. So what?"

"I've never been as casual about it as you are," Margot said, hoping she didn't hurt Ginny's feelings.

"So you think I'm a ho?" she answered laughing.

"Yes. You're a ho. Look, you're even knocked up." Margot cracked a smile.

"So, let me get this right." Ginny patted her growing belly. "You want to be celibate for the rest of your life?"

"You know how much I loved Kevin." Margot glared at her.

"It feels wrong to be with someone other than him. Except for when I'm with Chase, and then it feels right."

"What if you stayed with Chase more?"

"You're asking me to forget about Kevin."

"No, Kevin has passed away. You're alone now. I'm reminding you that there's this great guy who likes you. A lot. Some people never find that."

Margot considered this fact. She knew Chase was a rare breed. They saw eye to eye on everything. They were starting to finish each other's sentences. If she asked herself honestly whether she could really fall hard for him, the answer was yes. Which brought her back to the guilt. It was a wall she couldn't get past.

"This is not worth talking about. I always come back to the guilt. I hate myself for being weak and relying on Chase. I hate myself for not honoring Kevin with my actions."

"You're honoring him by living your life. For fuck's sake, Margot, we've established that. Be happy. He would want you to be happy."

"Enough about me," Margot said, exasperated. "How's the little one?"

Ginny, never one to shy away from talking about herself, or her baby bump, told Margot everything she'd been going through. It was enough to tire her out and she left a while later. In her wake, Margot's loneliness doubled.

Ginny was right, Margot and Chase were connected. There was no way to explain the dichotomy of her feelings, though. She could find no way to get over the pull of the past or ignore the inexorable present. It was starting to tear her apart.

The next day, still thinking about her conversation with Ginny, Margot broke the rhythm she herself had established. After a rare, exhilarating day at work, during which she'd managed to take down not one but two corporate executives who never saw it coming, she decided to surprise Chase. After work, she walked over to his shop and peeked in the window, expecting to see him working on a client or cleaning the place up.

Instead, Chase was standing around with a few people she didn't recognize. Clustered around his messy desk, they were drinking beers and laughing. Chase's arm was wound comfortably around a woman who looked close in age to him. Her bright hazel eyes and long, curly, sandy brown hair were vivacious. Her manner with Chase was familiar. Too familiar. She leaned up and kissed him on the cheek. His smile was that of a contented child.

Margot staggered backwards as though she'd been punched in the chest. All the air was squeezed out of her. Every moment she'd spent with Chase these past weeks suddenly seemed like a lie. They'd never made exclusive plans, they'd never said they wouldn't date other people, but she was sick to her stomach anyway. Of course Chase needed more than she'd been able to give. Of course he'd found it someplace else.

She watched his expression through the window. He looked so happy, so genuinely himself, he looked like he did when they played music together. Tears came to Margot's eyes as the depth of her sadness at this betrayal sank in. She'd let herself fall for him. She was a fool.

Margot leaned her head against the glass for a moment before she turned and walked away. Maybe she'd call Sam. He would understand all of this. He had been through it. How did he deal with being a widower in this universe? As she removed her phone from her pocket, she heard a familiar jingle of bells and felt a presence come up behind her.

"Hey, Margot!"

Chase had run and caught up with her. He must have spotted her in the window. Margot was mortified. "Hi," she answered.

"Do you have a minute?" he asked, sounding excited. "There's someone I'd like you to meet."

Margot's stomach was leaden as she pictured the effervescent woman.

"That's okay, Chase. I'm going to head home."

"Oh, all right." His arms fell to his sides and he looked crestfallen. "It's just that she's only in town for a little while."

"Who?"

"My sister. Caroline was passing through Portland and surprised me. I told her all about you and she wants to meet you. But if you're not up for it, I understand."

"Sister?"

"Yes." Chase looked confused. "Caroline's my sister. You knew I had a sister."

"Yes, but…" The image of Chase's arm around the other woman came back to Margot. She closed her eyes and took a deep breath. "I'm an idiot is all."

Chase's eyes grew wide. "You saw us in the window, didn't you? Shit, did you think we were, that I was… Margot, Jesus, I would never do that to you."

"I'm so stupid. I got so upset. I saw your arm around her, and I was sick. I know I haven't been able to give you everything you need, everything you deserve. I thought you'd found someone else, and I can't believe how much it hurt."

Chase took Margot in his arms and kissed her head. "I'm so sorry. I would never hurt you on purpose. It's okay, hon. It's okay."

Margot leaned into his chest, exhaling all the anguish of seeing him with another woman, trying hard not to cry. After a moment, Margot understood her own feelings more clearly and found it embarrassing. "I was jealous."

"That's a natural feeling. If I saw you with someone else, I'd be jealous too." He released her from his embrace and looked Margot in the eyes. "I want you all for myself." His carnal expression set off a charge of excitement in Margot's core. She kissed him rapturously. Chase held her to him, filling her with his adoration. Spontaneously, he walked her backwards and pressed her up against the cold brick wall of his building. They kissed like no one was watching.

Eventually surfacing for air, Chase smiled, and Margot laughed sheepishly.

"Now do you want to come meet Caroline? We're going to go get drinks next door."

"Okay," Margot said. "Thank you, Chase. Thank you for stopping me, for reassuring me."

"Listen closely with your heart, with your mind, with every part of you, to what I'm about to say." Chase held Margot's upper arms tightly and looked into her eyes with feeling. "Please hear me. I love you, Margot. Only you."

Margot's heart was about to burst through her chest. She'd almost let him go. She'd almost pushed him away. She was overcome with thanks that some good fortune was smiling down on her, keeping her close to him. She wanted to tell him everything. She wanted him to know, but it was so hard to let go. Courage blossomed inside her as she gathered strength from the moment.

"I'm so glad, Chase," Margot said, her hands trembling as she lay them upon his chest and looked into his earnest eyes, "I love you, too."

Chase's expression, as he absorbed her words, was enough to make Margot love him even more. For a moment they were locked together outside of time, and then Chase kissed her again. All his care, all his kindness, all his generosity surged from his lips and into her. She cherished him and admitting the fact was an unexpected release.

Caroline's kind, open smile lit up the room when Chase walked through the door with his arm around Margot. She set down her beer and rushed forward. Without hesitating, she threw her arms around Margot and kissed her on the cheek. "My brother is crazy about you."

"Caroline, this is Margot. Margot, Caroline," Chase said, in a belated introduction.

"I'm so excited to meet you," Caroline said exuberantly.

"I'm happy to meet you too," Margot answered smiling.

Chase introduced Margot to his other friends, Larry and Dorian. They'd all known each other in New York, before they'd each come to Portland. Then Chase said, "Come on. Let's take this party next door."

Caroline monopolized Margot's attention, sitting next to her in a booth and asking her a million questions. "What made you fall for the big lug?" she asked playfully.

"He tattooed me."

"No!" Caroline cried in disbelief. "Where?"

Margot glanced apprehensively at Chase across the table.

"Sis," he said protectively, "This is not the time…"

"Wait, Margot is telling me about how you tattooed her. You don't seem like the type, Margot, if you'll excuse the generalization. His other tattooed women have been a little more… obvious."

"Caroline," Chase protested. "She doesn't want to tell you about it here."

"It's okay, Chase," Margot intervened. "I don't mind." Turning back to Caroline, Margot started to explain about Kevin and Amandine and the tattoos she'd gotten both to deal with the grief of losing them and to honor them. Chase offered Margot his hand across the table and she held it tight as she spoke.

"He didn't tell me." Caroline's eyes were wide, horrified. "I'm sorry. I never would have asked."

"It's okay," Margot said. "I'm getting to the point where I can talk about them without bursting into tears." She unbuttoned the top two buttons on her blouse and showed Caroline a peek at her skin.

Caroline's eyes flashed with sadness for a moment as she looked at the beautiful lace design. "It's incredible. He's very talented, isn't he."

"He is. And kind. I'm lucky I met him."

"He's lucky too. His other gals have been a nightmare. You, though, you seem honest. And good. He deserves that."

"I'm sitting right here, Caroline," Chase said. "I can hear you."

"Be quiet, little brother," she reprimanded. "Your girl and I are talking." Smiling at Margot, Caroline put one arm around her, lifted her glass in her free hand, and said, "To the beginning of a beautiful relationship."

By midnight, Caroline had gone back to her hotel room, Sheila had cleared out most of the bar and was glaring at the stragglers, and Margot and Chase sat alone in the booth finishing the last of their drinks.

"I'm sorry about before," Margot said.

"Don't be. Like I said, I would have had the same reaction," Chase said. "What'd you think of Caroline?"

"She's vivacious. And sweet. I like her a lot."

"Me too. She's never been the kind of sister to call every day or anything, but she's always been there when I've needed her."

"Chase," Margot started.

"Yes?" he answered, taking her hand once more across the table.

"I'm ready to spend more time together, I think. I don't want to be together at my house, though, and I don't want you to get sick of me being at yours. And I might still need some space sometimes and don't want you to be resentful."

"We're moving at your pace, Margot. I'll give you whatever you need."

"Right now, I need…" She couldn't say it. She wanted to, but she couldn't let the words out.

"What?"

"You. I need you."

"Stay with me tonight, Margot. Stay with me every night, as long as you want. I'd have you by my side every moment if I could."

They settled up with Sheila, who winked at the blushing

Margot as they left, and headed up to Chase's loft, hand in hand. The moment the door closed, Margot turned and looked Chase in the eyes. She unbuttoned the rest of the buttons on her blouse, stepped out of her heels, and walked backwards towards the bed, never breaking eye contact.

Chase's look shifted from sweet to sexy instantly. His expression was full of desire, his eyes looked dark and intense. Margot knew his appetite for her was insatiable, and she wanted to feed him all night. He removed his shoes, and stalked her slowly, like a wildcat ready to pounce.

With her shirt unbuttoned, Margot let it slip from her shoulders, revealing her slender body to him. Her black lace bra shone in sharp contrast against her skin. She leaned back on his bed, still in her skirt, and with a look, invited Chase to her.

Following her to the bed, he stood before her, drinking her in. Margot kneeled on the bed facing him and lifted his shirt over his head. She unbuckled his pants, and slid them down, along with his boxers, and pulled him onto her, relishing the feel of his skin against hers. The spicy smell of his hair, the feel his stubble against her sensitive skin, the sound of his rapid breathing, these were the things about being alive that Margot needed to hold on to. He slowly lifted up her skirt and Margot's eyes opened wide with pleasure and surprise.

They moved with urgency. Chase breathed, "You. Are. So. Perfect." The tension between them grew unbearable. Margot's body brimmed with pleasure as she came undone, crying out his name, wishing their bliss would never subside. They were bound together in ecstasy.

Margot stayed with him that night, and again the next. She didn't want to be without him, and he appeared to feel the same. They found a dresser at a second-hand shop where she could put some clothes and Chase put up a hanger bar for things she needed to keep neat for work. Without discussing it, Margot and Chase moved her belongings little by little into his place, leaving empty the house she had loved for so long.

NINETEEN

A few weeks later, when Chase came home one evening grinning like mad, Margot knew something had happened. "What?" she asked, nervously.

"I got us a show."

"What?" she shouted, suddenly paralyzed with fear. "Why?"

"What do you mean why? We sound awesome and we should play our songs out."

"Chase, that's terrifying."

"Nah. It'll be fun. A band that was going to open for The Sparhawks cancelled. My buddy, who books shows for The State Theater, asked if we were ready and I said yes. We're on the line up."

Margot teetered on the edge of panic. "With The Sparhawks? Jesus. There's going to be like a thousand people there."

"Yep."

"We don't have a name yet!"

Chase shrugged his shoulders. "I told him to give me twenty-four hours and that we'd come up with something."

"Thinking of a band name is always impossible."

"That's why I'm taking you out to a fancy dinner. We're going to brainstorm about it over a lovely meal."

"Really? And where are you taking me?" Margot asked, unable to conceal her nervousness.

"It's a surprise."

"How should I dress?"

"Wear what makes you happy."

"I've wanted to wear that blue velvet dress again. Would it be too formal?"

"You're a showstopper no matter what, Margot. Wear it. People will think we're movie stars."

Margot giggled, but inside she was terrified. What was Chase thinking, booking a show so soon? On the other hand, they were good. The new songs they'd written had coalesced beautifully and Margot was proud of them. It might be nice to have people hear them play.

As for dinner, she'd have to go with it. It had been ages since she'd eaten anywhere that wasn't on her way home from work. She and Kevin had gone out all the time. It never seemed right without him. Where would Chase take her?

As Margot put on some make up, she studied herself. Her tattoos shone bright in the lights of Chase's bathroom vanity. Somehow, they looked more intricate than she'd remembered. The pattern work was elegant. Softly, Margot ran her hand over the designs on her shoulder and chest. They weren't raised anymore, since the tattoo had healed up perfectly. The white pigment Chase had chosen was almost pearlescent against her skin. It was dazzling. She'd still not shown the tattoos to anyone other than Ginny and Caroline, but it was enough to know that they were part of her now.

Margot called Ginny while she put on make-up. Dialing her number and setting it to speaker phone, Margot waited for her friend to pick up. Instead, she got Henry.

"Hi, Margot. It's Henry," he answered.

"Hi, Henry. Is Ginny around?"

"She is here but she's in the bathroom," he said, not bothering to disguise the humor he found in telling Margot this bit of information.

"Hey, don't tell whoever that is I'm in the bathroom! That's private!" Margot could hear Ginny yelling in the distance.

"Sorry," Henry apologized loudly. Then, more softly, he chuckled and whispered to Margot, "She's been feisty."

"Since birth, Henry. Nothing new," Margot stated.

"You're probably right."

"How are you holding up?"

"Fine. Just fine. I am interviewing for an actual job. I've been playing music so long I thought that was a living."

"What are you planning to do?"

"I'm a teacher, by trade," he said. "I'm going to teach middle school science again."

"Ouch!" Margot said. She couldn't think of any job more painful than teaching middle school.

"I actually enjoy the wee beasties."

"More power to you, Mr. H.," Margot commented. "Good luck."

"Thanks. I'll keep you posted." Margot heard a rustling in the background. "Here is Princess Ginny. Good night, Margot."

"Bye Mr. H., talk to you soon." There was a small clunk as the phone changed hands. "Hey there, Ginny. How're you feeling?"

"Shitty. I'm fatter than I've ever been. I've been hungry for vegetables and salmon, but eggs turn my stomach. I've always loved eggs! What the hell?"

"It's going to be all right," Margot assured her in a tone she might have used on a cranky child.

"Sure. That's what you say." Ginny laughed. "We found a little house, though. We put an offer on it."

"Oh, how wonderful!"

"We'll see if it goes through, but it's really sweet. It's got a big yard and everything." Ginny sounded pleased with the find.

"Good luck. I hope you get it. Is the baby doing okay?"

"Yep, she's doing great. I can feel her moving a little now."

Margot remembered that sensation with her whole being. She tried not to focus on the longing in her heart. "How wonderful. Do you need anything?"

"Other than my waistline back? No. I'm good. How are you?"

Margot hesitated for a second and then said, "I'm fine. I've been staying with Chase a lot lately. Sorry I've been out of touch."

"He's good for you. I'm glad," Ginny said emphatically.

"He's gotten us a show. It's nerve-racking."

"Tell me the details and I'll get tickets. We'll come see you. Henry loves live music."

Margot was skeptical. "He might not like this. We're loud."

"I want to come regardless. It's been over a decade since I've seen you play. Text me the details."

"Will do. Call me if you need anything."

"Okay," Ginny said. "Kisses."

"Bye," Margot said, trying to sound upbeat.

That evening, dressed in blue velvet and trepidatious beyond imagining, Margot climbed into Chase's car. When he pulled up to the Back Bay Grill, Margot almost had a heart attack. "Here? We're going here?"

"Yes," Chase replied, sounding hesitant. "Why? Isn't it good?"

"The food is incredible." Margot took a deep breath and steadied herself. "But it was Kevin's and my favorite place. I'm so sorry. I can't go in there."

"Oh, shit, Margot. I had no idea. I feel horrible." Chase looked mortified. "I'll call and cancel the reservation."

Chase took his phone from his breast pocket and started scrolling through to find the number. As she watched him in profile, his striking features twisted into contrite apprehension, Margot had a jolt of courage spike through her.

"Don't." Margot put out her hand and touched Chase's arm lightly. "It's okay. I'm all right. I didn't expect it, that's all. I want to go in."

"Are you sure? I can take you anywhere you like, you know. There's a thousand restaurants in Portland."

It occurred to Margot why Chase had chosen the Back Bay Grill. They were famous for one thing. "Truffle popcorn," she said, shaking her head. "That's why you picked this place, right? You remembered the popcorn from our movie night."

"Yes," he answered miserably.

"You've got a good memory."

"I remember every detail of every moment we've ever spent together. From the first time I saw you."

Margot nervously twisted her clutch over and over in her lap. "I remember too. I saw you outside your shop, patting your shirt pocket for a cigarette that wasn't there. Then you looked at me. It was like I'd been struck by lightning."

"Margot, I never want to hurt you. I never want you to feel uncomfortable. Tell me now and we'll drive away and we won't look back."

Margot looked out the car window at the façade of a place she'd loved and lost. It was time to reclaim it. "You know what? Let's go in and if it's too hard, we can leave."

"Are you sure? I don't want to torture you. That's not usually why someone takes a girlfriend out for dinner."

"Girlfriend?" Margot repeated skeptically. "Is that what I am?"

"Isn't it?"

Margot considered it. "Saying we're *girlfriend* and *boyfriend* sounds sophomoric."

"Kind of," Chase admitted. "What are we then?"

"I don't know," Margot said. "How about *confidants*?"

"It's different. I like it. Come, my lovely confidant, let's dine."

Chase, looking unbelievably sexy in his best suit and tie,

opened the car door for her. In every movement he made there was an easy grace, a confidence and purposefulness. It made him even more beautiful. "You're very handsome, Chase."

"Thank you, Margot." A sly smile spread across his face as he took her in. "I clean up all right."

Margot smiled as he offered his arm. Linked together, they entered the restaurant. Immediately, the host recognized her, moved around his podium, and took her by the shoulders and kissed her on both cheeks. "Margot. We've been hoping to see you again. We heard about everything. You have our deepest condolences. You know we adored Kevin."

"Thank you so much. I got the flowers you guys sent, but I wasn't in good shape and didn't write thank you notes. I appreciated that you thought of me, though."

"We're heartbroken for you."

"I hope this isn't awkward, Jameson. I missed you guys."

"There's nothing awkward about living your life, Margot," Jameson stated kindly.

"This is Chase Goodwin. He is my confidant. We're also playing in a band together, and we're here to brainstorm band names."

"You're a musician?" Jameson looked dumbfounded.

"I play drums and piano, although in this band I play the drums. Chase sings and plays guitar. We've got our first show in a few weeks."

"Congratulations. I'll ask the cook staff if they have ideas for band names."

Margot smiled at him and Jameson led them to a table. In a moment, he brought an overflowing bowl of the legendary popcorn over, along with an unexpected bottle of champagne.

"This is for you, Margot," Jameson said, holding out the bottle for her to view. "From all of us. Welcome back."

Margot's throat tightened and she suppressed a swell of emotion. "Thank you, Jameson. Thank everyone for me."

Jameson nodded, biting his lip. Then he mustered his

professionalism. He popped the cork and poured a bit of champagne in Margot's glass for her to taste. She brought it to her lips and swallowed, thankful the effervescence cut through the lump in her throat. She nodded and Jameson poured the full glasses. He smiled at Margot and took his leave.

Chase lifted his glass and Margot followed suit. "To Kevin," he said, softly.

"To Kevin," Margot answered. They clinked glasses and sipped the champagne.

"Five months ago, you wouldn't have been able to do this. You've come so far, Margot. I'm amazed by your bravery."

"Thank you for being so patient with me." Margot looked into Chase's earnest eyes. He was so kind.

"You don't need to thank me. I am grateful you trust me with your heart. Life is strange in all its twists and turns."

"It is." Margot thought about the twist that had brought her to Chase in the first place. "You know, I came to you for the tattoos for one reason alone. I wanted you to hurt me."

"Margot," Chase said, setting down his glass. "You know I would never hurt you."

"But you did. And it helped. The tattoo dulled the emotional pain I was stuck in. For a while it worked, too. The jolt back to reality reminded me I was still alive."

Chase looked even sadder. He didn't appear to know what to say. Margot didn't mind. She wanted to talk.

"The lace design was as much about symbolism as about pain. As the lace grew over me, though, I began to perceive your hand in the act of creation. So, what I'd thought of as a burial shroud for all I'd lost became a living thing instead. It's become a part of me through which my feelings were expressed. I've lost my mom, my dad, my husband, and my child. My history, my tether to life, everything I ever held dear. Yet somehow here we are, Chase. You and I are together. Ginny is pregnant. Life, flawed and miserable and beautiful and fragile and painful and glorious goes on despite us. I guess there's some comfort in that. Thank you for helping me see it."

"If I'd known your reasons for coming to me at the time, I would have turned you away," Chase said sternly.

"I know."

"Still, maybe I knew it, somehow, deep down. When I first saw you, vulnerable and broken and still fearlessly confronting Cassidy on a stranger's behalf out in the street, part of me fell in love with you immediately. I couldn't help it. You are so much more than a fragile beauty, Margot, although that's what people probably see at first. You are a force. I'll be thankful for every moment we have together creating music, finding pleasure, talking like this. I'm eternally grateful you crashed into my life that night."

"I am too." Margot raised her glass. "To honoring the past and embracing the future," she said, stoically.

They toasted once more. Jameson came over with a piece of paper in his hand and said, "Here are the kitchen's first thoughts about your band name. I'll arrange to close down shop early that night and come see you play."

"What?" Margot cried, "That's so sweet." She hopped up from her seat and hugged Jameson. "Thank you."

Jameson led her by the hand back to the kitchen. Everyone smiled when they saw her. Some of them set down spatulas and knives to come and hug her.

Some of the band names they'd offered were funny. They had "Wisk" and "Fryer" for kitchen related names, and "Pheasant" and "Guitar Man" and "The Flames" and Margot laughed easily surrounded by old friends. She and Kevin had gone to the grill once a week for nearly seven years, and although some of the people were new, most were not. This reunion was long overdue.

When Margot returned to the table, her eyes were sparkling. Chase looked up at her uncertainly, but when he saw her smile, he relaxed once more. She sat down and they discussed the band name at length, writing down some good options, mixing things up. Over dessert they came up with a name both of them liked.

Finally satisfied, they sat back and relaxed into the moment. Chase had not reached for Margot all evening. He hadn't tried to hold her hand, to kiss her, to stroke her hair. Margot noticed this restraint and wondered if it was because of Kevin's omnipresence in the room. Either way, it felt right, and Margot marveled at Chase's uncanny ability to assess what she needed in a situation like this.

As they left, they said goodbye and thank you to everyone, and Jameson saw them out. "Please come back soon. Both of you. It was wonderful to see you."

"Thank you for everything, Jameson. I can't tell you how much it means to me to know you guys have been rooting for me all this time."

Chase walked her to the car and opened the door for her.

"Can we go for a little drive? I'd like to see the water," she said once he'd gotten in.

Hesitating for a moment, Chase fixed her with a curious gaze. "I didn't think you liked driving any more than strictly necessary."

"I don't. I am sure I never will," Margot stated. "But I don't want to let fear hold me back any longer."

"All right. Promise to let me know how you're feeling and if you want to turn back at any time."

"Thanks, Chase. And thank you for a wonderful dinner. It was great."

Chase was pensive, staring out the windshield for a moment. "They all love you, Margot. I think they were glad to see you again."

"I think you're right. It was nice to go back."

"It's strange to picture you going there, back then," Chase said, uncertainly.

Margot reached out and took Chase's hand from the shifter. He met her look with a pained expression. She suddenly saw what his restraint had cost him. "Tonight wasn't easy for you either," she said. "I can see that. Thank you for holding back on your displays of affection. I noticed your restraint and it was very respectful. I appreciate everything about you."

"If I could hold you all day, every day, I would."

Margot squeezed his hand and a tear slipped from her eye. It flashed like a crystal as it fell into the darkness. "I'm still not there. I'm sorry."

"Don't apologize. When I met you, you were a living ghost. Since then, you've grown stronger every day. Confronting your past, little by little, you've proven to yourself that you're still alive. You're still here. Tonight was another step into the light."

"I miss him so much. It's not fair to you to say that or to feel it, but I miss him. He was my best friend. We were together for a third of my entire life."

"Of course you miss him, Margot. I'm not trying to replace him. I wouldn't have taken you here if I'd known how special it was to the two of you," Chase said miserably.

"I know. I'm glad we came, but it was hard."

———

They drove out to Higgins Beach, parked illegally, and took off their shoes to walk in the sand. The October night blanketed them in unusually warm air. With no humidity, it was a pure, simple comfort. The crash of the waves on the shore was rhythmic, like the fluid pulse of the world made tangible.

Chase held Margot's hand, while with her other she gathered up the velvet of her dress so it didn't drag in the sand. Her hair glinted platinum in the moonlight. The deep blue velvet dress, however, absorbed all light, bringing Margot into a oneness with their surroundings. Her beauty was beyond anything he had known. Hand in hand they walked the empty stretch of beach until they reached the far end where it turned inland into the estuary. At the water's edge, the black, still waters of the estuary reflected the stars.

Despite the beauty of the place, Chase was depressed. The moment Margot had disappeared into the kitchen at the restaurant, Chase had grown melancholy. Left alone at the table, feeling foolish, he wished he'd never suggested taking her out to dinner. She had reconnected with a part of her past and had left him alone in the present. It was selfish to feel so wounded, but he couldn't help it.

Naturally, she missed her husband. She still loved him, and she should. When she voiced those words, though, Chase felt her slipping away again. He was scrabbling for balance on a shifting terrain. The idea of losing Margot terrified him, feeding into his deepest fears of abandonment. The legacy of his parents' deaths reared its dreadful head and stared him down.

If he didn't control the fear of losing Margot, he would push her away by holding on too tight, and this time, the damage would be permanent. Margot needed more time, but what would she do when she was better and stronger? Would she leave him then?

"I'm sorry I hurt your feelings," Margot said, uncannily dissecting his emotional state.

"I'm only human."

"I know. And you're very kind."

"I believe in you, Margot. You're healing. Just because we heal, though, doesn't mean we forget. Kevin will always be a presence in your life, and therefore in mine. Our hearts are big enough to hold everyone we've ever loved. I'm sorry you lost him. I am. But I am thankful you've entrusted your heart to me. I adore you, Margot."

The water's ever-shifting patterns were mesmerizing, and they calmed his racing heart. The salty tang of sea air emboldened him. Chase took Margot around the waist and held her close. Margot smiled up at him and he kissed her lovingly.

Margot held him tight in her slender but strong arms. He

stroked her back and her hair, and kissed her forehead. She tilted her head back, brought her mouth to his, and kissed him deeply, passionately. The urgency in that kiss, combined with the touch of her body beneath the velvet, was enough to ignite Chase to passion. He ran his hands down her back, around her rear, squeezing her to him. He wanted to make love to her right there on the beach. He wanted to sink into her body, the deepest comfort he'd ever known, the keenest pleasure he could ever imagine. He wanted to possess her, to fill her, to help her forget her sorrow, to forget his own.

Instead, he contented himself with the kiss. For a long moment after, he held her against his body, unwilling to relinquish her to their own separate beings. He wanted to be one, to stay together, to hold her in the moonlight.

When Margot shivered against him though, for her sake he said, "Let's go home."

"Home?" she answered, as he wrapped her in his suit jacket.

Chase looked into her eyes, searching for an answer. "Yes. Come home with me and stay."

Margot nodded and smiled faintly. "Okay."

TWENTY

With the show less than a week away, Margot was queasy every time she thought of it. Could she actually perform in front of people again? She'd never had much of a problem with it, but this was different. She would be exposed, showing a side of herself that was unformed, not ready to be viewed by strangers.

Still, she and Chase had worked so hard. They'd written ten songs together, all of which were very respectable. Chase had written the guitar lines and the words. She had crafted rhythms to go along with them. They sounded tight. They'd recorded one of their final practices on Chase's phone and listened to it together. Margot was intent on smoothing the few rough patches out in what would be their last practice before the show.

"How was your day?" Chase asked when Margot walked over to the shop after work. He was finishing up a tattoo on an attractive lady with dark hair.

"Pretty good. I'm itching to play," she added, smiling. The woman, however, shot her a look that was pure venom.

"I'm almost done, babe. I'll be up in a sec."

"You know I like watching you work," Margot stated coyly, sidling up to the chair, smiling at the woman.

"Okay by me," Chase said smiling at her before turning back to his work.

"That looks nice," Margot said to the woman.

"Thanks," she replied curtly.

"There," Chase said, wiping the blood from her ankle. "I'll wash and wrap you, then we're done."

After the woman left, Chase cleaned up all of his supplies, threw away the used stuff, and disinfected the space. Margot watched him, smiling at her own possessive moment in exerting her claim on Chase before his customer.

"What was she like?"

"What do you mean?" he answered, looking genuinely perplexed.

"What did you guys talk about before I came in?" Margot pressed.

"Only what she wanted and where. Then I got to work. I don't talk much while I work, you know that."

"I know. I thought *she* might have."

"Maybe she did. I was paying attention to the design. It was pretty, I guess."

"It was okay." Margot looked at the ceiling.

"Are you jealous, Margot?" Chase asked, stopping his work for a moment and fixing her with a glare of disbelief.

"No," she replied, smiling. "Although I did have a minor moment where I wanted to beat my chest and yell 'He's mine!' at her."

Chase laughed and smiled at Margot. Once they were upstairs, Chase said, "Would you like to exert your claim upon me now?"

"Yes, please," she replied.

They made love with frantic abandon. Chase was powerful but tender, and Margot was enraptured. Afterwards, Chase dressed in dark jeans and a black t-shirt, walked barefoot over to his guitar and plugged it into his amp. He was so sexy Margot almost wanted to drag him back to the bed. Instead, she dressed and followed him across the room.

"Ready?" he asked after he'd tuned up.

"I'm terrified to play out."

"You're amazing," Chase reassured her. "I told you, babe. You're the best drummer I've ever played with."

"What if I mess up in public?"

"You won't. And if you do, who cares?"

"I care," Margot stated petulantly.

"Why? Don't let the fear of mistakes paralyze you, Margot. Let's have fun."

Skeptical, Margot played her best and kept the remainder of her fears to herself.

The day of the show, Margot left work early. She hadn't told anyone at work about it, but she thought Jim would get a kick out of her leading a double life. On her way out, she stopped by his office.

"Hey," she said from his doorway.

"Hi there, Margot. You leaving?"

"Yep. I've got a show tonight."

"What show do you watch?" he asked, looking up from his computer screen.

"Not that kind of show," she said, smiling. "I play the drums in a rock band. We're loud. We're opening for a big name act at The State tonight."

Jim looked shocked. "Well holy shit. So, you're a rock star?"

Margot laughed out loud. "Not yet."

"It's the craziest thing I've ever heard. I'll definitely be there. Break a leg, or whatever."

"Thanks, Jim," Margot said, laughing. "For everything."

"You've come a long way, my friend. Kill it tonight."

The theater filled up fast. Margot's heartrate spiked as she peeked from backstage at hundreds of people. Afraid she'd be sick to her stomach, she headed to the greenroom, but it was crowded with guys. Chase was drinking beer with them like he'd always been there. He adapted to every situation with grace. Margot was a nervous wreck in comparison.

"Hey," she heard behind her and she jumped in her skin.

"Hi," she answered, turning around toward a youngish man.

"First time?" he asked genially.

"In a while," she acknowledged, smiling bashfully.

"I'm Jake. I run sound. Your test sounded good earlier. You're going to be fine."

"Thanks, Jake. I'm Margot."

They shook hands. "Twenty minutes, Margot. Go have a beer. You'll relax in no time."

Jake, with his bright blue eyes and curly blonde hair, smiled kindly and walked away. He looked like a grown-up version of The Little Prince. It was pretty sweet. Had the music scene changed this much in the past decade? Was she going to be accepted without reservation, without feeling like she had something to prove simply because she was a woman? The thought was like warm honey.

"There you are," Chase said, smiling his winning, easy smile as she entered the greenroom. "You all right?"

"Yep."

"Want a beer?"

"Yep."

"Okay," he said, and got one out of the fridge for her. "Here, Margot. Everything is fine. You look the part, by the way."

Her black mascara and eyeliner were thicker than usual. Her eyes felt heavy, and the makeup had made her feel like a different person. She needed to channel that difference now. She wasn't Margot, accident victim and widow, bereft mother of Amandine. She was Margot the drummer, an equal creative force in a collaborative project with a man she loved. They clinked bottles and drank their beers.

What seemed like a moment later, they were called upstairs, where they took the stage to the applause of a three-quarters-full audience.

Chase nodded and smiled at them, took his guitar, checked to make sure it was still in tune, and said, "Thanks for coming out. I'm Chase, this is Margot, and we're Latitude." He nodded to Margot.

Mastering her trembling hands, she clicked off a beat for their opener and rolled into the song without hesitation. They played flawlessly. The energy of the music propelled Margot from her self-doubts and into the now. She could only be in the moment while playing music. It was pure joy to forget herself, to forget the place, to forget everything she'd lost, and instead to lose herself in the complexity of the rhythm, in the sweetness of the songs, as it all came together.

They blasted through their first four songs without a break, exactly like they'd practiced. People were hooting and clapping, although it didn't register with Margot as to why. She took a swig of her beer, nodded to Chase who looked intensely focused, and he started off with the complex melody of their next song. He faced her instead of the audience now, playing for her, playing for only the two of them. Everything disappeared as Margot joined him, playing off his riff, building into the chorus. Only then did Chase turn away, towards the mic, towards the audience, to sing the words she remembered hearing as though from a dream months ago. Margot watched him in awe, his charisma and talent blazing away before the wild audience. He was incandescent.

Their set ended to a standing ovation, with people cheering and clapping wildly for them. The audience had swelled to capacity. Phones were flashing as people took pictures and videos. Margot stood up, her sticks in her hand and waved to the audience. The stagehands helped them take their equipment off stage during the intermission where the other band mobbed her. "Holy shit," a guy she vaguely remembered from the greenroom said. "That was amazing. You guys should tour with us. I'm serious."

"I know. You guys are a force," said another guy with shaggy hair. They both stood close to her, making her feel small and overwhelmed.

"Thanks," she managed to say.

"Will you stick around? We wanna talk after we play, okay?"

"Okay," Margot replied in a daze.

Chase found her amidst the chaos backstage and threw his arms around her waist. He swung her around in a circle and said, "You were amazing. That was totally incredible. It was fucking flawless."

"You were incredible too," she said, breathlessly, as he put her down. "I love our songs, Chase. You are such a great writer and such a great player. I'm so lucky."

For a moment they held each other's gaze, fixed in the moment, the entire world around them slipping away.

"So am I," he agreed. "So am I."

The Sparhawks played next and their sound was so full, so tight, it was joy incarnate. Margot loved watching from backstage, with Chase's sweaty arm draped around her. His scent was so musky, so manly, so hot, part of her wanted to lure him to some dark corner so she could have her way with him, but she forced herself to remain in the moment, listening to the music. She was utterly alive. It was an awesome experience.

The Sparhawks led them to the greenroom after the show and there they talked about music, touring, life in a band, tattoos, and car accidents. Margot spoke honestly about her experiences.

"Jeez," said Toby from the band. "It would be hard to go on tour after something like that. You spend so much time driving from place to place in the bus."

"I think a bus would feel different," Margot admitted. She had surprised herself with her candidness, with her ability to discuss the past without getting emotional. It was a first. "Besides, I'm getting a little better all the time."

"Well, you're a phenomenal drummer," said Danny, the drummer from The Sparhawks.

"He never says that about anyone," added Toby.

"It's not about complementing people for the sake of niceness. I speak my mind," Danny clarified. "And Margot is one of the most talented drummers we've seen. You know it."

"We're serious. You guys should totally tour with us. We lost the other band, as you know. Fighting, drugs, all that. It was stupid. They were immature. What do you say?"

"I could leave, Margot. I rent out the space anyway." Chase looked exhilarated. "What about your work?"

"I think Jim's been waiting for me to take some time off. It sounds terrifying but everything in life is terrifying if you stop to think about it for too long."

"That's the truth," interjected Danny solemnly.

"We'll talk a little more and let you know," Chase said. "When would we start?"

"Local bands have filled the spots in shows for the next two weeks, but after that, we'd need someone. We've got bookings in Europe too, to sweeten the deal. You might even get a record deal out of it."

"Jesus, that would be a dream come true," muttered Chase. He looked expectantly at Margot, trying to gage her temperature.

"Fuck it," she said. "What have we got to lose?"

Ginny and Henry stayed for Latitude's debut and texted Margot afterwards saying Ginny was tired, so they couldn't stay, but that they'd loved the show. Margot and Chase met them the following morning for brunch, excited to tell them about the tour.

After the initial greetings, Margot told them the news about Latitude.

"Holy shit, The Sparhawks want you to tour with them?" Ginny said, way too loud.

"Tone it down there, sailor!" Margot looked around the tiny restaurant horrified. "You've got a kid to set an example for."

"She's going to come out swearing a blue streak, then,"

Henry said playfully, inviting an elbow to the ribs from a scowling Ginny.

"You guys are amazing together," Ginny said in a serious tone. "Your music is incredible. I'm glad you're finally playing again, Margot. You sound better than ever."

"Tour will be fun, don't you think?" asked Chase.

"I do," Margot agreed. "It will be a learning experience. When I was at Berklee, all I wanted was to play in a successful band that toured and recorded. I worked so hard, but it never seemed to matter. I never found the right people to play with. Chase, with you it's natural. I don't have to try so hard. It feels right."

"The crowd picked up on that too," Henry said. "They loved you. You guys knocked it out of the park."

"Thank you, Henry," Chase replied, earnestly. "From one musician to another, it means a lot."

After they ordered their food, they continued talking.

"What are you doing for daycare?" Chase asked.

"Henry was going to teach, but we think for the first year or so he is going to stay at home. My job pays more than the teaching gig and with his music I think it will work out."

"Daycare is expensive. I'd rather raise my own child than pay my entire salary to a stranger to do it," Henry commented.

"Right on," said Chase. Everyone looked at him and burst into laughter. "What? Even I know that."

For the first time in public, Margot snuggled up next to Chase and let him put his arm around her. It was natural, overdue. Henry and Ginny shot each other a glance which Margot was sure referenced a conversation they'd had about her.

"Yes, we're in love," Margot said quietly. "I'm finally ready to admit it. Chase understands that I will always love Kevin, but like he said, we've got room enough in our hearts for everyone."

"I'm so happy for you," Ginny said, getting a little misty. "We figured since you were staying together a lot that things were good."

"I think I'm ready to sell the house," Margot said, eliciting a gasp from Ginny. Chase raised his eyebrows but let her continue. "I can't be there anymore. It's too sad, too full of the past. I don't know what I'll do when we get back from tour, but we'll see."

"I know how much the place meant to you and Kevin," Ginny said, sadly. "You're the bravest person I know."

"It's time to let go," Margot said. "It's time for some other person to fall in love with that place."

Everyone was quiet for a little while, so Margot resuscitated the conversation. "So. Do you guys have any names picked out?" Margot said, trying to deflect the subject from her personal life.

"Yes, we do," Henry said. "Ginny, can I tell them?"

"I guess." Ginny narrowed her eyes. "This is all top secret though. And I don't want to know if you don't like them."

"It's a deal," Margot agreed. Sunlight filled the tiny restaurant with a warm glow, a comfort Margot was only too happy to accept. Her heart was lighter than it had been in ages, as she gave herself over to the present moment, here with her friends, her lover, her life.

TWENTY-ONE

Margot sold her house during the tour and she and Chase had to fly back for the closing. She called Ginny and told her to take whatever she wanted before everything else got sold. Ginny was hesitant. "It's your stuff," she'd said uneasily. "I don't want to take your stuff."

"I'd rather you have it than some strangers," Margot said.

Ginny finally agreed and Henry moved the nursery furniture and some other everyday objects into their new house. Margot moved the few things she'd decided to keep into Chase's loft, trying to hold her emotions at bay. She'd already let go of everything that mattered. This was just stuff.

On their last day, before she signed the paperwork, she went and said goodbye to the house. Chase waited for her out on the steps because Margot wanted to be alone.

She went inside and her footsteps echoing on the barren floors sounded too loud. Now that the place was empty, it seemed utterly cavernous. There was no warmth left, no life, nothing to hold onto. Kevin's presence had moved on. That made it incrementally easier to let go, but Margot still had to work to keep from losing her shit as she moved from room to room.

In Amandine's nursery, Margot paused, looking across at the painted clouds on the wall. Nothing would ever be the same. No version of her life moving forward could resemble what might have been. Margot needed to accept that.

"Goodbye, my sweethearts," she said, into the still, cool air. "I love you. You are always in my heart."

She and Chase finished out the tour with a whirlwind of gigs, and since The Sparhawks were a well-known indie band, Margot and Chase garnered a little following of their own along the way.

One night, after a particularly rockin' show, a guy came up to Margot at the bar.

"You guys killed it tonight," he said. He had that aloof rocker air that Margot could spot anywhere. He was probably a musician too.

Since Margot was used to being zeroed in on by random guys after their shows, she shrugged and said a non-committal, "Thanks."

The guy reached into his pocket and drew out a business card. When Margot read the word Matador across the top, she went weak in the knees.

Chase saw her waver from a few stools away. He swooped over thinking something was wrong. "What's going on, Margot?" he asked, angling his body between Margot and the man.

Margot shook herself from her moment of awe. "This is Zane Ruiz. He's with Matador." She handed the card to Chase who didn't seem to comprehend the situation.

Zane put out his hand to Margot first and then to Chase and introduced himself formally. "We've been hearing good things, so when I heard you guys would be in town, I thought I should check you out for myself. We're interested."

"Interested in what?" Chase asked.

"In signing you guys."

In a most uncharacteristic moment, Margot cried out,

jumped off her bar stool, and hugged the impassive Zane. If he thought the two of them were nuts, he never said.

———

They recorded the ten songs they had and named the album *Inside Out*. On the cover they put a picture of Margot from the back, overexposed, with the ocean sweeping out in front of her. The white lace tattoo shone bright against her skin, glowing as though it had always been a part of her. Chase loved the cover. It brought together all the things he loved the most in life.

When Chase and Margot finally returned to their old reality, to their old lives, to their old jobs, nothing at all had changed. Nothing except for them. After a week of pretending they still fit in, Chase invited Margot out to dinner at the bar.

"Do you still want to be an accountant?" he asked her after their second drink.

Margot didn't hesitate. "No," she said. "I absolutely don't."

Chase, however, was more hesitant to give up the career he'd built for himself. "Do you think I should keep tattooing?"

"Do you love it?" Margot asked.

"I do. Art and music have always been intertwined for me."

"Things at the shop went well while you were gone," Margot said. "You make plenty of money renting out the space, right?"

"Right."

"Maybe you could only take on jobs you're really into artistically, instead of tattooing everyone who walks through the door. Block out special time for special projects."

"I guess that could work," he said, brightening. "It's not about the money at all. That's all set. Things are paying for themselves. It's about the art."

"It's a privilege," Margot added. "To be able to do the work we want to do rather than working because we have no choice. The privilege of creating on our own terms is precious. Let's agree not to take it for granted."

Chase nodded, thankful he'd found someone who could understand this so well. She was a creator too, and they were in it together. Chase was looking forward to some of their local shows and he couldn't wait for the release of their album. It was being mastered, and Matador had set a date for distribution. At the release show, they'd headline at a big venue in Boston. Then they'd headline on another tour. It was surreal.

"I'm ready to write some new songs," Margot mused aloud. "I love our stuff, don't get me wrong, but I hear our songs in my sleep. I want something new in my head."

"I've got some ideas," Chase said. "I'll play them for you when we get home."

Margot's slow, easy smile set off fireworks in Chase's heart.

———

The next night, Margot and Chase went to see Ginny and Henry and the new baby. Margot wondered how she would feel being at their house, but Ginny was so happy, Henry doted on the baby, and the three of them together were adorable. She couldn't have been more thrilled for her friend.

After dinner, Margot sat peacefully on the couch. Cradled gently in her arms was baby Grace, swaddled in a familiar soft white blanket. The room was quiet and peaceful, as all four adults were taken with the simple joy of watching a sleeping baby. Eventually, Ginny fixed Margot with a serious look that seemed totally incongruous to the moment.

"What?" Margot finally asked quietly.

"Henry and I would like to ask you guys something. We want you to be Grace's Godparents," Ginny said.

"Really?" Margot looked up at Ginny, then at Chase, who sat next to her on the couch. His arm was wrapped around her and he squeezed her to him. Nodding, he smiled encouragingly.

"Please," Ginny said forcefully. "Margot, you've been watching out for her since the minute I found out I was pregnant. I have a feeling you'd do anything for her. You've always been like a sister to me. It would mean so much to us."

"We would be honored," Margot said, her voice unsteady. She looked down at Grace's tiny head, her eyes shut tight, her little fists tucked to her chest. What did babies dream about?

Kissing Grace on the head, cherishing the feel of her soft, wispy hair, the baby smell of her unmistakable, Margot knew Ginny was right. She would do anything for this child. If she couldn't have her own angel Amandine, so fragile, so precious, so beautiful, then this was the next best thing: A Goddaughter to love.

Preparing for a wedding with a baby proved as difficult for Ginny as it would have for any new mother. As her Maid of Honor, Margot did everything she could to help her friend. Henry's jobs were to secure the reception site, find musicians, and rent tents, furniture, and dishes. He'd been done for months.

Ginny, however, had taken her detail-oriented approach to a whole new level. The bridesmaids would all wear strapless, coral-pink cocktail dresses; the groomsmen would wear dove-grey suits. The centerpieces were wildflowers from a local farm displayed in vases Ginny had collected from the Goodwill, and the food would be catered by a friend of a friend's company. The consternation aroused from the guestlist alone would have been enough for a lifetime, but Ginny's mom seemed hell-bent on ensuring every relation within a thousand-mile radius would receive an invitation. Ginny couldn't even imagine doing the seating charts.

When the day finally came, with its balmy September heat, the wedding took place in a big antique barn overlooking the bay in Damariscotta, before sunset. The colors in the sky were a glorious riot, and Margot now understood Ginny's choice of color scheme for the dresses and the flowers: they matched the magnificent sunset sky.

Lanterns were strung from every beam inside the barn;

Christmas lights festooned every rafter. The place seemed straight out of a magazine. Ginny had been skeptical of the setting when Henry had first suggested it, but the idea had grown on her.

Ginny glowed with joy as she spoke her vows and Henry's kind eyes glittered. They were magnetic in their sweetness, and the entire congregation was overjoyed when husband and wife finally kissed. Margot remembered the night when she'd seen Henry play music for the first time. She'd thought his band would have been perfect at a farmhouse wedding. She'd been right. They played their exuberant bluegrass tunes at the reception, mostly without Henry, although he sat in for a few songs later in the evening.

As she and Chase spun around the dancefloor, Margot stared up at the romantic lights. Had this been two years before, she would have forced herself to come, she'd have been sitting alone at a table, frozen with sadness, possibly waist-deep in scotch. Instead, she was dancing happily to bluegrass with a man she loved. It was absolutely right.

Thoughts of Kevin and Amandine were still ever-present in her mind and Margot had realized long ago that they always would be. Lately, though, she'd begun to make peace with her longing for them. The grief had simply become another part of her, like the tattoos had, and it was no longer debilitating. It had lightened and been transmuted into the lodestone in Margot's moral compass. Why should love be a weight in her heart? Rather, Margot now believed love was a thing of light, free as a bird, soft as a cloud, and should never be the source of pain. As she danced, swept along in Chase's strong arms, her feet barely touched the floor.

Thankfully, Margot was now comfortable showing her tattoos, for the coral strapless dress had left her little choice. All evening, strangers and acquaintances alike had complimented the elegant designs. There was something familiar about lace, something poignant that resonated with a lot of people, especially at a wedding. Chase's artistry was evident, and Margot always gave him the credit for its beauty.

Ginny's smile throughout the entire evening was joy itself and Grace was held non-stop by her grandparents and parents alternately. Now, she slept peacefully in the arms of Henry's father, who sat back and watched her with a contented smile as the festivities swirled around him unnoticed. How Grace could sleep through this wonderful racket, Margot had no clue.

At the end of the night, Margot and Chase danced to one last slow song beneath the soft glow of lantern light, holding each other tight.

"Margot," Chase whispered into her hair.

"Yes?"

"This is the part of the night where I'd get down on my knee, pop a ring out of my pocket, and ask you to marry me, but I don't think that's what you want. Am I right?"

Margot froze in mid-step as a fierce sadness squeezed her heart. Holding Chase's gaze with wide eyes, she didn't want to say the words in her heart, but Chase needed to hear the truth. Softly, she said, "I already have a husband, whether or not he's here in this realm. I'm sorry Chase, but I can't have another."

Margot expected to see his hurt, his heartbreak, some kind of jealousy in his eyes. Instead, she saw only the purest love and complete acceptance. Chase loved her for who she was, for what she was, without limitation, without reservation.

"That's exactly what I thought, sweetheart. I understand. But would it be okay if we did something different, something special that binds us in this love, in this life?"

"What, like vows?"

"It could be something like vows. Or I was thinking maybe tattoos."

"How about both?" Margot answered. "Could we do our vows now?"

Chase looked so relieved; all the tension left his body and

was replaced by his lovely smile. "I can't think of a more romantic moment."

So, bravely bearing the lace patterns of her matriarchal ancestors' bridal veil, etched lovingly into her being, Margot took new vows. In the middle of the dance floor, she and Chase stood still as the few remaining couples danced enchanted circles around them, binding them. Chase took Margot's hands in his own and held them to his heart. "My darling Margot, I, Chase Goodwin, promise to love you, to cherish you, and to give you my fidelity as long as we both shall live." He brought her hands to his lips and kissed them.

"Oh, Chase," she said, her voice quavering with emotion. She brought his trembling hands to her chest, and said, "My sweet Chase. I, Margot DeWitt, promise to love you, to cherish you, and to give you my fidelity as long as we both shall live."

"May I kiss you, darling?"

"Yes," Margot asserted firmly. "You may."

Chase looked deep into her eyes and said, "I love you." Before she could respond, they were enveloped in a kiss, deep and passionate and full of love, a kiss with all the magic of the evening in it, for good measure.

The presence of all those who had come before her, of all those who had loved her, and of those whom she had loved, was tangible in the air around them, a blessing on their informal union. Thus woven together, Margot and Chase left the dancefloor as the music faded, their arms entwined, ready for whatever the rest of time would bring.

TWENTY-TWO

The buzz of the machine evoked so many different feelings for Margot. Now, as she sat in Chase's chair once again, the scent of alcohol sharp in the air, the drone of the needle was like a familiar song. Margot closed her eyes, letting a wave of Kevin's and Amandine's love wash through her being. Breathing deeply, perfectly at peace, she was not shocked when the needle once more pierced her skin. For the first time during a tattoo, Margot did not focus on the pain. Opening her eyes to the new love before her, she focused on Chase instead.

The unique line Chase was tattooing on her inner wrist, just above the thrill of her strong and steady pulse, was mesmerizing. As she'd learned from Kevin, everyone's heartbeat is as different as a fingerprint, unique to each person, a reflection of the life in one's veins, of the shape of one's heart. This line, in a full spectrum of colors, was Chase's ECG signature. It signified Margot's return to life, her return to color, her return to music, and most of all, her return to love. She adored it, and the fact Chase now bore the unique signature of Margot's heartbeat made it all the better. Her gaze wandered up, alighting upon Chase's lovely features. He was smiling as he worked.

Every so often, as he shifted positions, Margot caught a glimpse of his tattoo, in the same exact spot as hers, above his pulse point, only his was done in white, an homage to Margot. When Margot had asked him why white, he'd said, "Every other tattoo I have is in color. This one's for you, for us. I wanted it to be special, to stand out."

"So just when I've gone for color, you switch to white?" she asked in mock incredulity.

"For me, white isn't about the ghosts of the past. It's about a clean slate. About starting over. That's the gift we've given each other, Margot. The gift of another chance at love. A way to live a full, abundant life."

Once she'd understood, Margot was honored. Chase was his own person, a creative force to compliment her own. Their love was in perfect balance, the yin and yang so casually referred to in every black and white symbol so taken for granted by the western world. But when Margot stopped to think about how Chase was the sun and she was the moon, how with every moment they were together they became more of a compliment to each other's best qualities, and how without that balance, they had both grown listless and lost, she was overcome with gratitude to have found him. Thankful to have the balancing forces of her universe finally intact, Margot sat back in the chair and let her pain become one with her joy.

THE END

Don't miss out on your next favorite book!

Join the Satin Romance mailing list
www.satinromance.com/mail.html

THANK YOU FOR READING

——

Did you enjoy this book?

We invite you to leave a review at your favorite book site, such as Goodreads, Amazon, Barnes & Noble, etc.

DID YOU KNOW THAT LEAVING A REVIEW...

- Helps other readers find books they may enjoy.
- Gives you a chance to let your voice be heard.
- Gives authors recognition for their hard work.
- Doesn't have to be long. A sentence or two about why you liked the book will do.

ACKNOWLEDGMENTS

Getting a tattoo has been on my list of things to do for a while. Not having personal experience with a tattoo, however, meant I needed to "phone a friend" in order to get the details right. Thankfully, Nick "Bellows" of Gold Star Tattoo was willing to help. Thanks, Nick, for answering my endless questions with patience, humor, and philosophical depth. I appreciate your advice and guidance deeply. Rock on.

This book wouldn't be what it is without the insight of my incredible editors, Carly Hayward and Barbara Bradley. Thank you both for your masterful work and honest feedback.

Every once in a while in life, someone takes a chance on you because they see your potential. Nancy Schumacher, you took a chance publishing my first book and you continue to support my career as a writer. Thank you. Your confidence and encouragement mean so much to me.

Joshua and Bob, my dear friends-become-family, thank you for enthusiastically supporting my work. You're always there to talk me through the tough times and to celebrate the good. I am so thankful for you both.

Erica, thank you for your honesty about the first draft of this book. You were totally right about everything. Honesty takes courage, and you have my deepest thanks.

And lastly, to T, E, and S, having you in my corner keeps me in the ring. Thank you for showing me what true love is.

ABOUT THE AUTHOR

Emma Hartley is an author and artist living in picturesque Maine. She has been writing and making art since childhood and has been insatiably curious and industrious her whole life. Emma was a double major in English and Fine Arts and holds a Masters in Art and Design Education. This devotion to art is apparent in her in her novels, manifesting itself in the work her characters enjoy. Emma's  other interests include playing drums in an indie rock band, gardening, and exploring every square inch of the Maine coastline.

www.emmahartleyauthor.com

facebook.com/emmahartleyauthor

instagram.com/emmahartleyauthor